This carved replica of Ralph the bear sits outside the shop next to the highway. He has been there since 1991 dispensing wisdom to the traveling public. Ralph doesn't always follow his own advice; he much prefers talking to thinking.

OTHER BOOKS BY THE AUTHOR

My Big Dinosaur Book (For Mature Children)
Waiting for the Stage
Ralph, Conversations with a Bear

WHAT OTHERS ARE SAYING ABOUT THIS BOOK

"The *Council of Bears* rips the misty veil from the hitherto secret society of bears...a riveting, probing exposé. Now we know what bears do when they are not eating or sleeping."

H. Lorenzo Wrongbuckle, Park Visitor

"The story is cute, but certain passages concern the rutting behavior of bears and are not suitable for very young children. Parental guidance is advised."

Twyla Pinchley, Moral Crusader

"Vivid and fascinating...packed with passion, intrigue, and lusting...set in a wilderness setting where there's lots of trees and stuff."

B.G.M., Friend of Pete
(Once read 'Call of the Wild')

"Way better than that book about Ralph. This book packs a wallop. It's overflowing with passion, rage and treachery...bears as they really are when nobody is watching. Boffo! Way to go, Pete."

Second Growth Sam
Olympic Park Nuisance Bear and Special Counsel to COB

"Put in terms that an engineer can understand, the *Council of Bears* explains bear behavior far better than the Bernoulli equation explains the flow of water. Merrill's writing has enough pressure, density and velocity to satisfy even the most jaded of readers."

Paul Halvorsen, Engineer

"Some of this is partly true."

M. Ronald Rumpsley, National Director of Wildlife Statistics
Office of Bear and Cougar Assaults and Incursions
Tabulations, Compilations and Recording Unit (NDWSOBCAITCRU)

"Good grief, another book? I haven't finished the first one yet. No wonder the old fella hasn't been seen wandering around the neighborhood for the last couple of years."

Larry Gordon, Pete's Neighbor

"Every bathroom should have a place for the *Council of Bears*. No matter where the reader leaves off it's easy to pick up the story on your next visit. Keeps you coming back for more."

Graffito, Found written on a restroom wall

"Compelling...does not disappoint."

Flossie Shortclaw, COB member
Self-proclaimed "Expert on Everything"

COUNCIL OF BEARS

*RALPH AND MACDUFF SHAKESBEAR
IN OLYMPIC NATIONAL PARK*

BY
PETE MERRILL

AUTHOR OF
Ralph, Conversations With a Bear

WITH ILLUSTRATIONS BY THE AUTHOR
SUPERVISED AND APPROVED BY MACDUFF
SHAKESBEAR HIMSELF

Peter A. Merrill, Sr.
14103 E. Highway 106
Belfair, Was 98528

Note for Librarians: a cataloguing record for this book that includes Dewey Decimal Classification and US Library of Congress numbers is available from the Library and Archives of Canada. The complete cataloguing record can be obtained from their online database at:
www.collectionscanada.ca/amicus/index-e.html
ISBN 1-4120-4291-7

Cover Design by Pam Merrill, Outlook Writing and Design – Belfair Book Production by Melinda Halvorsen.
Printed in Victoria, BC, Canada

TRAFFORD

Offices in Canada, USA, Ireland, UK and Spain
This book was published *on-demand* in cooperation with Trafford Publishing. On-demand publishing is a unique process and service of making a book available for retail sale to the public taking advantage of on-demand manufacturing and Internet marketing. On-demand publishing includes promotions, retail sales, manufacturing, order fulfilment, accounting and collecting royalties on behalf of the author.
Book sales for North America and international:
Trafford Publishing, 6E–2333 Government St.,
Victoria, BC v8t 4p4 CANADA
phone 250 383 6864 (toll-free 1 888 232 4444)
fax 250 383 6804; email to orders@trafford.com
Book sales in Europe:
Trafford Publishing (uk) Ltd., Enterprise House, Wistaston Road Business Centre, Wistaston Road, Crewe, Cheshire cw2 7rp UNITED KINGDOM
phone 01270 251 396 (local rate 0845 230 9601)
facsimile 01270 254 983; orders.uk@trafford.com
Order online at:
www.trafford.com/robots/04-2098.html

10 9 8 7 6 5 4 3 2

To my daughter, Melinda, whose refusal to be intimidated by a computer allowed this book to appear between covers. To Pam for providing the covers and to Betty for her suggestions and advice. To all three for their infinite patience.

Introduction

It has been said that if the North American black bear had been treated with respect and consideration in the early days instead of being made into steaks and stew meat by the likes of Daniel Boone and Davy Crockett he might have become one of man's best friends. Just like dogs are, only bigger, but I'm not sure this is quite true. It's hard for me to imagine a bear patiently scratching at the back door waiting to be let inside for dinner. He would be more likely to simply dismantle the door, eat everything in the kitchen, including the cook, and go to sleep on the nearest soft bed. Telling a black bear that he's been "bad" doesn't cut it either. This is not to say that the feral *Ursus americanus* doesn't have some redeeming qualities, it just takes patience to bring them out.

Ralph and Macduff Shakesbear, a pair of black bears — grandfather and grandson — once lived up in the backwoods behind my property. I made their acquaintance by accident and became a friend, and even a confidant, during a series of adventures in the early 1990s. Ralph, an adult bruin of strong opinions, had been raised in an extended family of highly educated bears known as the "Shakesbears". The bear family got its name after Ralph's great grandmother Ophelia found a discarded set of the works of William Shakespeare in a garbage can. All of the Shakesbear clan had been brought up reading the Bard. Young Duffy, in fact, could recite passages from the books whenever circumstances suggested.

The uneducated Toonerville bears, who lived about ten miles to the northeast, considered Ralph's family "stuck up" and it was the Toonervilles who had given the Shakesbears their name. Intended to be derogatory, Shakesbears wore the name proudly, spoke flawless English and took a special interest in the affairs of people. Apparently I was the only person Ralph actually talked to, however, and I quickly found that he didn't have a high opinion of human "beans" as he called them. My patience was tested on many occasions during our association, and more than once had brought me into near conflict with the law. In 1999, Ralph, citing the growing pressure of encroaching civilization, persuaded me to transport him and Duffy to the Olympic National Park, a haven where they thought they could live in peace.

In 2002, three years after their departure, I wrote about our adventures in a book called *"Ralph, Conversations With A Bear"*.

I assumed that I had seen and heard the last of them. Little did I know.

CHAPTER ONE
Noises in the Night

It was the slamming of the car door that woke me up, along with the acceleration of an engine as a car drove off. There was no use in jumping out of bed to see what was going on, since whatever was going on had already gone on. I fixed one eye on the clock, which stared back at me with the information that it was 3:45 A.M., way too early to get up.

I turned over and went back to sleep.

Years ago when my display of carved figures over in front of my shop was new, such noises in the night would bring me out of bed in a flash, concerned that someone was about to rip off my statues or abuse them in some way. Since no one had bothered them for fifteen years I'd come to assume that nobody ever would, so in my somnambulate state I dismissed the noise as being the paper man, who usually comes by at some god-awful early hour. In any case, by morning I had completely forgotten the incident.

There are seven carved figures over there across the highway — six people and one dog — which represent a group of western characters waiting for the arrival of the stagecoach. Somewhat removed from them is the statue of a black bear that is seated in an easy chair with his legs crossed, holding a sign up in the air. Admittedly this is an unusual pose for a bear, but Ralph, as he is known, is a very unusual bear. There are messages on Ralph's sign, which I change every three or four days, most of them quotations gathered from a vast range of sources from Socrates to Santa Claus.

Some of them are actually original with Ralph himself.

Two days after the noise in the night I went over to change Ralph's sign and noticed what appeared to be a postcard in his lap. Now, notes to Ralph are not all that rare. They are generally complaints from some passer-by who objects to the latest verbal indiscretion the bear has committed, like a message that said "LOOSE WOMEN TIGHTENED HERE", a crack I caught hell for back before I learned to be more careful. Everybody around here knows that I'm the guy who puts those quips up there, not Ralph or his grandson Macduff, as I used to pretend, so I'm the guy who takes the heat. Of course Ralph sometimes gets mash notes, too, like Valentine cards and even love poems, but I'm sure those are actually meant for me.

Anyway, there was a postcard in Ralph's lap. I gave it a cursory glance and saw that it seemed to be from a child who was just learning to write. In the address space, in smudged pencil, was written "old pete at bareplace rode 106". That's all. There was an uncancelled stamp on the card, placed upside down and in the wrong corner, and in the space for the message were the words "PLEZE CUM SAME PLAICE. BRING BOOKS DUF". Planning to look at the card more carefully later, I carried it into the shop, where I left it on the workbench, dismissing it from my mind as just another practical joke from my neighbor Larry. I put up a new sign — HEAVEN'S FOR CLIMATE, HELL'S FOR COMPANY — that didn't seem outrageous enough to stir up my more sensitive readers, and went back across the road to rest, completely forgetting to look at the card, as so often happens these days. Any old guy over eighty who says his mind is still "sharp as a tack" is blowing smoke, or more likely, has forgotten how forgetful he is.

It wasn't until sometime in the middle of the next night that I remembered that I had forgotten to read the card more thoroughly. As I mulled the matter over in my mind certain things disturbed my sleep, and I began to question my original notion that it had been left by my neighbor. Larry was simply far too penurious to spend thirty-seven cents on a practical joke. I couldn't remember the exact words on the card, but in my unstructured, half-asleep state I seemed to recall them as being vaguely similar to a message I had received during my adventures with the two black bears, Ralph and Duffy, back when we were trying to escape up to the mountains. I tossed restlessly in my bed until the drumming of the rain on the roof heralded a new day.

As I scanned the morning paper over my meager breakfast of bran and raisins, I realized that my subconscious was being disturbed by something other than the bleak prospects of world peace. I couldn't quite put my finger on what was bugging me until an article related to modern children being unable to write the English language properly brought to mind the misspelled words on that postcard in Ralph's lap. As I read the article I remembered my years of travail trying to teach Ralph's grandson how to spell which, in turn, reminded me that I had planned on going over first thing that morning to read the card more carefully, which I decided to do just as soon as I finished the paper. By then my mind was fully occupied with the weighty problem of solving world and regional dislocations and getting the two breakfast dishes washed, which reminded me that I must take out the garbage, which then brought to my attention an overflowing gutter, and after I found a ladder and got that problem fixed it was almost lunch time. But before lunch I thought it best to rest a bit.

After a little nap I went across the highway to get a screwdriver to fix the knob on the back door and came across the postcard on the workbench. I took it back to the house, forgetting all about the screwdriver, and sat down to take a closer look at the thing. In small script under the crude message about the books was a note that read, "The park ranger gave this to me. I think it's for you. Fred." Very curious, I thought. I carefully examined the picture of a big grizzly bear standing on his hind legs on the front of the card and turned it over to scrutinize the crude message again: "PLEZE CUM SAME PLAICE. BRING BOOKS DUF".

This thing sure looked to be the genuine article — a message from my long-gone friend, Macduff Shakesbear, who was living up in the national park with his grandfather Ralph. If it really was from Duffy it appeared that he had been working on his handwriting, if not his spelling. But what was I to make of the other message? And what about Fred? Did I know somebody named Fred? How did he get into this mystery?

It had been long enough since I had driven the bears to the mountains that I had forgotten where I put those three volumes of Shakespeare that Macduff had left in the truck. I guessed they were the books he was talking about. They must still be over in the shop somewhere. I was beginning to think it more and more likely that the cub bear had indeed sent the postcard. Who else would know about the books?

Cub bear? What was I thinking, anyway? A lot of time had passed since I had last seen the little rascal and bears grow up fast.

4

Duffy was probably a full-grown young stud bear by now. Maybe it wasn't such a good idea for me to go looking for him again. Who knew what I might run into? My better judgment told me that this one innocent little piece of cardboard could change my whole comfortable existence into a new chapter of confusion and disorder.

It wasn't like I was just out looking for trouble though. If this message was legitimate, Duffy was sending for **me,** not the other way around. Memories of adventure and turmoil came flooding back as I recalled my previous efforts to try to get Duffy and Ralph out of my backyard as it were, outwitting the law, racing down the highways with an unstable load of bears in the back of the little pickup truck and trying to outrun minions of the law.

What was the name of that nosy sheriff? Ed? Yeah, that was his name. Fred Edd. What had become of good old Fred Edd? Ohmygod, FRED EDD! Could this be the Fred on the postcard? I hadn't seen Deputy Edd patrolling the highways in my vicinity for so long I had forgotten he existed.

I made a discrete phone call to the county seat where the nice lady from the sheriff's office told me that Deputy Edd was still with the department, and was now assigned to the night shift at the northern end of the county. When she asked if she could take a message for him I assured her that my call wasn't important, and that I would catch up with my friend later.

The northern part of our county abuts the boundaries of the Olympic National Park where I supposed my bear friends were still living. It was logical to assume that the county sheriffs worked closely with the park rangers, and that Deputy Edd was frequently in and out of the park. Everything seemed to be coming into focus.

Not knowing any other way of getting a message to me, Duffy had attempted to send me a postcard which he probably stole somewhere. He didn't know my address so he just wrote "bareplace on rode 106", which is the state highway that passes my house and shop where the statue of old Ralph is still holding his signs. Duffy had likely just left the card near the ranger's cabin hoping somebody would pick it up and mail it.

I began to feel a bit like Sherlock Holmes, although my powers of deduction were straining to find a conclusion to this mystery. So then, I surmised, on one of his visits to the park rangers, Deputy Fred Edd had somehow come into possession of the postcard, had recognized the crude address and, on one of his night patrols, had either dropped the card off in Ralph's lap, or had asked one of his colleagues to do it for him. It didn't seem likely that Edd would have gone out of his way to do me any special favors, since we had never been very friendly. Maybe he'd mellowed since our last encounter. Either that or he was still plotting to bring me up on that old rap of consorting with wild animals.

Before I had a chance to forget, I went across to the shop and looked for the three Shakespeare books that I had stashed after my last encounter with the bears. I found them way up on a high shelf, all covered with dust and cobwebs, *All's Well That Ends Well, Love's Labor's Lost and Much Ado About Nothing.* I wondered if the titles portended anything, but couldn't seem to make a connection, except maybe for the last one. Before leaving the shop I remembered to pick up that screwdriver I'd forgotten on my earlier trip. When I got back to the house I'd forgotten what I needed it for.

If Duffy was asking to see me I needed to do some serious

thinking before I made any rash moves. Did I really want bears back in my life again? I began a mental list of all the things that had happened to me back in those "good old days" when two bears were in control of everything I did.

On the positive side of the matter was the curiosity I had maintained over the years about what my two friends had been doing since I last saw them. Perhaps I had never acknowledged to myself just how often I thought of them, although my thoughts seemed more often to be about our narrow escapes than our pleasant encounters, of which there had been all too few. Even after three years of separation most of my remembrances of our times together revolved around disputes, conflicts and disagreements, but I liked to think most of those problems were caused by Ralph's uneasiness about the encroachment of "human beans" in general, and had nothing to do with his relationship with me. It would be interesting to know if living way out in the wilds of the national park had improved his temperament any. Shoot, I thought to myself, what harm could come from visiting them for an hour or two?

What harm, indeed, my more rational brain asked? That old curmudgeon Ralph had been living away from human contact for a long time now. Suppose he had reverted to the wild? Perhaps he had even forgotten who I was. I didn't know anything about the nature of a bear's memory. If I walked up to shake his "hand", likely as not he would bite it off.

Then again, I thought, that postcard message came from Duffy, not Ralph. Duffy wouldn't ask me to visit him if he thought Ralph was planning to beat me up. My hyperactive imagination was taking over again. Ralph had once been my friend; why should I suppose

7

he still wasn't?

And so it seemed I had talked myself into going back to look for them. For better or for worse, I was committed. I would pick a nice day when nothing else was scheduled and go, and my memory being what it was, I would take along a notebook to record my adventures.

In the words of Julius Caesar, "the die was cast".

CHAPTER TWO
On the Edge of the Cliff

The message from Duffy had reached me in the middle of March and the weather was lousy. Those little logging roads that criss-cross the forests surrounding the park would still be covered with snow. But by late April with the coming of milder weather and the lessening of the spring rains, my thoughts turned seriously to the mission to which I had committed myself: to find my friend Macduff, grandson of Ralph B. Shakesbear, the last remaining member of the Shakesbear family of black bears who once populated the unkempt woodlands that I called my backyard.

Of course it wasn't really my backyard at all, but the land adjoining my backyard, and it was totally uninhabited, owned by a big logging company that was waiting for the trees to get big enough to cut down. For twenty-five years they had been nibbling away at the area, which was gradually but inexorably being converted from a tangled wilderness into a growing collection of housing developments, each divided up into five-acre plots that nowadays were called "estates". The increasing number of garbage cans that accompanied this kind of suburban development would normally be sufficient incentive to keep bears interested in such a place, but it was not enough for Ralph. He had been having more and more run-ins with dogs, motorcycles, sheriff's deputies and rifle-toting woodsmen. Mostly it was the sheer press of humanity that had finally driven the old bear and his small grandson to seek refuge in a less crowded environment.

Ralph had appealed to me for help, and in a moment of weakness I agreed to transport the two bears the forty miles to the Olympic National Park where they might be free of the encroachment of civilization. Ralph had heard that there were opportunities in the park for an enterprising bear such as himself; that a wealth of ursine companionship was available and, as the deciding inducement, he learned that bear hunting was not allowed. Legal hunting, at least.

Duffy had mentioned on his postcard that I should come to the "same place", which I took to mean a spot on an old logging road a couple of miles beyond the causeway at the upper end of the lake near a stand of small second growth trees where I had left the bears years earlier. There we had found a small clearing where we held our last meeting and said our goodbyes. I could still picture the place exactly, though I doubted it would look the same. The backwoods in this country can change in a very short time. It's the temperate zone equivalent of a tropical jungle, and things grow fast here in our well-watered climate.

As the time for my departure approached I began to have second thoughts about the whole idea. There was no way of letting Duffy know that I was coming, or when to look for me. I pictured myself sitting up there in that little clearing, day after long day, waiting for one of the bears to happen by — a truly fruitless prospect on the face of it. Ralph probably didn't even know that Duffy had sent for me, and he wasn't likely to have any interest in seeing me again anyway. The whole scheme seemed to be a dumb idea. Then I reminded myself that practically everything that I'd ever done with those bears was a dumb idea. Why should I change now?

On the morning of the twenty-first of April — a day that lives in the memory, if not in infamy — I packed a lunch, put the three Shakespeare volumes in a plastic grocery bag and set off on my quest to locate Duffy. I couldn't help but believe that Columbus started out to discover the New World with more assurance of success than I had.

The beauty of the lovely spring day was awesome. The trees and roadside vegetation were stirring with new life. Buds were swelling, the leaves of the willow and alder unfurling — "the season all aglow" as the poet would have said it. As I skirted the lake, sparkling there in the morning brilliance with a hint of breeze ruffling its surface, my gloomier thoughts resurfaced, distracting me from the beauty of the scene. Somewhere between the bright blue of the lake and the snowcapped peaks in the distance, in the dark green tangle of forest lying between them, I pictured a small black bear sitting on a stump in a little clearing of second growth evergreens, maybe reading a book, and awaiting the appearance of a friend from another day, summoned for purposes yet to be revealed.

My poetic reverie ended abruptly as the paved road became an unimproved gravel track, and I was jolted into reality by the first serious chuckhole. Enough of daydreaming, I told myself, it was time to pay attention to driving and navigation. The splendors of nature would have to wait. Over the bridge and up the hill I went, closing in on my destination. As the road climbed steeply and narrowed ominously I realized that on the right side the terrain dropped off in a sheer cliff. How come I hadn't remembered this treacherous spot from my earlier trip up here?

Perhaps because I had an excited pre-adolescent cub bear on

the seat beside me in the cab of the truck, and Old Ralph in the back with his big snout stuck through the little window, breathing on my neck and giving me advice and instructions. Under the circumstances I suppose I might have overlooked the fact that between my tires and the edge of a 200-foot cliff was a maximum of about two and a half feet of solid roadway. It was way too narrow to turn around so I proceeded on hoping that up ahead somewhere was the place I was looking for. If I actually found Macduff up here I was going to insist we find another meeting place.

The farther I drove the more convinced I became that I was on the wrong road, and had there been room, I would have turned the car around and headed out. Duffy would be out of luck. Rounding another curve the terrain leveled out and I began to breathe easier. Up ahead was the kind of vegetation that three years earlier would have been about what I was looking for — small trees about ten years old, on land that had been logged within the past fifteen years or so, maybe forty acres of it. This had to be the place I decided, but I couldn't see a way to get into it. The access road was overgrown.

I slowed the car and proceeded carefully, trying to peer into the thicket with little success since the growth was extremely dense. Eventually I reached the end of the scrub trees and was mightily relieved to see that there would be room for me to turn the car around. Up ahead the road narrowed again, continuing to climb, and not too far in the distance I could see snow. There was no way I was going any further, afraid I'd get stuck and would have to back out. Trying to follow my tracks out backwards on a very narrow road was not a pleasant prospect for a fellow whose neck was none too limber. Frankly I was beginning to seriously wonder why an old guy would be up here by himself in the first place, limber neck or not. Why was it that I got myself into these uncomfortable situations whenever bears were involved?

Turning the car around, I pulled as close to the side of the road as possible. I shut the engine off and then, without knowing quite why and feeling a tad stupid, I blew two short blasts on the horn. I guessed this was to let Duffy know I had arrived should he be around. I got out of the car and looked off to the east, dumbfounded by the magnificent panorama spread out before me. I was standing at the edge of a sheer rocky cliff overlooking a part of the national park where trees were never cut and where highways did not go. Snow-topped peaks were at my back and to the left. Off to my right and far in the distance, the deep blue of the lake reminded me of the path I had come. Except for the barely audible sound of the river in the valley far below, the silence was absolute, without even the usual mutter of a distant jet plane to corrupt it. The breeze was sweet, the air warm and fragrant.

The whole spectacular vista had seemingly been placed there exclusively for my pleasure. I was the only human there to view it; it was mine alone. I'm convinced that for a time my senses were so overwhelmed by the natural splendor of it all that I actually forgot why I had gone up there. With a need to relax my frazzled nerves I crossed the road and sat down on a log to rest and absorb the magnificence of it all, the sun warm on my back. Thoughts of problem bears, treacherous mountain roads, and the mundane cares of the world receded from my consciousness. All seemed so pleasantly right that for a few minutes I might actually have experienced what the mystics call an "out of body" experience. I seemed to be floating silently and effortlessly over the vast landscape, riding the thermals like a bird, the warm air carrying me higher, ever higher, unvexed and serene. Soon I became aware of a large eagle flying off my left wing. He swiveled his great white head in my direction.

"Well, old man. How do you like my view?" he asked. Funny, I thought, in a detached sort of way. I would have imagined that an eagle would have a squeakier voice. This one sounded more like a bear.

The eagle faded away and I began to sense that something was not right. My arm had gone to sleep; my rump was sore. I moved to ease my discomfort and discovered I was still sitting on a log overlooking the valley. Had I heard a voice? Where had the eagle gone?

"Hey, dude. How do you like the view?" the voice repeated. I turned my head toward the car behind me. There was nothing unusual to be seen, but that voice had certainly sounded familiar.

As my wits slowly re-gathered themselves, comprehension returned. "Is that you, Duffy? Come out here where I can see you. You're the guy I'm looking for."

A pair of hairy ears appeared over the trunk of the car. They looked like bear ears, but they couldn't belong to Duffy, he wasn't that tall. As I watched, the rest of the head popped into view, and I could see that it **was** Duffy, and he wasn't even standing on his hind legs. Wow, how the little fellow had grown! He came out from behind the car, grinning broadly, and there was absolutely no question about it. He had that big old sloppy grin that I remembered so well; his mouth was open and he was making happy

14

little grunting sounds. He shuffled across the road in that high-rumped, pigeon-toed gait that bears have, and as he approached he lifted up on his hind legs so that I could see the unmistakable Duffy trademark — that inverted white crescent on his chest.

Stretching to his full height and with just a bit more exuberance than I might have preferred, he threw his paws around me and planted a cold, wet slobbery kiss on my cheek. While he was still not as tall as I was, Duffy surely outweighed me. Standing uncomfortably close to the edge of the cliff I managed to get a good grip of the fur on his back and survived the greeting. I wiped my face with my bandana. Duffy didn't seem to notice.

"You got my message. Way to go, man!" he blurted, in a voice much deeper than when I last had seen him. I supposed this was the adolescent bear voice, not quite the deep basso profundo of the full-grown bear, like Ralph, but commanding authority nonetheless. "This is cool, man. I've been up here watching for you for most of a month. I guessed you probably weren't coming. What took you so long?"

"Your message was confusing. I couldn't figure it out. I don't even know how it got to me. You've got a lot of explaining to do, Duffy, my boy."

"Did you know you've been sitting there fast asleep for the last fifteen minutes?" asked the bear, ignoring my questions. "You're lucky you didn't roll over the cliff. It's a long way to the bottom. You gotta be more careful."

"Speaking of which," I said, "I don't remember the road being so close to the edge. Is this the same place I left you?"

"Yeah, it's the same place all right, except the loggers moved the road. Wanted to make room for more trees, I guess. They never stop messing around with things up here." Duffy sounded a lot like Ralph, who seldom missed a chance to criticize "human beans" about anything they did.

"Where's Ralph? Didn't he come with you?"

"Old Grandpa doesn't climb hills any more if he can help it. Anyway, I think he's got one of his meetings today. What day is it?" asked Duffy, with apparent disinterest.

"It's Tuesday."

"Tuesday? Yeah, today is COB day. He's at the COB meeting."

"COB? What's COB?" I asked.

"Stands for Council of Bears. It's an organization that Ralph started. Naturally, he's the head of it, along with everything else in the park," said Duffy, with a hint of annoyance.

"Do you mean to tell me that Ralph is running the park?"

"No, not the whole park, just the bears in the park, which is bad enough. Did you bring the books?" Duffy didn't seem to want to talk about Ralph.

"Well," I said, "I hope you were talking about the Shakespeare books you left in the truck when I brought you two up here. They're in the car."

"Way to go, dude! I haven't found much to read up here. Just what I get out of the ranger's garbage can. Mostly it's triplicate copies of blockbusters like 'rainfall totals during September and October, 1999'. Real stimulating stuff. I read a few newspapers — mostly what campers leave behind. Trouble is they use the paper to start their campfires with, so I don't always get the whole story on things. If they use the front page to get the fire going, all I get is the

16

'continued on page six' stuff on the back pages. I have to guess at a lot of things. It doesn't matter much, I don't suppose. Most of the bears up here can't even read. They don't know diddly-squat about anything. Never even heard of Shakespeare, if you can believe that."

"Too bad," I said. "There's nothing worse than a bunch of provincial bears."

I think Duffy missed my whimsy, as usual.

"I'll get the books." Duffy quickly shuffled over to the car and opened the back door with practiced ease, as if he'd been doing it all of his life. He rummaged around in the rear seat and backed out with the shopping bag hanging from his lower jaw. His eyes squinted with pleasure as he sauntered back across the narrow road.

"Good man," he said with feeling. "This is the best thing that's happened to me since that lady ran off and forgot her copy of *Lady Chatterley's Lover* on the camp table."

I was sure I already knew the answer to my next question. "Dare I ask what caused her to run off?"

"Let's just say that I have adapted to my new environment," he said, with a look of innocence. "We ought to get off the road here. Go over into the trees. Sometimes those rangers get to spying around with binoculars. I have a feeling some of them don't like me much. Not long ago I saw myself referred to in one of their reports as an 'adolescent bear with proclivities toward detrimental and inappropriate behavior'. It was written by an apprentice ranger named Pinky Upton who used a lot of big words to impress his boss. Pinky was a college kid, and scared of everything in the woods. We used to call him 'Pucker' Upton. He'd pucker up if he came across a tree frog. Bears really freaked him out. He didn't last very long. The rangers gave him a bad progress report; said maybe he had more aptitude as a bank teller. Most of the rangers are okay, though. I help 'em out when I can."

I was still trying to picture Duffy helping out the rangers as he motioned for me to follow him across the road. "We'll get out of sight here — out of harm's way. Actually we aren't in the park right here anyway, so the rangers don't have any say. The forest rangers do, but not park rangers. Just the same, it behooves a bear to be cautious. You know the bear motto, 'Danger is everywhere. Caution counts'."

Behooves, I thought. How many bears would use a word like behooves? Came from Shakespeare no doubt.

"What happens if somebody comes up here and sees my car?" I asked. "What'll I tell 'em?"

"From what I remember about you from the old days you'll have no trouble thinking of something. Tell 'em you're an ecology professor looking for mushrooms, or you're a biologist studying beetle bugs. That's always a good scam. You remember the sheriff, don't you? Sheriff Edred, or whatever his name was. You flummoxed him real good."

"That's a nice word, Duffy. You Shakesbears never cease to amaze me. For a species of animal not known for its verbosity you and your old grandpa do pretty well. Flummoxed, indeed."

"Grandma Ophelia started it all, you know. You've gotta admit reading the Bard helps increase one's vocabulary. I'm not sure he used 'flummox' though. I don't remember ever seeing it. He'd say 'confusion worse confounded' perhaps, but not flummoxed."

"Whatever you say, Duffy," I said.

18

We found a little spot where there were some fairly large trees. Duffy marched around in a small circle smashing down grass and weeds. Then he sat down, his back against a hemlock. "Set a spell, old man. Rest, we'll talk."

For the first time I noticed that Duffy was wearing one of those fanny pack things around his middle. "Where'd you get that thing?" I asked.

"Oh, a guy went off and left it in his camp. It looked kinda handy so I saved it. It really isn't big enough, though. I can barely get the belt buckled."

"I don't suppose he took off in a hurry when he left?"

"He seemed like he was in a hurry. I smiled at him but he was having trouble getting his car started. His wife was in the back seat yelling at him, which wasn't helping. I guess he didn't need this thing too much — he never came back. It's kind of handy to carry stuff in. I'll put my books in it."

"Duffy," I suggested, "show me what kind of smile you gave him." Turning to me, he wrinkled up his top lip and displayed a magnificent set of canine teeth.

"Just as I thought," I said. "You know you're going to ruin the reputation of this park, Duffy. That 'grin' of yours would do credit to one of those Hollywood horror movies. Didn't Ralph ever describe the concept of the nuisance bear to you? You're apt to find yourself way up in the backcountry of the park with a collar and a radio around your neck. Relocated bears don't get a second chance, you know. It's one strike and you're out, man. National parks take a dim view of nuisance bears. They scare away the customers. And that reminds me, Duffy, whatever became of the old bear named

Pixley Poomer? He got darted by a ranger while he was halfway inside a garbage can down in Hoodsport. Ralph said he was on the payroll up here. He had a daughter named Peaches. You remember her?"

Duffy brightened at the name. "Sure I know Peaches. Peaches and I are very good friends. She's the mother of the twins."

"What twins?"

"My twins," said the young bear with pride. "Dromio and Luciana."

"You've got children? Cubs? Little Duffy has babies? Pardon my flabbergast, Duffy. I still think of you as a cub yourself."

"Bears get started on these things early. The twins are over a year old."

"That's their names? Dromio and Luciana? What kind of names are those?"

"They come from Shakespeare's *Comedy of Errors.*"

"Where do they live?" I asked.

"Over near Mt. Rose somewhere. I'm not exactly sure."

"What do you mean you're not sure? Don't you ever see them?"

"No, we're bears, you know. Not people. We do things differently. Men bears are just around to get things started, if you get my meaning. They don't hang around."

"I know people like that," I said.

Duffy chuckled. At least it sounded like a chuckle.

"How is Peaches? You still see her don't you?"

"Well, yes," said Duffy. "We try to see each other once a year, if you know what I mean."

"And how about the old man? Old Pixley? Is he still around?" I asked.

"Naw, Pixley got so old and mangy he couldn't even scare the tourists anymore. Broke his heart. Lost all his zest for life and he just walked off into the sunset. Nobody ever saw him again. We all thought that was a noble thing for him to do. Of course, the way I heard it the rangers were talking about 'putting him down', as they say, so he just beat 'em to it."

"Duffy, there's a notebook in the bag with the Shakespeare stuff. I brought it up to take notes. I'm getting so I can't remember anything any more. I've got to write this stuff down so I don't forget it." He handed me the notebook. I found a pen in my pocket and poised to write. "What did you say you named your kids?"

"Dromio, that's the boy, and Luciana, she's the girl. They're twins. Gimme the book. I'll write it for you." He scribbled the names in the notebook with a flourish and gave it back to me. The names were written in perfectly legible English. Duffy noticed the look of amazement on my face.

"Been practicing," he said. "I use the tables down at the campground when nobody is around. It's kinda fun. I copy the words off the newspapers. There's not much else to do around here in the off-season."

"What's the off-season?" I asked.

"It's when all the tourists leave. There's nobody in the campground then. I have the place pretty much to myself."

"Don't you guys hibernate in the winter?" I asked.

"Oh, yeah, sometimes when it gets real cold. I have a place underneath the ranger's storehouse where I go. It's cozy under there."

"What about Ralph?"

"Ralph has a cave up the river a couple of miles. Old Pixley Poomer used to live there. It's all fitted out real fancy. He's got a big log in there fixed up like the chair in that statue you made of him down on the highway. The old fool sits up there like Napoleon, giving orders to everybody. He's the self-appointed boss of all the bears in the park, and he's got the big head, let me tell you. He set up this thing he calls the Council of Bears. Made himself President. COB, it's called. There are some bears in the park that say COB stands for Conceited Old Bastard. They don't like taking orders from Ralph. Say he's gotten too big for his britches."

"You told me about COB. This doesn't sound like the old Ralph I used to know," I said.

"You'd be surprised what a little power does to a bear," lamented Duffy.

"People, too, I might add. Maybe I ought to have a word with him," I said.

"I suppose it wouldn't hurt," said Duffy, with some sadness, "but not today. He's very busy. In executive session, making new rules. Passing ordinances, as he calls it. Remember how he used to gripe about environmentalists and bureaucrats? Well it seems like he's joined them."

"What a shame," I said. "I think I liked him better the other way. Before I forget, Duffy. Do you have any idea how your postcard got into the lap of the Ralph statue down at my place?"

Duffy looked puzzled. "I mailed it to you. I put it in the box over at the ranger's house a long time ago."

"What kind of an address did you put on it?" I asked.

"I just wrote 'bareplace, road 106'. Everybody knows where that is."

"Well, not exactly, Duffy. I doubt the post office knows where that is." I told Duffy about the puzzling note from Fred.

"That's that sheriff guy. He comes up here to drink coffee with the rangers sometimes." Duffy's face lit up. "I bet he took it down to your place."

"That's what I suspect, but I don't know why he'd do me any favors. You remember how he chased us all over the place a long time ago?"

"Yeah, he's kind of excitable, but he's not such a bad guy. Just lazy is all."

"Here's another question for you, Duffy. Since you seem to have learned to write as well as I can, why did you use that schoolboy scrawl and bad spelling on the card?"

"I had to write that way or you wouldn't have known who it was from," he said.

"Makes good sense and you're absolutely right. I wouldn't have guessed. That's good thinking." I noticed Duffy sniffing the air, his nose twitching. He was watching the edge of the clearing.

"Does the sheriff bother you bears?" I asked.

"Naw, he's a county guy. He doesn't have any authority around here. Anyway, it's illegal to mess with bears in a national park unless you work for the federal government. Then it's okay. Someday I'll show you all the federal regulations about bears. You wouldn't believe them." A young deer walked into our clearing and stood quietly watching us.

"You knew that deer was coming didn't you? How do you do

that?" I asked.

"Shoot, man, I'm a bear. I have to know that kind of stuff. That's why I have this big nose."

"Can you talk to deer, Duffy?" I asked.

"Deer don't have any smarts. Doesn't do any good to talk to them. Keep watching now, there's a coyote about to show up. He's tracking the deer." The deer bolted off through the trees, her tail aloft, and was instantly out of sight. A coyote trotted into view.

"She went that way, man," said Duffy to the coyote, pointing in the wrong direction. The coyote curled his lip in a canine version of a sneer, and followed in the direction the deer had gone. "Coyotes are jerks. They eat bear cubs, you know. They do if they can catch them, that is."

"I'm sorry to hear that," I said.

"Don't be sorry. We eat coyotes, too, when we can catch them. You have to be pretty hungry, though. They're plenty tough unless you can get 'em when they're real young."

I didn't tell Duffy that I already knew most of what he was telling me from my reading on the subject of bear behavior. I thought it time to change the subject.

"Tell me about your grandpa, Duffy. What's he up to besides being self-important?"

Macduff shifted nervously, almost as though he didn't want to talk about him.

"You know how things go with bears during the rutting season, don't you?" Duffy seemed embarrassed.

"Sure," I said. "I bet I know what you're leading up to. Ralph is the big dude now, right? The dominant bear? Makes some problems for you I suppose."

"'Problems hardly covers the matter. Grandpa damned near killed me last season. He was trying to have his way with Peaches, you know. That's why I sent her up to Mt. Rose. Otherwise those cubs would have been his, not mine. Now that I think of it they may not be mine anyway. I don't know why his behavior should surprise me. That's just the way we bears are. The big dude runs the show; he gets to service all the ladies if he can manage it. That's the reason old Pixley Poomer left. He was head bear until Ralph showed up. To be sure, Pixley was over-the-hill, but he was still in charge. Ralph beat him up during the rut of '01 and broke the old bear's spirit. He's just too damned bossy, even when it's not rutting season."

"Do you think Ralph would talk to me?" I asked. "We used to be pretty good friends. Would it be safe?"

Duffy pulled up a handful of new grass and munched on it. "Oh, yeah, he'd be glad to see you. He still talks about you all the time. You're the reason he's the big expert on people matters at the COB meetings. You'll probably have to make an appointment, though. I'll see if I can work it out."

"Do you belong to COB, Duffy?"

"No, it's mostly just for the old geezers. Any of us can go but all they do is sit around and talk and complain. They never accomplish anything, but it makes them feel important. Last meeting they were talking about garbage again."

"You got a garbage problem up here, too?" I asked in surprise.

"The old bears are complaining that it's too hard to get the lids off the cans. They don't seem to realize that your government has spent years trying to invent cans that bears can't get into. Bear proof, they call them. Costing 'em millions of dollars. The old bears say they'd take care of the garbage problem free of charge if they could just get into the cans. Save the government a bundle."

"I can imagine how far that went," I said sardonically. "Garbage is a very serious business with governments. And the untidy nature of the bear family as a whole is well known to the park bureaucracy. I read a 'position paper' on that very subject once."

"Yeah, I read it too," said Duffy, "but it was about Yellowstone bears. They're a slovenly bunch. Our campground is very neat. Ralph has passed an anti–littering ordinance. We have to tidy up after ourselves. That's another reason the bears hereabouts don't like him."

I couldn't think of a response. I was trying to grasp the concept of a tidy bear. It appeared that Ralph had indeed gone over to the enemy.

We sat in silence, soaking up the warmth of the sun. It occurred to me that it must be getting along toward afternoon, and I remembered that I had brought along a lunch for myself.

"I've got a lunch with me, Duffy. You want to share?"

"What have you got?" he asked, with interest.

"I've got the ever popular peanut butter and jelly sandwich. I've got an apple, a banana and two Oreo cookies."

"Apple would taste good," said Duffy brightly.

"It's in the front seat of the car. Can you get it?"

Duffy chuckled. "Now there's a truly dumb question," said the young bear on his way to the car. "I check out the contents of cars in the park all the time. I'm an expert."

"Yeah," I said, "I should have known." Duffy returned with the

26

lunch. As I ate the sandwich the bear downed the apple in one bite, and began to eye the banana, his nose twitching.

"Go ahead, eat the banana. This sandwich is enough for me. If I had any idea I was going to find you I would have brought more food."

Duffy consumed the banana, hide and all. "That's okay," he said. "The grass is coming up nicely this year. There's plenty to eat." He peered at me expectantly. "An Oreo might taste good though."

"Help yourself, but just take one. I have to have the other for my dessert." He smiled and neatly picked one cookie from the bag. I was amazed at how dexterous and delicate Duffy had become in manipulating his claws.

"By the way, Duffy. Did you know I wrote a book about you and Ralph? About when you guys lived down near my place?"

"Really?" he said, without much surprise. "Ralph always said you were writing something. You ever get it finished?"

"Yep, it's all done. I've got some copies in the back of my car. Want to see it?"

"Sure I want to see it," said the bear, rising to his feet and starting toward the car. "Getting into a car trunk is a little harder than opening a door, though. Sometimes we do a bit of damage. You know, scratches and things. Maybe you better open it yourself."

We walked to the car. I used the key, raised the lid and gave Duffy a copy of *Ralph, Conversations With A Bear*. For the first time since we'd met he showed genuine excitement.

"Neat," he said, "pictures and everything. Can I have it?"

"Sure, you can have it. Here's a copy for Ralph, too." I gave him another book.

"Oh, man, Grandpa is going to wet his pants when he sees this. Did you put in that part about when you brought us up here in the truck?" Duffy was doing what appeared to be an excited little two-step.

"Yeah, Duff. It's all in there. Even the part about you stealing the computer and Ralph's collision with the motorcycle. Probably some stuff in there you didn't even know about."

Duffy was rapidly turning pages and exclaiming about the photos. "Here's the part about that nutcase Oddball the environmentalist. This is neat, man. Grandpa won't believe it. When he shows this to the old dudes at the COB meeting he's going to puff up like a poisoned pup. He'll really be Mister Big now."

Duffy was seated on the ground, racing through the pages. "You've even got that poem I wrote. This is awesome, dude. Far out!"

It was good to see the young bear so excited. Duffy hadn't seemed to be his usual exuberant self this morning. He seemed bored and listless.

"Hey, I just had an idea," said Duffy breathlessly. "How about you leave that notebook with me and I'll write some more things? You know, about what's going on up here in the park. Maybe about Gramps and his COB buddies. There's stuff around here you wouldn't believe. Maybe tell about what goes on during the rut? Man, I could break this place wide open. Whataya think, dude?"

"Dang, Duffy. I just came up here for a little visit. I'm not planning to get myself into another big project. You can have the notebook. I'll even give you the pen, but leave me out of your plans. I don't have another book in me, man."

"The book's in **me** maybe. Let me give it a try. Whataya say, old buddy?" I'd never seen the young bear so exercised. It was as though he had suddenly found a mission in life. His enthusiasm was wonderful to see, but I was just a mite fearful that I was about to get conned into something I didn't want to be a part of.

"You take the notebook and write all you want, Duffy. If I get back up here sometime I'll see what you've done. Beyond that I have no plans."

"It's a deal, dude. We'll **make** plans."

For the next hour and a half I sat in the grass of our secluded retreat in the high reaches of the Olympic National Forest listening in amazement while my newly energized friend Macduff outlined grandiose plans for the writing of what was to be an exposé of the lives of black bears in the national park.

"This is uncharted ground," he proclaimed. "I will spare nothing. The secrets of bear life will be revealed in all their raw power. Nothing left out. Nothing held back."

His passionate pacing and his histrionic gesturing brought back memories of his grandfather Ralph in the old days, midst one of his tirades on political correctness. Quite frankly, I was awed by Duffy's display of emotion and fervor. I also wondered if he had been reading too many headlines from the National Enquirer, or maybe book advertisements from the back pages of True Romance magazines.

Eventually Macduff paused to catch his breath and I was able to fit in a question. "Forgive me for asking, Duffy, but where do you plan to market this blockbuster? You recently told me that none of your friends know how to read."

"Sell it to **your** friends, man. I bet there's big interest among human beans about the secret, untold affairs of bears. Hey, that might be a good title, *Bear Affairs*. Whataya think?" he took a new breath. "And when the bear population learns that the book is available they might just want to learn to read. Better yet, I could hold classes and read the book to them. Call it 'Duffy's Book Club' or 'Duffy's Literary Hour'. Give the bears something to do besides going to those dumb COB meetings."

I knew that I had to act quickly to head off any ideas that I would be an active participant in Duffy's cockeyed plans, but I didn't want to discourage the young bear from testing his creative wings. I'll give encouragement, I thought, but not offer help. Passive participation will be my role. Even that could get me too deeply involved, but I was willing to chance it.

Duffy was already scribbling entries in his notebook in a generous scrawl. "Better try to write smaller, Duff, you're going to have that book filled before I can get up here with another one."

"I can get lots of paper out of the ranger's trash. You know how government people are. They write everything in triplicate and then throw two copies away. I can write on the backsides of their statistical reports. I'll get the government to supply my paper."

I noticed that the afternoon sun was approaching the tops of the mountains off to the west and realized it was time for me to go. When the shadows arrive in the mountain valleys, darkness comes quickly.

"Duffy," I said, "when I come up here again we've got to have a different place to meet. It's too hard to get up here. This road is no fun to drive on. Where can we go instead?"

"I just thought of the name of a chapter," my young friend said, ignoring my question. "How does 'Sensuality on the Slopes' sound? That would be a chapter about Peaches and me on Mt. Rose. Maybe I'll take some ideas from *Romeo and Juliet.* Jazz it up a little."

"Duffy, did you hear what I said? About a place to meet?"

The bear was clearly more interested in composing an outline to his upcoming masterpiece than in working out the logistics of our next meeting. He reluctantly tore himself away from his work.

"Okay, yeah, I know just the place, but we'll have to drive. I'll get in the back."

Oh God, I thought. I was flooded with memories of the last few miles of our drive up here three years earlier. Duffy, a lot smaller then, was sitting on the seat beside me in the little pickup, steaming up the windows and taking up all the space. The old bear was in the back, breathing on my neck. Bear breath, I found, is of about the same essence as dog breath.

"How far do we have to go?" I asked, apprehensively.

"It's not far," said Duffy. "Just this side of Big Creek Park. It'll take ten minutes." He put his notebook and pen in his fanny pack with his other books, opened the rear door and tried to get comfortable in the back of my car while still chattering away about chapter names and lurid plot lines.

The problem of transporting a bear in a passenger car should be immediately apparent to anyone who understands a bear's anatomy. Bears have very short back legs attached to a long body that

31

connects with front legs that are perhaps even shorter. This arrangement facilitates a bear's natural gait, which is a four-legged walk often called a lumber, a trot or a gallop. While a bear is perfectly capable of walking on its hind legs, it is not its preferred method of locomotion. Standing up, to a bear, is for looking over the tops of things or for reaching stuff on trees, like apples, or for frightening people. A bear that tries to run on two legs hops along comically, like a crow. Speed becomes a problem, and I think I might even be able to outrun a bear on two legs, although I don't plan to try.

So when Duffy climbed into the back of my car and tried to sit on the seat his head hit the ceiling and his feet barely touched the floor, a very awkward and uncomfortable position. I suggested he lie down on his back, which he did, but then, of course, he couldn't see out the windows. He had to describe the route I was to take to our new rendezvous spot, which we found without incident, although I had to tell my friend to get his head down when we passed a couple of cars. The spot he selected appeared to be an abandoned section of an old road with a turnaround at the end that would do nicely as a secluded place for future meetings. I stopped the car.

"How does this sound?" asked Duffy, excitedly. "*Desire in the Dogwoods: Secrets of the Springtime Rut.* Oh, man, this is great."

"Okay, Duffy. If this is the place, you hop out and I'll be on my way." I opened the door and the bear backed awkwardly out of the car. He seemed to be trying to brush detritus off the seat. "Never mind that, Duffy. I'll clean things up when I get home."

I had visions of those big non-retractable claws of his tearing furrows in my upholstery. "Could you put the notebook away for a minute, Duffy, and answer a couple of questions for me?"

"Sure thing," he said, stuffing the book back into his fanny pack. "Fire away."

"Well, here's the problem," I said, seriously. "Since I have no sure way of ever getting a hold of you, suppose we set a date, and I'll meet you here in this spot at ten o'clock in the morning. Unless it's raining, that is, in which case I won't be here."

"Those sound like the kind of muddle-headed plans that I might come up with," said Duffy. "Can't you do better than that? Why don't you just give me your telephone number, and I'll call you when I need you?"

"How are you going to do that?" I asked, as Duffy began to dig around in his pack. I shouldn't have been surprised when he retrieved a cell phone so small that it was barely visible in his huge paw.

"Where in the world did you come up with that?" I asked him.

"I think it was in a BMW convertible. Kids are careless these days. They don't really know the value of things. They went to bed in their tent without putting the top up on their car. That was really dumb, don't you think? They should be more careful. All the signs around here warn about the bad habits of bears. They ought to know better." Duffy seemed to be doing his best to make it sound like it wasn't his fault that they had lost their telephone.

"Did they leave in a big hurry like the guy with the fanny pack?" I asked him.

"Actually the last time I saw them they were over at the ranger's cabin reporting the loss of their telephone. They were talking real loud, and demanding that some action be taken."

33

"Duffy," I said, "I would think that by now you would have worn out your welcome around here. How do you get away with this stuff?"

"I help the rangers a lot. I patrol the campground at night, you know, and make reports to the rangers if anything bad happens — take down license numbers and so on. They appreciate the help."

"Do you report thefts, too, like telephones and such?" I asked.

"Well, yes, usually," said Duffy in his most sanctimonious voice. "But sometimes I have to make a decision about who needs stuff the most. I make my reports based on need. I figure a guy who drives a BMW convertible probably has two or three of those little telephones. He wouldn't hardly miss one of them."

"You're a bear with a high sense of moral duty, Duffy," I said, "a credit to your species. I'll try to remember that if any of my friends plan to visit your campground."

"I do like to think of myself as knowing right from wrong," he remarked, sounding like he really believed it.

"Okay, Duffy, here's my telephone number," I said, scribbling in his notebook. "But just in case your batteries run down or something, I'll put the date in here, too."

I took a small calendar from my wallet. "Let's say Tuesday, June 18th. We'll meet right here at ten o'clock unless it's raining. If it is, I'll come on the first dry day. How's that?"

"That's no good. Tuesday is the day COB meets. Ralph won't be available."

"Okay, make it Wednesday the 19th then."

"There's just one other problem," said Duffy seriously.

"What's that?" I asked.

"That's in the middle of rutting season. I'm usually pretty busy."

"Oh, hell, take half a day off. You can spare that much time."

As I started the car and prepared to leave Duffy had his notebook out composing chapter headings for his book.

"Hey," he said, crow-hopping alongside the car, "how does this sound, 'Dominant Bears Do It Best' or 'Coupling in the Conifers'? Whattaya think, dude?"

CHAPTER THREE
Roadside Follies

As so often happens, that beautiful day in April was followed by weeks of drizzle and rain. Thoughts of bears and the affairs of bears faded from my mind. To be sure, as soon as I had arrived home from my trip to the park I had gone straight to my kitchen calendar and put a big circle around June 19th, writing "Duffy" in prominent letters. And because it was so far in the future, and making allowances for my unreliable memory, I also made note of the date in all of my appointment books, of which I have several.

My daily routine around the place was mostly uneventful. My utopian plan, which was to quit making those bear signs as soon as I finished the book about Ralph, had backfired badly. I found that the book had only increased interest in this roadside attraction and, far from being shut of it, I realized that I was probably stuck with the job for the rest of my natural life. When a young kid stopped by to say he'd love to make up quotations for me, I couldn't believe my good fortune. I was sure that my sign writing days were numbered.

"Son," I said, "you've got yourself a job." And I never heard from him again.

So I put up a sign that said "SIGN WRITER WANTED" to no avail. In desperation I finally stopped changing the signs, leaving the same one up for over a week, and got calls to see if I had died. And so, in the interest of neighborhood harmony I labored on, putting up new witticisms every three or four days, but original ones got ever harder to come by.

One morning in May, in a fit of frivolity, I raised a sign that read "FOREPLAY BEGINS AT BREAKFAST, SHE SAID", a line from a novel I read once. While I felt good about my daring and creativity, my timing couldn't have been worse. I was standing in the doorway of the shop admiring the sign when a car went slowly by, stopped and backed up. I immediately recognized the driver as being Twyla Pinchly, one of the area's most determined Christian crusaders, and an unusually prolific and quarrelsome writer of "letters to the editor". Naively thinking that she wished to buy a book I put on my most welcoming grin, and prepared to be congratulated.

Twyla, a woman of considerable age (roughly matching my own), alighted from her machine dressed in her usual bright red coat, matching hat and sensible shoes. She approached with purpose as I smiled broadly, hoping she'd notice my newly restored front teeth.

"Mr. Merrill," she said, with a bit more severity than I would have expected, "I have read your book and thought most of it was cute."

"Thank you, Mrs. Pinchly," I replied with appreciation, although "cute" was not exactly the result I had been aspiring to when I wrote it.

She rushed right on, "However I urge you not to let success cloud your judgment. The sign you have just put up is offensive to Christian sensibilities."

"I'm sorry to hear that. What is it that you dislike about it?" I asked, affecting surprise.

"That word, there," she huffed, pointing to the sign. I knew full well which word she was talking about, but I was hoping to get her to say it right out loud.

"Which word, Mrs. Pinchly?" I asked, in all innocence.

"I think you know which word. That first word is distasteful." She made a face as if eating a sour pickle.

"It has overtones which are contrary to God's commandments. It is obscene." She fairly spat the words. Mrs. Pinchly was working herself into high dudgeon.

"I am sorry you feel that way Twyla," I said, a note of earnest concern in my voice. I used her first name thinking it might mollify her. "This is no more than my subtle way of encouraging men to be nice to their wives. Where's the harm in that? I'll bet there are men going by here right now wondering what I'm trying to say, and when they get down the road a ways it'll come to them. Something they probably haven't thought of before. Look at it as my own little contribution to domestic harmony." My attempt to mollify had misfired.

Mrs. Pinchly continued to fume. "That can be done in better ways. Think of the children going past here on the school bus who will read this. You cannot imagine the corrupting influence of such things." She was reaching into her handbag. "Please take some time to read this pamphlet," she said, handing me one of those little tracts that evangelists always seem to have handy. "It will improve your thinking, and give you a clearer vision of what is appropriate in the short messages you write on your signs. I will pray for you. Praise God." She turned on her heel and marched back to her car without even telling me to have a nice day, which, in today's discourse, I consider to be downright un-American.

38

The pamphlet was entitled *Commandments of the Lord, The Road to Salvation*, which redirects those of us who are in danger of being "lost" to the path of righteousness. The book looked like heavy going to me, so I put it in my pile of "to do" tasks and prepared to go over to the house and rest.

Just as I started across the road my friend Phineas drove up, his dog Maximo in the co-pilot's seat. A tall, stooped citizen with a great shock of white hair, he was a frequent visitor. Maximo, or Max as he was known, was his constant companion. A big hairy wolfhound of uncertain lineage, he sat right beside Phineas on the front seat. Unless you looked carefully you would swear that it could be Phineas's wife riding along with him, though I wasn't sure Phineas was even married. The dog, being only slightly shorter  than the old man, kept his eyes fixed on the road, as would any dutiful spouse. I often thought that if they were to switch places, Max would be perfectly capable of driving the car. Phineas visited me at the shop on a regular basis to discuss politics and world affairs, though I had no idea why. It probably had something to do with the signs I put up on the bear, many of which were uncomplimentary remarks about politicians. As he came in and seated himself on my visitor's stool I told him about my recent encounter with Twyla Pinchly.

Phineas was from Maine and he had a quaint "down East" accent — a difficult accent to put into print "Yeah, old Twyla lives just up the hill from me," he said. "We call her old 'Praise the Lod' Pinchly. Everybody in the neighborhood has one of them handbills like you got theah. She's all the time makin' the pitch to get us all 'saved', but it ain't worked yet for none of us, as I know of. I stated to read the scriptyahs once, like it says. Got bogged down in all them begats in the first chaptah; had to give it up. Did you know theah's some old guy in theah lived nine hundred yeahs? Can you beat that?" Phineas chuckled. "Say, by the way, you know why Twyla always weahs them bright red clothes?"

I told him I had no idea.

"So if Jesus wants help on somethin' and needs her in a hurry, she'll be easy to find," said Phineas with a chuckle. "At least that's how I look at it."

For the next half-hour Phineas filibustered me on the inequity of federal taxes and the incompetence of certain local politicians, while I grunted occasional agreement. Eventually we heard a bark from out in the car.

"Maximo's getting restless. When he makes one bawk like that it means he needs to git to the bathroom. I guess we betta be getting on home," said Phineas.

As he climbed into his car I saw the old fellow studying the bear sign carefully. He rolled down his window. "Say if I get yer meanin' just right, maybe I'll try that. Somethin' I hadn't thought of before. Well you take care of yourself, and be sure to read that little book Twyla gave you. If she stops by again, give her my regawds." He eased his car onto the highway as Max looked intently down the road to make sure no traffic was coming.

Bear matters came up again suddenly as I was resting my eyes on a drizzly afternoon in early June. The phone rang and an unfamiliar gruff voice asked me what I was doing. After several "whats" and a lot of "who is thises" I realized that I was talking to one of the bears, probably Ralph. The caller was nearly impossible to understand, and I suspected that the older bear was using Duffy's little cell phone, which would come nowhere near to reaching from his ear to his mouth. When I told him that I couldn't understand what he was saying he raised his voice until he was fairly shouting, which did nothing to improve clarity. I thought I did hear the word "book" several times, which gave me a clue what the subject matter was, but I couldn't follow the conversation. Soon there was static and the phone was apparently dropped. Eventually I heard more loud talk and finally what seemed to be Duffy speaking.

Ralph never did get the hang of the telephone.

"Dammit, Ralph, give me the phone. You don't know what you're doing!" I heard more clattering about, some scratching sounds, and finally, silence. After some heavy breathing I was relieved to recognize an intelligible voice. "Ralph, telephones weren't made for bears. For God's sake, don't you understand? They're made for people. A bear telephone would have to be two feet long." I could hear grumbling, and what sounded like a snort or a snuffle.

"Hello, hello, is anybody there?" It was Duffy's voice.

"Is that you, Duffy?" I inquired. "What's going on? What do you want?" It was difficult to know if he could hear me due to all the background noises including more static, some more scratching sounds and undecipherable voices.

"Yeah, it's me. Ralph just left, thank God. Damned old fool thinks he knows everything. He wants you to bring some of his books when you come. He's going to teach some of the old geezers at COB to read. Good joke, eh?"

"Maybe I can spare five, Duffy. Will that be enough?"

"Sure," he said, "but bring more if you can. I'll sell them to the campers".

"You **sell** things to campers?" I asked incredulously. "How do you get away with that?"

"Wouldn't you buy something from a bear if he asked you to?" he asked with a chuckle.

"I hadn't thought of it before, but I suppose I just might. Duffy, you're a scoundrel. Say, how's the rut going?"

I couldn't hear his answer as our connection began to fade. "Hey," he said, "if you have a tape recorder bring it. Another notebook, too." One last word came through which sounded like "nineteenth". The line went dead. Our conversation had ended.

Well, I said to myself, all of this certainly gives me something to think about. My bear friends had apparently gone into some kind of business. Ralph was teaching bears to read and Duffy was selling goods to tourists. I began to see complications, and wondered how long it would be before the park rangers connected all these bear doings to me. So far they had no reason that I knew of to suspect my involvement, but sooner or later one of them was going to get a hold of a copy of that book with my name on it.

Then there was the deputy sheriff connection. Fred Edd, even though he wasn't the brightest bulb in the fixture, must have remembered my previous fraternization with bears down on Highway 106. Maybe it wasn't such a good idea for me to go back up to the park on the nineteenth. I just might be walking into trouble. With a couple of weeks to think it over, I told myself that I had time enough to work things out. Of course I knew full well that there was no way I was **not** going to go. In my softheaded way I imagined that I should get up there, and counsel those two miscreants before they got themselves into deep trouble with the federal government. I was the one who had taken them up there, and I felt responsible for their welfare.

The day was approaching for my return visit to the park, and I realized that I had better start preparing myself for what I might find when I got there. I knew that Duffy's cell phone was probably dead, so I would take along a battery charger on the chance that it might work with his instrument. He had asked for another notebook, which was easy enough, and then, most interestingly, a tape recorder, to what purpose I could not imagine. For a moment I considered taking a six-pack of beer for Ralph, just for old times sake, but discarded the idea. No use getting him hooked on beer again. I'd be running up there all the time to keep him supplied, I thought, remembering how I used to trudge up the hill behind my shop every week carrying a half-case in my backpack. The beer always had to be in longneck bottles, too, which added to the weight. That was before Ralph had learned to drink from cans.

By the second week of June I began watching the long-range weather forecasts to see if rain was expected for the nineteenth. I wondered why I had made such an indefinite plan. It was a dumb idea to say that I would only come if it wasn't raining. Around here it rains most of the time. We probably have more words for rain than Eskimos have for snow. We have mist, heavy fog, drizzle, morning drizzle, occasional showers, intermittent showers, scattered showers, afternoon thundershowers, occasional rain, heavy rain, intermittent heavy rain and torrential downpours. Not only that but in the space of a few miles, or a few hours, we can have some of each. On the nineteenth I might be in a morning drizzle down here at my house, while my bear friends up by the park were in one of those occasional showers that last all day long. I could make the long trip up there for nothing. The best I could do is just wait for the big day, and quit fretting about it.

I reminded myself that Ralph wanted some more copies of "his" book because, according to Duffy, he was planning to teach reading at his COB meetings. The very idea of old Ralph teaching a bunch of elderly, illiterate bears to read struck my fancy. I couldn't help but feel complimented that he was planning to do his teaching from my book rather than from the more poetic prose of Shakespeare, from which he himself had learned to read. Of course this meant that Ralph would be reading from a text in which he was the central character and unqualified hero, which probably had more to do with his choice of books than the fact that I was the author. Clearly there was to be a measure of self-promotion included with his literary lessons, which was typical Ralph. I was trying to figure out a way to be a witness to one of these reading sessions. Maybe Duffy could work something out for me.

In the meantime I watched the weather reports.

CHAPTER FOUR

Alpha Ralph, King of the South End Bears

On the evening of June 18th I tuned into the local forecast and listened attentively as a hyperventilating TV weatherman extolled the virtues of his station's "pinpoint and digitally enhanced Doppler radar satellite images." All of his impressive technology indicated that tomorrow's weather would be "parley" – in their excitement weathermen often have trouble with their elocution – cloudy in the morning hours, with scattered showers and possible afternoon thunderstorms over the Cascades and the Olympics. There seemed to be something for everyone in his forecast and, best of all, no mention of the dreaded word rain.

Although I had planned to be on the road by 9:00 A.M., I overslept, and by the time I left the house I was thirty minutes late. The morning was gray and the radio weatherman was chattering about scattered shower activity, which differed in some way, apparent only to forecasters, from plain old scattered showers.

Because of my late start I didn't have time to put together a lunch, so I threw together a bag of fruit and hit the highway, moving fast. Just before I reached Potlach State Park I saw Deputy Fred Edd headed south, probably going off duty. He was wearing his big sunglasses. Likely as not he didn't recognize me because he didn't respond to my wave, which may have been just as well. I quickly reduced my speed trying not to be too obvious about it. I doubted that Deputy Ed took the time to pinch people for speeding when he was on his way home anyway.

I'm always nervous when I go to my meetings with the bears, and this morning more so than usual. I hadn't laid eyes on Ralph for three years and I didn't know what to expect, although I knew he would be different due simply to the passage of time. I read somewhere that bear years are about the same as dog years, and if that was so, then Ralph was more than twenty years older than the last time I saw him. Lots of changes come about in twenty years, and I already knew that in Duffy's opinion, at least, Ralph had become too self-important. I wondered if I could deflate him without getting myself in trouble. I vowed to proceed cautiously. I would feel my way along.

Just before the turn off to the bumpy, partly hidden road leading to our rendezvous spot I noticed shower activity on my windshield. I crossed my fingers hoping that it wouldn't turn into something more unpleasant, like frequent showers or morning thundershowers, instead of the afternoon thundershowers that we'd been promised. Nothing of the sort happened, in fact I soon saw patches of blue sky and decided to put the prospect of real rain out of my mind.

Getting my car situated out of sight without scratching up the finish in the tangled undergrowth proved to be a problem. I knew that I must get the car well-hidden. Fairly new sedans found in remote locations tended to attract unwanted interest when spotted, as did old junky ones, but for different reasons. When I got parked to my liking I realized that my bear friends were nowhere in sight, which really shouldn't have surprised me. I certainly couldn't expect them to come running to greet me like grandchildren galloping out to greet grandpa on his weekly visit. They were smarter than that. Nevertheless, I was disappointed, thinking that having made the effort to come all the way up there on this special mission, I should get a more auspicious welcome.

The bears were doubtless back in the bushes, sizing up the situation, making certain the coast was clear. So, I sat in the car for a while and waited. Then I got out of the car and waited. I stood around identifying flora, and counting ants, and waited. I ate an apple, chucked the core into the bushes, and waited, consulting my watch, and noting that my bear friends were now forty-five minutes late. I decided to give them twenty minutes more and then I'd leave, certain that if I didn't connect up with them now, I had no way to get in touch with them again. Duffy's telephone was dead, and another mailed message was a long shot, since it wasn't reasonable to expect Deputy Edd to deliver another letter to me. I'd run out of ideas.

So then, I thought, this is how it ends; it's farewell my friends. Maybe someday you'll find a way to contact me again, but I simply can't keep coming up here just to drive aimlessly, with no plan in mind.

I sat on the front seat of the car with the door open, working myself into a state of depression. Except for the sound of an occasional car passing on the distant highway, the forest was quiet. A crow called twice from a tall fir, was answered by another from farther away and then there was nothing but silence. I looked at my watch and saw that my self-allotted time was up. As I reached to close the car door I was startled by a sound that instantly took me back nearly fifteen years to the afternoon when I heard a bear noisily eating blackberries inside a dense berry patch. At the time he was out of my sight, but actually no more than ten feet away. This was a similar noise, but it sounded a lot more like a bear eating an apple core than a bear eating berries. I prayed that this was the same bear, but got ready to slam the door shut if it wasn't. I spoke softly and hesitantly, "Ralph, is that you?"

Back came the reply, "Que pasa, old man, sorry we're late." Ralph appeared out of the underbrush and moseyed slowly across the road. I noticed a slight limp before he sat down in the dirt and peered at me with interest. His first words were hardly the warm welcome I was expecting, "I see you haven't grown a new crop of hair, yet."

"By George, it's good to see you Ralph," I said, alighting from the car. "I was beginning to think you weren't coming." I was so pleased to see the old bruin that I lost my composure. I petted him on the top of the head.

"Hey, hey," he said, pulling away. "Don't pet the bear. Bears aren't dogs, you know."

"Sorry, Ralph, I got carried away. It's just so darn good to see you old friend. Where's Macduff?"

"At the moment Macduff is running off a cougar that was fixin' to have you for lunch."

"What do you mean?" I asked in alarm.

"Big cougar named Bubba. Mean bugger. He's been watching you for the last half-hour. He couldn't figure out how to get around your car, or by tomorrow you'd be written up in the papers. Don't worry, we ran him off. Duff is just making sure he keeps going."

"I guess I owe you Ralph. Thanks."

"You got any more apples in there?" Ralph was looking in the car through the front window. I hastened to get one out of the back seat. He ate it, bear-style, in one bite.

"Good," he said. "Makes for a nice change in diet." Ralph shifted gears. "These damned cougars are out-of-control around here. Ever since your stupid legislature made it illegal to kill 'em, they're multiplying like cats, which is what they are."

Big Bubba has plans for an early lunch.

"I do know that, Ralph, and I'm well aware of how fast cats multiply."

"We bears are planning a pre-emptive strike whether the rangers like it or not. We've had enough of their troublemaking. The anti-cougar committee meets tomorrow; we've got to move on this matter."

Duffy hadn't been kidding when he said Ralph was full of himself. He seemed positively pompous. But I wasn't in any mood to discuss politics.

"You're looking real good, Ralph, a little more gray around the muzzle, maybe. How have you been feeling?" I asked, fudging a little. Actually Ralph had put on quite a bit of weight, and I had noticed the limp again when he came across the road.

"Feelin' old. Got the rheumatism, and I can't go uphill worth a damn. Otherwise I'm fine."

"Join the club, Ralph, you're talking my language," I said.

"Did you bring the books?" he asked. I thought I detected mild enthusiasm when he mentioned the books.

"Yep," I said. "I brought you five copies. That's all I can spare. Duffy said he wanted some to sell to the tourists but I didn't think that was a good idea. What do you think?" I asked.

"Duffy is walking on thin ice. Whenever anything gets screwed up around the campground the rangers immediately suspect he's involved. There is no doubt that he could sell books, but some of those tourists aren't real fond of pushy bears. Duffy's going to end up with a dart in his ass if he's not careful. The young sprout won't listen to me; maybe you ought to talk to him. I'm afraid he's headed for trouble."

Ralph sat on the ground and leaned back against the car. He sighed wearily. "Thank God the rut is over," he said. "Don't know whether I can handle another one. It's getting so it's hardly worth it anymore. Pretty soon Duffy's going to have to carry on the family honor, if he lives long enough that is."

I thought this might be a good time to get information from Ralph without having Duffy around to throw our conversation off track. Ralph seemed to be relaxed and in a reflective mood.

"Duffy tells me you're Mister Big around the park. Is that so?" I asked casually, trying not to sound too judgmental. "Got things pretty well organized, have you?"

"Boy, you have no idea how bears were being pushed around here when we arrived. Some day I'll read all the anti-bear regulations to you. You won't believe them. Old Poomer let the park bureaucrats get away with murder. Did you know that a camper can't even bring anything smelly into the park anymore? The rangers say smelly stuff attracts bears. You ever hear of anything

50

dumber than that? Of course smelly stuff attracts bears. What's wrong with that? They say if a camper gets caught with something smelly he'll get fined fifty dollars. The smelly stuff gets confisticated and the poor bugger gets kicked out of the park."

"You mean confiscated, don't you Ralph?"

"Whatever," said Ralph, not pausing for breath. "Bears like to smell stuff as much as people do. It's damned discriminatory, that's what it is. The rangers put lists everywhere saying what kind of smelly stuff is prohibited, like soap and perfume and buckets and washbasins. Hey, listen to this! They won't let you bring beehives into the park either. Did you ever hear anything stupider than that?"

"That stuff is written by lawyers," I said, "and they try to make sure everything is covered. You just can't be too careful. You never know when somebody might bring a beehive into the campground. Then all the bears in the park would come down and tip it over and eat all the honey and wreck the hive and the bee man would say that nobody told him not to bring a beehive into the campground. He'd sue the government and there would be hell to pay. And it's tax payers like me who would do the paying."

"Do tell," said Ralph, wearily. "Here's something else you probably didn't know. I've got this memorized it's so good. They put up these signs with facts about black bears and what to do when you see one. Listen to this: 'Keep calm; avoid eye contact; wave your arms; stay upwind so they can smell you; identify yourself as a human so they won't see you as prey; bears are nearsighted; the bear will probably leave you alone.' This stuff must have been written about Toonerville bears."

"Ralph," I said, trying to sound forceful, "I'm going to stay downwind and look you right in the eye when I tell you this. The first time that I ran into you in that berry patch I didn't know whether I was upwind or downwind. I didn't make eye contact or wave my arms. And I damned sure didn't stay calm. I ran at top speed, until I slipped in your damn bear poop, fell on my ass and gave myself up for dead. Perhaps you remember the incident?"

The old bear snorted loudly, "Ah, those were the good old days. I remember it well. You didn't identify yourself either, as I remember. I probably should have asked for your social security number."

"Tell me about this COB business," I said, trying to change the subject. "Duffy tells me you've got a bear organization up here."

Ralph puffed up, becoming very serious, "You've heard the expression 'nature abhors a vacuum', haven't you?"

"Sure," I said. "Baruch Spinoza said that. Seventeenth century Dutch philosopher."

"No need to show off," said Ralph, grumpily. "You sound like Duffy. Anyway, when we first got here old Pixley Poomer was the dominant bear. The dominant bear, you know, is in charge of things. Well, talk about vacuums. Poomer was a walking vacuum. He didn't know diddly–squat about anything. Olympic Park bears were in total disorder. They had no organization, no coherence. Anarchy prevailed everywhere."

"Good grief, Ralph, you've just described the very nature of bears, if you'll forgive my impertinence. I've memorized a passage from my own readings about bears, to wit: 'Bears are solitary, independent creatures, not given to socialization or interaction'. From what I've gathered they don't even like each other very much."

52

"You're not talking about Ralph B. Shakesbear bears, my friend. We might not like each other much, but by God we're organized."

Ralph slapped his knee vigorously. "I'm whipping my bears into shape around here, and COB is my instrument of change. COB stands for 'Council of Bears', you know, elders of the clan who make the rules."

I thought it time to venture a question that just might be a bit sensitive. "How did you get to be in charge, Ralph?" I asked tentatively.

"Damn, you clearly haven't done **all** your reading, my friend. A bear becomes the dominant bear by will power and physical prowess." Ralph was on his feet now showing the kind of vigor he used to demonstrate in his younger years. "You beat up everyone in the clan who thinks they're tougher than you, which is just what I've done."

I was beginning to think that Ralph was indeed becoming too big for his britches. I wasn't sure that I was comfortable with the "new" Ralph. There was an untamed element that I hadn't been exposed to before, except for that time when he had the run-in with the kid on the motorcycle.

"Are you in charge of all the bears in the park?" I asked. "Even the ones on the other side of the mountains?"

"Well, not exactly," said the old bear. "Over on the other side there's an uncivilized bunch called the West Mountain Bonecrushers. There's a story that they tried to come over onto this side years ago, and raised all kinds of hell before they were run off. There isn't anybody still alive who remembers it. Don't know if it's true or not. There's another bunch up in the high country too.

They're not real friendly, and they speak a different dialect. I'll get them organized when I find time."

I didn't say it right out loud, but I couldn't help thinking that what I was witnessing was a bit of ursine empire-building with Ralph The Great, King of Olympic Black Bears running the show. It was a scary thought.

Suddenly something exploded from the underbrush in a great shower of rocks and dust, and Duffy appeared, galloping down the road with his tongue hanging out. Breathing heavily, his eyes bright with excitement, he skidded to a stop just short of running over us.

"I chased that cougar half-way to Mt. Ellinor. Howdy, dude," he said, looking at me.

"Did you get his number, Duffy?" asked Ralph.

"Yeah, it was big Bubba, just like we thought," Duffy said matter of factly. He looked at me. "Did you bring the stuff?"

"I brought a new notebook and a recorder," I said, "and by the way, Duffy, I put my name on that tape recorder so you won't forget where it came from. There's an extra tape in the bag, too, so you won't run out."

"How about the books?" Duffy asked.

"Your grandpa says no books for you, lad. He's afraid the rangers might not understand the concept of a pushy bear selling books in the campground."

"Man, I could make a lot of dough," said Duffy, with disappointment. I noticed that he still had on his fanny pack. Apparently he had outgrown the old one, since it looked like he had extended the belt with somebody's suspenders.

He saw me looking at it and explained, "Ran into a logger over near Dry Creek. He said I could have his suspenders."

"I didn't know loggers were so generous," I remarked. "Especially with an item so essential to keeping their pants up."

"He didn't complain much, but I told him I'd put him back down if he'd let me have them," said Duffy.

"See what I mean?" said Ralph. "The kid's headed for trouble. You can be sure that that logger has complained to Dudley Do-right by now. I'll bet he's already made a report to the park administration, and it's working its way though channels as we speak. We'll hear about it eventually. You can be sure it's gone into Duffy's file — his growing file, I might add."

"Dudley Do-right?" I asked. Ralph noticed my quizzical look.

"He's our 'by-the-book' park ranger. His real name is Ronald Rumpsley. He's our local version of Dudley Do-right. It doesn't matter where you go in the park service, there's always one of them around. Some of the other rangers call him 'Right-Angle Ronnie', he's so damned square. He was the guy who posted all of those rules around that say it's against the law to bring beehives into the campground."

"Yeah, beehives are smelly, you know," said Duffy. "Smelly stuff isn't allowed in campgrounds. Mustn't wear perfume in the park either, or a bear might eat you."

I was sitting in the driver's seat of my car with the door open. Ralph and Duffy were sitting comically, bear-fashion, on the ground. We looked like a trio of farmers who had gathered to talk about spring planting, or the price of butterfat. I offered my friends some more fruit from my cache, lending an even more rustic touch to the scene as they munched their vittles.

Duffy piped up with an observation. "Man, if righteous Ronnie were to show up right now, we'd all go to the hoosegow." He pointed at me. "You'd get slapped with a 'feeding the bears' and a 'consorting with wild animals' rap, and Ralph and I would be labeled as 'nuisance bears' for cohabitating with human beans. We'd all go up the river big time. A haul like that could make Ronnie's career."

"We're outside the park," observed Ralph.

"We're in the national forest, but it doesn't matter anyway. Those are state laws," said Duffy. "Even old steady Eddy could bust us."

"Well," said Ralph, "he'd have to take me at gunpoint. You can bet I wouldn't go easily into that good night, as the poet said."

He rose wearily and dusted off his backside. "I'm going to mosey along. I've got to get ready for the cougar committee meeting tomorrow. Before we can move on this thing we'll need a resolution, and I've got a few arms to twist. Some of the elders don't see any need to squabble with the cougars; claim they've never been bothered by them. How do you stand on the issue, Duffy?"

"I'm foursquare against cougars. That Big Bubba has been stirring up trouble for too long. He's got to be removed, or none of us are safe. We must smite him hip and thigh."

"More Shakespeare?" I asked Ralph, quizzically.

"Old Testament," said Ralph, limping off down the road. "Get back when you can, old man. Keep in touch."

"Hey, Ralph," I yelled, "you forgot the books." The bear stopped and turned slowly. "Do you want me to sign them?" I asked.

"Hell, no, I'll sign 'em myself," he said. "I can't carry them, though, give them to the kid. Duffy, put 'em in your fancy sack. Leave them up at my place on your way home."

"Take care of yourself, Ralph," I said. "It's been good to see you again."

The old bear vanished into the forest without a sound.

"You notice the limp?" asked Duffy.

"Yeah," I said. "He says he's got a touch of rheumatism."

"Rheumatism caused by an old cougar wound, remember?"

"That's right," I said. "About the same time that he had that collision with the kid on the motorbike behind your place before we moved up here."

"And the birdshot in the butt," Duffy reminded me.

"The old boy has had his share of adventures," I said.

"You don't know the half of it. Someday I'll tell you the rest of the story." Duffy sat down in the road again.

"Ralph tells me the rut is all over for the year. You two didn't get into another fight, did you?"

"No," said Duffy. "I stayed as far away from the old coot as I could. He's too tough for me, rheumatism and all. Got any more apples in there?" Duffy pointed to the back seat.

"Take a look. Get me an orange while you're at it."

We sat in silence for a time. Duffy inhaled his apple as usual, while I peeled my orange. He ate the peelings.

"Did your phone battery go dead?" I asked.

"I guess so."

"Give me the phone and I'll see if my charger will work." He rummaged around in his bulging pack and handed it to me. It was quickly apparent that I wasn't going to be able to help him. "This

57

one's no good, Duffy. Sorry."

"No matter, dude. I'll keep looking. Lots of people up here don't lock their cars. I'll find the right one sooner or later."

"Remember what Ralph told you, lad. Don't ask for trouble."

"Fear not, old boy. Like I said before, stealth is my middle name." Duffy was making paw prints in the dirt and then erasing them.

"By the way," I asked him, "is there any chance I can get to watch one of Ralph's meetings?"

"No way, man," said Duffy solemnly. "The other bears wouldn't even show up if they smelled you around the place. Most bears don't like hanging around people, unless they're looking for something to eat. Wouldn't do you any good anyway. They talk bear, not English. You couldn't understand them."

"Well, I'll be danged," I said. "I never thought of that. I didn't even know there was a bear language. What's it sound like?"

"Oh, it's a lot like grizzly and polar bear," he said in an off-handed way. "Distantly related to dog."

"That's not very helpful, Duffy. Say something in black bear for me."

"Okay, listen up." Out of the young bear's mouth came a torrent of rumbles, snuffles, growls, barks, snorts and a whole lot of what seemed like mumbling of the sort I had first heard from Ralph before he became proficient in English.

"What did you say, Duff?"

"I said the reason you never expected us to have a language is because you human beans are very self-centered and think that nobody but you has the smarts to develop language. You are pitifully ethnocentric. In bear, ethnocentric is pronounced 'baarnupfolagula'." It sounded like Duffy was getting ready to throw up. "You might want to add that word to your vocabulary."

"Well, I'll be damned," I said. "You bears never cease to amaze me. Does any one else know that bears have their own language?"

"Oh, only about 600,000 other bears in North America," said Duffy condescendingly. "That is, if you don't count the ones who are illiterate, and the Siberian and Norwegian bears who talk different."

My young friend had put me in my place, but I'd already decided that he didn't need to worry about me wanting to learn their language. I wouldn't be any good at the snuffle snorts and huffing rumbles.

"That's the reason I wanted you to bring that tape recorder up here," Duffy explained, "so I can record one of Ralph's meetings. I'll translate it for you in my notebook, and then when you get ready to write your next book we'll have some good material. This kind of thing could bring a better understanding between bears and human beans. It could be the biggest thing since Winnie The Pooh."

"Yeah, you bet Duffy," I mumbled. "Maybe someday I'll get you membership in the U.N. In the meantime why don't you see if there're any more apples in the back seat?" Duffy found two more apples and I started to eat mine as he finished his.

"How you doing on your exposé of the spring rut? Making any progress on your book?"

"Yeah, I got the first chapter done. You want to read it?" he asked, excitedly. "It's a real bodice-ripper."

"Why don't you let me take it home with me, Duffy? I'll bring it back next time I come. Say, what do you hear from Peaches?" I asked. "How are the kids — the cubs, that is?"

"All good," he said. "Peaches is reading Shakespeare to them. They're quick studies."

"Luciana and Dromio, right?"

"Yep, Lucy and Dromio. They're true Shakesbears," said Duffy with pride.

"Well, I've got to get going, my boy," I said. "Anything you want me to bring you next time?"

"Some more apples," said Duffy. "Bring a whole box. Some sweet potatoes would taste good, too."

"Apples, maybe. Sweet potatoes, no, too expensive. Let me look at that telephone again. Maybe I can find a charger. Where would you plug it in?"

"That's no problem," said Duffy airily. "Anywhere in the campground. Men's room is a good place. In the middle of the night, of course."

"You're very considerate to use the men's room, Duffy. You've been well brought up."

I noticed that the young bear had been sniffing around in the underbrush, particularly near an old rotten stump. He clawed at the  base of it until he had excavated a fairly large hole. I supposed that he had found an ant's nest.

"Look here, old man. I've fixed a hole where you can hide stuff. Any time you have something you want to bring us you can put it under here. Stuff like, you know, food. Wrap it up in plastic so it won't get all wet, and so that nobody else smells it. This would be a neat place to exchange things if our phones are dead, too. Anytime you come up, look in here. Okay? Stuff things way back in so they will stay dry. Be sure to wrap the food good, or the damned raccoons will get it."

I gave Duffy my apple core. "Okay, Duff, that's good thinking. Let's make a date anyway. When should I come back?"

"Come back at the end of summer. The tourists will be leaving; kids have to go back to school. Things quiet down."

"Okay," I said, "that's September 23rd, right? How 'bout ten o'clock in the morning? Same place."

"Okay, unless I tell you otherwise," said Duffy. "If it's raining come the next day."

"It's not going to rain on September 23rd," I said, for want of anything else to say.

"Don't forget to mark the calendar — September 23rd, the autumnal equinox."

As I headed out on the highway I noted that we had made it through the whole day without any rain. There'd been nothing but a little sprinkle activity.

CHAPTER FIVE
Passion In The Pines

When I got home I put up a "Ralph" sign that said, "A SMOKING SECTION IN A RESTAURANT IS LIKE A PEEING SECTION IN A SWIMMING POOL". This kind of a message is popular with the coarser element of my readership, which I suspect is actually the major part of it. The next time I saw Twyla go by she was staring straight ahead, her jaw firmly set. I supposed that I had lost her as one of my regular readers. It didn't take much to offend her.

Even though I tried to forget bears, at least until our next meeting in the fall, they continued to be on my mind. I began to question whether Ralph and Duffy, aside from their unique ability to speak English, were really typical members of their species. Though I had done a fair amount of reading on the subject of bears, I began to wonder whether I really knew what I was talking about, so I sought additional information in libraries and on the Internet.

The first book I picked up nearly soured me against ever going near my friends again. It was written by a man who had spent a good part of his life investigating bear attacks on humans. When I read the story about a lady who was trying to play dead while a black bear was chewing her arm off, I was decidedly unnerved. This was the kind of vicious behavior that could be expected from grizzlies, but surely not from black bears, like my gentle friends Ralph and Duffy.

The author of the book, taking direct aim at the likes of me, decried the tendency of writers of children's books and other fictional whimsy to anthropomorphize bears and other wild creatures in such a way as to lull the population into believing that they were harmless. Smokey Bear, Yogi Bear, teddy bears of every description, and even Winnie the Pooh, were portrayed in books and on television as lovable and cuddly creatures whereas in truth, according to the author of this book, bears were dangerous and not to be trusted.

Fortunately, most of us are able to distinguish between fictional bears and real ones so it has not yet become necessary for the federal government to put warnings in children's books, like they do on stepladders and washing machines. Just suppose that A.A. Milne, in the interest of teaching realism to young children, had written that Winnie the Pooh, in a fit of anger, chewed Eeyore's hind leg off and let all the sawdust fall out. It was too awful to contemplate.

In any case, just to be on the safe side, I've decided to include a disclaimer right now, which I hope will absolve this author of any liability that could cause him or his heirs financial or emotional hardship:

DISCLAIMER

Throughout this book, the author has utilized a technique called anthropomorphinization, which means the "giving of human qualities to animals". It has been used since Aesop wrote his first fable about the snake talking to Adam. Readers who are in any doubt about their ability to tell real bears from fake ones are cautioned to read the following notice carefully. It might be well to paste it to the windshield of your car while traveling through the national parks.

WARNING!

In light of the information herein provided about the unpredictability of wild animals, the author of this book encourages his readers—especially the children—to use extreme caution around bears. They are not to be trusted. In encounters with bears always let the bear be the one to start a conversation. If he fixes you with eye contact and seems reluctant to talk, get into your car and roll up all the windows. Keep your arms inside the vehicle. Also remember that some bears do not like to have their pictures taken. Be sure to ask for permission first and always have adult supervision when you try to spell a big word like anthropomorphinization.

Fortunately for me, and my continuing relationship with my friends, further reading gave me a less malevolent picture of the life of the typical black bear. I learned that their life span in the wild (where practically all of them live) is somewhere near twenty years, though I suspect, given the increasing hazards of modern living, it is rare for one to live that long. I had met Ralph back in 1991 when he was already well-read and well-spoken, a mature bear who was wise to the ways of the world. At the time, Ralph professed not to know how old he was, but guessed maybe he was about ten. He said his mother never mentioned age, which I have come to learn is not unusual, since bears really have no interest in time except as it affects eating, sleeping and rutting. If my figures were right and if the life expectancies were correct, Ralph was pushing the limits.

Evidence of aches and pains seemed to support this, and though the old bruin was showing some physical decline, I was happy to see that his mental vigor remained undiminished. He was still his usual curmudgeonly self, and seemed to have found his niche as an elder statesman among the bears in the national park system.

Not long ago a friend of mine sent me a story from a California newspaper that I later passed along to Ralph for comment. It concerned an old bear that lived in a culvert near the twelfth green on a golf course somewhere down south. His name was Arthur, and because he got most of his meals from the garbage cans around the golf links, he was soon labeled a "nuisance" bear, subject to all the bureaucratic indignities that attend such a classification.

The story said that Arthur weighed 550 pounds, which must be close to the black bear heavyweight record. It wasn't mentioned in the article, but those of us familiar with ursine habits know that a bear who has nothing to do except sit around in a culvert eating generously out of gourmet garbage cans on a golf course is apt to bulk up considerably. Probably the only exercise the old fool ever got was practicing his putting after the other golfers went home.

Anyway, it seems that Arthur had a bad limp that attracted the attention of the animal rights people who are ever on the alert for creatures with any sort of disability whether they deserve to have it or not. So they informed the state wildlife authorities about the bear with the bum leg. The state, busy with other matters and not wishing to get involved, said the bear looked okay to them and that they didn't have any place to put a 550-pound bear anyway.

Then the Humane Society and the California Bear League — whatever that is — got into the act and threatened to sue the state on animal cruelty charges for not attending to the limping bear. The state panicked, darted old Arthur and put him in the animal "hoosegow" up near the state capital where they gave him a full battery of diagnostic tests, which showed he had arthritis and lumbago, probably from sitting around in damp culverts. Now Arthur was not only a nuisance bear but a "disabled" nuisance bear as well, which caused the Americans With Disabilities Act to kick in.

But before the Department of Health, Education and Welfare joined the act the PAWS people, who ran a resort for retired circus animals in a small central California town, offered to have Arthur come join the lions and elephants.

Arthur, California nuisance bear

They even built a $20,000 compound for him, complete with a big hot tub to ease his aches and pains, but that wasn't the end of the story. Local Indian tribes heard about Arthur and showed up saying that the black bear was a "sacred" animal and demanding that he be released. The state said "no way" because Arthur was now a "Fed" bear that could no longer survive in the wild. This caused the People for the Ethical Treatment of Animals to open fire, accusing the state of animal cruelty and insisting that the Attorney General investigate, or face legal action. At last report the state bureaucrats were doing what bureaucrats always do; they were studying the matter.

After hearing this heartrending story, Ralph's only comment was that if he ever got caught in a mess like that you can bet he'd demand that they put a putting green in his $20,000 compound along with the hot tub.

I soon discovered that far from getting bears out of my mind, I was spending way too much time reading about them. I found that the most serious social issue dividing people and bears is not bear attacks, as one might think; it is the great American garbage can. Bears simply cannot resist refuse. They can smell an odoriferous backyard garbage can from a great distance, and will go to almost any lengths to investigate its contents.

Ordinary bears are only interested in the foodstuffs they find. Both Ralph and Duffy, on the other hand, learned to read from literature found in garbage cans. It's safe to say that the Shakesbears considered themselves a cut above the average bear because they used their garbage foraging habits to develop their minds rather than merely to fill their stomachs. It's remarkable given the number of garbage cans that they'd been in that they'd avoided the fate of so many of their kind; that of being labeled nuisances, shot with tranquilizers and relocated or, more likely, simply shot, period. Now that they lived up in the park with its inflexible rules and regulations about garbage and other smelly attractions, Ralph and Macduff seemed reasonably safe from such an end. I just hoped they wouldn't become too complacent.

I checked on the Bear League (originally known as the Bear Protection League) down in California and discovered that it spent a lot of its time on "nuisance" bear matters, like educating bears to stay out of garbage cans. They used aversion therapy techniques that involved shotgun blasts, rockets, pots and pans, and bullhorns. I made myself a note to tell Ralph about these things. Perhaps he could incorporate them into his COB meetings.

Clearly I was having no success in getting the bears out of my mind. Even in the middle of the night they seemed to roam around upsetting my sleep. In fact, in a somnambulate state one night I suddenly remembered that I hadn't looked at Duffy's notebook — the one with the first chapter of his blockbuster bear novel in it — since I had come back from my last visit. Worse yet, I couldn't even remember bringing it home, although I clearly recalled him giving it to me as I sat in the car. I was certainly going to be out of Duffy's good graces if I had lost it, but I figured it would be easy enough to distract him and get him off on some other project. Unlike most bears who are sedentary creatures, Duffy was constantly in motion, his post-adolescent interests were wide-ranging, and his attention span distressingly short. Just examining the contents of his fanny pack provided ample evidence of this; it was crammed with books, a useless telephone, recorders, pens and his notebook, telephone numbers, notes and addresses. He didn't have a camera yet, probably because he hadn't found just the right model in somebody's unlocked car. I had complete confidence that I could get the young bear to gallop off on another tangent and forget about his intended writing project if I found it necessary to do so.

Then a week or two later when I was cleaning out my car I found Duffy's notebook in the glove compartment. On the cover was written:

"Macduff S. his book. Hands Off"

His handwritten warning reminded me of the emphatic way we would label our possessions when we were school kids, so nosey classmates, especially girls, wouldn't get at our secrets and perhaps learn our innermost thoughts.

Several pages of comments and notes to himself followed, a couple of which I thought especially interesting: "Ranger Ronnie followed me across the bridge last night banging on a metal pot with a big spoon. I guess he thinks he scares me, he didn't know that I was leaving anyway." Another entry said, "I saw P (that must be Peaches) she said the twins have left home — actually she kicked them

Duffy begins the Great American novel.

out. P said she'd like to have me visit next spring. Hot Damn!"

When I had finally worked my way through all the unrelated items and arrived at the beginning of Duffy's epic I decided to finish washing the car and to go into the shop and get comfortable before proceeding. As I glanced at the title page of the young bear's manuscript I congratulated myself on my foresight — this was going to be a challenge.

PASSION IN THE PINES
Secrets of the Unchained Wilderness
A novel of Lust and Intrigue
By
Macduff Shakesbear

The dull moonlight filtered through the mossy boughs illuminating the slumbering buttercups. The weeping geraniums wept silently. Small creatures paused inexpectently, their slow sense piquanted by the changing of the humidity, a primalistic urge responding to forces beyond their intelligibility.

Aloft in his secure perch the owl hooted, heralding the portent of he knew not what. Perhaps the approach of a new season, maybe the resumption of spring. The forest waited with excrution, expectant and redundant like a coiled spring aimed, waiting to be discharged against the darkness. The land was still, clutching its bosom, fingering its skirt, shifting slightly in its pinions.

So far Hemingway and Shakespeare had nothing to fear.

Bruno, the resting boar raised his massive head slowly, twitching his nostrils nervously. A faint but familiar fragrance caressed his olfactories. He shifted his position in his snug den of scotch broom restlessly. There was no mistaking that faint but powerful smell. It was an oder to quicken the pulses of even the most jaded of male bruins. It was the MUST! The first of the season **MUST**. *The first sign that the rutting season had arrived. It was from an easterly drection a long way off, truly from a great distance, but the drection was right and the flavor of the essince was identifiable. Surely it eminated from the opening love valves of his beloved Lucy Anne, queen of the Rockmount clan of bears, mother of at least five of his children and perhaps many more. Bruno raised himself from his bed and shook himself vigorously. Ah, Lucy Anne, Lucy Anne, I'm comeing to you Lucy Anne!!! Bruno felt a stirring of his loins....*

Oh, my god. Love valves? Stirring of the loins? Duffy wasted no time getting up to speed, but he really needed to look in a garbage can for a good dictionary. (I have corrected some of his worst spelling mishaps to improve clarity.) Ed.

Urged on by primal instincts that he could never comprehend, Bruno faced east and began his annual journey of fulfillment, stoping frequently to

70

sniff the air and remind himself why he was making this trip. Once he thought he had lost the scented trail only to rediscover it again as the breeze shifted. Visions of Lucy Anne's warm haunches, her sweet breath and her loving caresses motivated him through the difficult passages. He was being propelled on his quest by ancient and mysterious forces, tugging at him like the Pole of the earth tugs at the needle of the compass. Twice he thought he caught sight of other bears traveling in the same direction, younger bears no doubt, with visions of prideful conquest, about to test their skills in compitition with Bruno, the old boar for years the unmatched lord and master of his clans harem. Thoughts of past triumphs passed through the old boar's dim memory as he tried to recall how many other sooters he had bested in uncounted rutting seasons. The mere thought of doing battle with young upstarts caused the hackles on his neck to rise, a low growl rumbled in his throat.

Onward he easted, the miles vanishing under his stedy trot, with each step the musty bouquet of Lucy Annes charms growing stronger. One last hill to climb, one last rise to top and Bruno would be in the enchanted valley secure in the arms of his beloved Lucy.

Bruno caught the strong hormonal essence of Lucy Anne where she had straddled a huckleberry bush leaving behind the heavy heavenly MUST that drives boars into paroxysms of ecstatic pleasure. Three more steps and he would view his prise. Bruno parted the bushes and gazed into the green valley.

Oh, the horror! Oh, the abomination! Bruno stood transfixed in disbelief. Down below him on the verdant plane was his lovely Lucy chewing on a mouthful of tender grass while being serviced by a sleek young boar with a smirk of satisfaction on his face!

It took a moment for the scene to register on a brain dulled by the long exhausting overland questing trek, but register it did and with a monumental roar Bruno stood to his full towering height and launched himself down the steep hillside like Sir Galahad on afterburners. There was no way that Bruno was about to relinquish dominance of his clan to a fuzzy face, shiny-coated skinny young punk bear with a smirk on his face.

The first titanic battle of the new rutting season was about to begin.

END OF CHAPTER ONE

Wow! I was tempted to hold the notebook under the faucet to cool it off. This was truly steamy stuff. My mind raced. Was the story autobiographical? Could that old bear be Ralph and the smirking youngster be Duffy himself? Should I encourage the budding author, or should I put the notebook back in the glove box and forget it?

As I sat on my stool in the shop with Duffy's opus still clutched in my hot hand my friend Phineas drove up with his faithful canine co-pilot, arriving on one of their intermittent visits. The old fellow unfolded himself from his vehicle and instructed Maximo to sit tight, telling him he would only be a minute. Max appeared to give the instruments a careful check to make certain that the car was safely in park, and then he stared straight ahead, prepared to wait.

"What do you think of O'Conner and Smith passin' that excise bill on draft beah? How'er they goin' to get away with that?" asked Phineas, before he was halfway through the door of the shop. This was his accustomed way of starting a visit — abruptly and mysteriously.

With my mind still on the spring rut I had no idea what the old guy was talking about, and I regarded him with puzzlement.

"Danged if I know Phineas, but they'll get away with it alright, they're politicians."

"Now theah talkin' about pullin' all them dams out of the Snake Rivah. Can't see how that's going to help any. Hard to figure them guys." This sort of leap from one subject to another appeared to cause no hardship to Phin's overactive mind, but it confused the hell out of me.

"Oh, they'll probably get over it," I said, as he headed off on another tangent.

"Went back to my high school reunion two weeks ago. Aroostock High, Class of '35. Ain't many of us old timahs left. Saw my old girlfriend Betsey Lou. She don't look too much different. She's aged real good."

"That's fine," I said, in a distracted sort of way. "How's the potato crop this year?"

"Got that blight again. Might wipe out the whole crop. Old Senator Billabong's gonna get a ridah hooked to that housin' bill, take care of it. Billabong and Snellhauser, they's big in crop payments, ya know. Say, you heard the Indians up theah want us to give the whole state back to them? Want us to pay them for it too."

"Hey, Phineas," I said, not wanting to get myself too far removed from the Duffy matter. "Read this story for me. See what you think." I handed him Duffy's notebook.

Phineas sat down on my short little visitor's stool with his knees up around his chin. He slowly commenced reading, moving his lips as he went. I busied myself at my workbench trying to avoid watching lest I embarrass the old fellow, who was moving his finger along with the words to keep his place. I could see that reading was

73

not his favorite activity. Duffy's puzzling prose was anything but easy to unravel, and Phineas was nearly in over his head.

"This is kinda hard goin'. What's this word heah?" he asked, pointing to 'excrution', one of Duffy's manufactured words.

"I'm not sure, Phin, you've kind of got to skip over some of the words. Just try to read for content."

"You didn't write this did you?" he asked, suspiciously. "You got a mess of awful funny words in heah."

I continued with my whittling as Phineas labored on. Maximo maintained his vigil in the car, his attention focused on the traffic.

Phineas lowered the notebook with a heavy sigh. "Man, this is hard readin'. It's about beahs, ain't it?" he asked genuinely puzzled. "You didn't write this did you?" he asked me again.

"No, a friend of mine did."

"We got a lot of beahs up in Maine. I used to be around them all the time, but I ain't seen anything like what this guy's talkin' about. Hardly anybody goes around beahs durin' the matin' season. Tain't safe. Beahs go crazy. I remember a damned nearsighted old beah tried to mount Maximo's mothah once. No, on second thought, it was his grandmothah. She looked a lot like Max. I got my 12 gauge out, but couldn't get a good shot at the danged beah without I hit old Blue — that was her name, Old Blue — so I fired over the beah's head as close as I could get and he run off. He didn't even get to finish his business, I reckon, 'cuz Old Blue's next litter was puppies, not cubs."

"What do you think of the story?" I asked, trying to get Phineas back on the subject.

He looked at me closely. "This heah's what I call a pot boilah.

Who wrote it?"

"A bear friend of mine wrote it," I said matter of factly, without looking up from my work.

Phineas chuckled. "Yeah, sure. I've known a lot of beahs, but I've never known one who can write. Beahs can't even write poetry, let alone pot boilahs," he laughed.

"Well, anyway, what do you think of the story. Is it any good?" I asked without contradicting him.

"No worse than a lot of the stuff they put on television. Needs work, though. Tell your beah friend not to use so many big words, and that business about the big beah running downhill with his afterburnahs on don't work. Black beahs can't run downhill worth a dang, not even with afterburnahs."

"Thanks, Phineas, I'll tell him the next time I see him. He needs a lot of encouragement. By the way," I asked him, "did you get a look at the book I wrote? It's about bears. Some of it's about the bear that wrote that story," I said, pointing at Duffy's notebook. I handed him a copy from under my workbench. "Mostly it's about that old bear sitting outside in the chair."

"Ralph, is that his name? Ralph?"

"Yep," I said. "He used to live up in the backwoods not too far from your place." Phineas seemed to be edging toward the door. "He's moved away now. You take the book and read it. Tells all about him."

Phineas brightened up a bit. "I used to see a beah up theah once in awhile."

"That was probably Ralph. He lives up in the Olympics now." I began to think I was talking too much. Phineas was smiling strangely. Perhaps I'd better cool it. I'd never told anybody about the bears before. Not in a serious way, at least. Maybe Phineas wasn't the best place to start.

"I was just kidding about a bear writing that story, Phin, it was really written by a friend of mine who thinks he knows all about bears. I'll tell him I showed it to you. Let him know what you said about the afterburners."

Maximo barked twice and Phineas looked relieved. "We gotta' get those bozos over in Olympia to quit trying to raise taxes. Max says it's time to eat. Bettah get movin'. Looks like the military's got a grip on those guys in Washington, movin' them troops and all." Phineas headed out through the shop door, talking as he went. "Whataya think about that farmer wantin' to put that dike up on the river? Thanks for the book."

He looked up at Ralph's sign. "I DON'T LIKE POLITICAL JOKES", it said, "TOO MANY OF THEM GET ELECTED".

"You got that right," he said, giving me a nod. "That's a good one," he said.

Max watched attentively as Phineas went through the steps of getting ready to drive. Looking both ways up and down the highway, he gave the old man the go sign and away they went.

CHAPTER SIX

Escape From The Barrel

Around here in the summertime, a season that is all too brief, owners of shore side residences can expect visits from hordes of relatives, and most of the friends they have ever known. When the weather gets warm and pleasant they suddenly remember that you live right on the beach and recall how much fun it is to frolic in the saltwater and barbecue stuff on your deck and carouse about in carefree abandon. Under such conditions it was easy to forget my two bear friends who were probably up in the high country taking naps anyway.

And so it was that on a hot day in the middle of July I celebrated my birthday with a multitude of admiring friends who came out to see how I had managed to live so long while taking so little care of myself. As the party began to pick up momentum, word was brought to me by one of the small grandchildren, who was playing whatever the politically correct version of cowboys and Indians is nowadays, that there was a phone call for me. I went inside to check it out. The only person in the house was a portly, middle-aged fellow called Pooh-Bah who showed up every year as a guest of a distant cousin of mine named Dickey Spindle, who knew when my birthday was and simply arrived every year on speculation, correctly assuming that there would be some sort of a celebration going on. Pooh-Bah, or Poob, as I called him, didn't much care for sunshine or swimming, so he spent most of his time inside the house drinking gin and watching reruns of sitcoms on television.

"Hey, Poob, one of the kids said I have a phone call. Did you take it?"

"Yeah," he mumbled, "a guy named Ralph called. He said somebody's in jail. I couldn't understand him very good, the dang TV makes so much noise. He said he'd call back, I think."

"Look, here, Poob," I said, picking up the remote controller. "Do you see these little buttons on this thing? Here's one that says 'mute' and here's another one that says 'power'. Either one of them makes everything go quiet."

Pooh-Bah was slurring his words badly. He had clearly been doing serious damage to my gin supply. "I couldn't hardly understand him anyway," Pooh-Bah grumbled. "The guy's got a speech problem, mumbles real bad. I think he'd been drinking. He was slurring his words." Poob was so engrossed in an ancient episode of F Troop he seemed uninterested in discussing the matter with me any further.

"Are you sure he said he'd call back?" I asked, with annoyance.

"No," said Pooh-Bah simply.

I returned to the revelry outside, determined to winnow deadwood from my guest list before next summer. The phone call was from Ralph, that much was certain. But where had he found a telephone, and what was the business about somebody being in jail? Before the party ended and cousin Dickey had loaded the dead weight of Pooh-Bah into his car, my troubled mind had conjured up a variety of scenarios to fill in the missing information. For obvious reasons, every one of them ended with Duffy being locked up somewhere. It seemed inevitable. Somehow Duffy and jail just seemed to go together. For a long time they had been headed for a

78

rendezvous.

At about four o'clock in the morning the insistent ringing of the telephone awakened me. As I gained consciousness I could see that it was not far from the mid-summer's early dawn, and what was left of the night was brightly lit by a full moon. It took me half a minute to gather my wits and find the phone. I immediately recognized Ralph's gruff voice on the line.

"I got him out of jail. He's up in the mountains."

"Is that you, Ralph?" I said, with a note of annoyance. "Do you have any idea what time it is?"

"Yes, I do, it's nighttime."

"What's going on? What's happening?" I was slowly regaining my senses. The long day of partying and a very short amount of sleep were making it a challenge to get a grip on things. "Is it Duffy?"

"Of course it's Duffy. Who else do you know up here?" Ralph sounded out-of-sorts. "Damn fool got himself caught in the barrel trap. Rangers were going to dart him in the morning and then do all those indignities to him. I sprung him loose."

Now I was wide-awake. "Good work, Ralph. How'd you do it?"

"Just broke the snap off the hasp and opened the door. Whacked him on the butt and told him to stay up in the mountains until he got some sense."

"How'd they get Duffy to walk into a barrel trap?" I asked. "I thought he was smarter than that."

"Those rangers aren't so dumb. They get some of that female bear must and spray it around inside the barrel. Damn fool young bears fight over who gets to go in first. Duffy's got too many hormones for his own good. He beat out the other bears and sprang the trigger. It's just lucky I heard about it from old Bartley Numnuts. Bartley thought it was funny. He's been in traps so many times he's got numbers tattooed all over himself. Got a tag in his ear, a collar around his neck and red paint on his ass showing the rangers that they don't need to bother trappin' him any more."

"Bartley told me about Duffy being inside that trap out behind the generator plant. Soon as it got dark I went right over and let him out. The rangers are going to be pissed. They were planning to come back in the morning with their darts and measuring tapes and radio collars and tattoo stuff. They pull out a tooth now too, ya' know. That's supposed to tell them how old a bear is, and they measure his collop, which is a fancy way of saying fat. You remember that collop business, don't you?"

"Yeah, I remember the collop business, Ralph. You nearly had your collop measured once or twice back in the good old days."

"Good old days, my ass," grumped Ralph with a snort. "By the way, who was that dork I talked to this afternoon? You let drunks hang around your place?"

"That was a guy named Pooh-Bah. He shows up with Dickey every year to drink my booze and celebrate my birthday."

"You need to find a better class of friends."

"Listen up, Ralph, I've got some questions. First of all, where'd you get the telephone?"

"It's Duffy's telephone. He showed me how to use it. The kid's

80

actually good for something every once in a while. Finally got a battery charger somewhere. Stole it, no doubt."

"Where are you calling from?" I asked.

"I'm at my place, up past the Beaver Burn. Someday you'll have to come up for a visit. It's where Poomer used to live. Got it fixed up real good."

"How come the rangers are trapping bears? You guys been causing trouble?"

I could hear Ralph snort. "Not my guys," he said. "It's the young bucks who are getting too big for their britches. Duffy's kind of a ringleader, I'm sorry to say. I'm putting this matter on our agenda for the next COB meeting. Either the kids start shaping up around here or they'll all get trapped and transported to the backcountry, Duffy included. When he comes back he and I are going to have a heart-to-heart talk. I don't expect to save his bacon again. This time of year the park's crowded with tourists and the rangers get real edgy. They freak out if somebody reports seeing one bear, let alone a whole bunch of 'em raising hell around the campground."

"How come you called me about Duffy's problem, Ralph?" I asked. "What did you expect me to do about it?"

"I guess I kind of panicked. I had a cockeyed idea you might have some pull with the rangers."

"Not a chance, old boy. I don't know a soul up there," I said. "You have more pull than I do. Do you remember telling me about old Pixley Poomer and how he was on the park payroll? Told me that he got paid off in dog food if he just hung around the place to entertain the tourists. Why don't you go over to the ranger's place and make a deal with them?"

81

"No way," said Ralph wearily. "Poomer didn't have any teeth, and he had to have all his claws pulled out before he could get the job. I'm not going through that kind of abuse."

Our signal was getting weak. Duffy's batteries were probably about to go dead. "You'd be a lot better off, Ralph, if you'd suck up to the rangers. Get 'em on your side. Think of the possibilities, man."

"I'm not a man, dude, I'm a bear. A damned good one, too, and planning to remain so. I have no intention of joining your human circus."

"Have it your way, Ralph, but before we lose the signal, give me your telephone number."

Grabbing a pencil I struggled to get it written down before I lost him. "710-8963," I thought I heard him say as his voice faded away. I repeated the number.

"One more question, Ralph. How is a big bear like you able to manipulate a tiny little cell phone? I can remember when you told me you couldn't even operate a pencil."

There was a scratching of static and the line went dead.

A week later an official-looking letter appeared in my mailbox. Written on the letterhead of the National Park Service, it informed me that on July 26th a portable tape recorder with an adhesive label on it bearing my name and address had been found in the campground. It suggested that if I would come to the ranger station and identify this item it could be returned to me. The recorder must have fallen out of Duffy's overloaded fanny pack. I debated whether it was worth the effort to go all the way up to the park to get it.

The second paragraph of the letter put a different slant on

things: "*This instrument,*" the letter read, "*was found after a disturbance near campsite #48 late on the evening of July 19*[th]. *Noise complaints came to this office concerning campers partying in a campsite where excessively loud recorded music was heard—music that exceeded 60 decibels measured on the A-weighted scale at 50-feet. (See Code of Federal Regulations, Title 36, Vol. 1, Sec. 2.12, Audio Disturbances). (36CRF2.12). Upon the approach of the below—named officer the offending party (or parties) disbursed hurriedly and were not apprehended. Several nearby campers, including complainant A.J. Roperstein, age 82, retired audio engineer, estimated the noise level to be in excess of 120 decibels and seemed to be what is known as 'Rock and Rolling or Rapping' music. Please contact this office at your earliest convenience in order to clear up this matter.*" The letter was signed by M. Ronald Rumpsley, Park Ranger (Supervisory), Staircase Campground.

This had to be "Right-Angle" Ronnie, the Dudley Do-right of the local ranger staff, who Ralph and Duffy had described to me as being the straight arrow, "by the book" man. Checking out the date of the alleged campground disturbance, I discovered it had been exactly one week after Ralph had liberated Duffy from the bear trap and sent him to the high hills to contemplate the error of his ways. It sounded to me like Duffy had quickly returned to his old haunts and his disturbing habits.

As I had told Ralph when I last saw him, I didn't know any of the park staff. Perhaps this would be a good opportunity to make their acquaintance. I decided to call Ranger Rumpsley and make an appointment.

In the meantime it might be well to do some creative thinking.

CHAPTER SEVEN
Mystery in Campsite #17

Not knowing how to reach the ranger's cabin in the campground I called the division headquarters of the National Park Service and was patched through to Ranger Rumpley's quarters.

"Rumpsley, here, how may I be of help?" I thought I heard the suggestion of stuffiness in the ranger's voice as I identified myself and requested an audience. We agreed that one o'clock on the next Tuesday afternoon would be convenient for both of us. I was determined to keep an open mind about Ranger Rumpsley. I'd always attempted to avoid forming opinions about people I had never met based on the judgment of others, especially when the "others" are a couple of decidedly biased black bears.

It was on a "partly cloudy, scattered shower" kind of day that I made the trip up to the park again — for the third or fourth time since I had reconnected with my bear friends. I had no thought of seeing either Ralph or Duffy, but I fully expected that I would learn something new about them, and it was likely to be something bad. I also hoped to learn about how a national park campground was managed.

Staircase takes its name from a crude cedar stairway built by the first explorers in the area when they discovered they couldn't negotiate the cliffs along the river west of the present day campground. The staircase is long gone, but the name remains. It is one of the most popular spots in the park, being close to populated areas and easily accessed by paved roads. It has all of the amenities to be found in a "Federal Recreation Facility", including bear-proof garbage vaults. Thousands visit this bucolic spot every year, many coming in their thirty-foot RVs which they park, unfold awnings and TV antennas, then sit inside and watch nature shows celebrating the glories of the great outdoors. Government publicists refer to the Olympic National Park and its surrounding national forests as a two million acre recreational wonderland. Ralph and Macduff occupied only a tiny potion of this vast space, but I was beginning to think that they had a disproportionate effect on its well-being.

Being early for my appointment with the ranger, I parked and took a leisurely stroll through the campground, which seemed to be completely full. I was pleased to note that there were a few visitors actually roughing it in real tents, sandwiched here and there between the motorized recreational behemoths. I also smelled fragrant cooking odors emanating from numerous outdoor grills, and wondered idly if the campers might be violating the "attractive odor" restrictions designed to discourage bears from visiting campsites. I decided that aside from the couple of bears I knew, few of them were likely to be visiting campgrounds in broad daylight.

The ranger's headquarters at the campground was nothing more than a rustic cabin that provided a place for the ranger to hang out, answer questions, issue backcountry hiking permits and collect fees from visitors. Inside there was the usual counter

covered with brochures, maps and booklets, along with a large number of pamphlets explaining the things that are not allowed within the park. A casual inspection revealed that the items on the prohibited list far outnumbered those on the list of permitted activities. As I approached the little building I had already formed a mental image of Ranger Ronald Rumpsley, picturing a tall, athletic, straight-backed man in a starched uniform with a Sam Brown belt and a "Mounty" hat. In my mind's eye he was even wearing polished boots. Mine was a vision right out of central casting, more befitting the image of the Canadian Mounted Police than what I knew to be the outfit of our everyday park ranger. I stepped through the ranger's door precisely on the stroke of one o'clock, determined to show the kind of precision and punctuality that was likely to impress any man who "went by the book".

Clearly I had wasted a lot of time creating this image. At first glance Ranger Ronnie "Right-Angle" Rumpsley didn't appear to be even remotely similar to what I had imagined. Our campground ranger was quite young, somewhat portly, and a trifle rumpled, even through his shirt and trousers appeared to be properly laundered and pressed. He did have the Smokey Bear hat, but it was hanging on a hook on the wall and his hair, barely shorter than the legal length, might have been combed by the wind. I noticed the corner of a red bandana sticking out of his back pocket. Contrary to my expectations this Ranger Rumpsley actually looked like a regular guy. I was shocked. I had expected spit-and-polish.

Then I learned that this wasn't the ranger at all, but the ranger's aide, Wilmer Archibald, a student in wildlife management from The Evergreen State College, who was serving as Rumpsley's summer intern — a "park aide" as they are known. I introduced myself and mentioned my appointment with the ranger.

"The ranger had to step out for a moment to help a camper adjust his TV disk," said Wilmer with a smile. "He'll be back presently. Please make yourself comfortable." He indicated the single wooden chair in the outer office.

Seating myself I noticed a large bound volume on the top of the desk with the title, PARK REGULATIONS, written in prominent letters. I hoped that the rangers wouldn't find a reason to throw the book at me. The thing was big enough to kill.

"So," I said, by way of making conversation, "you're a student at Evergreen? You ever run into a fellow named Oddware Stumple? He used to go to school down there. I met him out in the woods several years ago when he was doing some kind of research on illegal garbage dumps."

"Stork Stumple?" asked young Archibald. "Sure, everybody knows Stork. He teaches there now. I had a class from him last year. I guess you probably know why they call him Stork, right?"

"As I remember he looked more like an owl than a stork. Quite a character," I said. "He used to drive an old Volkswagen with signs all over it, and a chimney sticking out of the top."

"Yeah, that's the guy. The old Volks is still parked down near the campus. I think it's on the National Register of Historic Junk. It's become the official campus graffiti site. Kids write stuff all over it."

"Has it still got a 'FREE TIBET' sign on it?" I asked.

"Absolutely," said Wilmer. "That's still one of Stork's favorite causes."

"What does he teach?" I inquired, not knowing quite what to expect.

"Street Protest As a Tool of Social Reform: Effective Methods and Techniques. It's a four credit class."

"What do you do in a street protest class?" I asked, even though I was pretty sure I could have guessed the answer.

"It's mostly field trips, observing protest marches, street riots, stuff like that. You write lots of reports. For your final test you have to organize a march. The bigger the march the better your grade. Me and three other guys did a 'STOP EATING BEARS' march in McCleary — right down Main Street in the middle of the parade during the Bear Festival. The local cop ran us out of town. Stork said we would've gotten a better grade if we'd had more bullhorns, and if we could have sprayed the cop with pepper. As it was we didn't even get our pictures in the papers. I got a B-minus. If you can get in a big protest, like the WTO or a war riot, and get pinched, you get a better grade. Some of the kids joined a group called 'Rent-A-Mob' down in San Francisco. They're going to be career protestors. I couldn't afford it."

I was about to comment on my own interest in saving bears when the ranger came through the door. "Sorry I'm late, he said. "Had a little TV emergency down at campsite #27. It's hard to get good reception in some of those older RVs, especially on the 'Shooting Star Turbo 28'. They're a nice rig, but the older ones have dead spots in 'em. I've been trying to get the administration to put cable outlets in all the hookups, but I'm afraid money is too tight just now."

He turned to the young park aide. "Archie, get on down to the generator shack and get the trap set up. Make sure it's baited right and test the door. See that it doesn't hang up. I have a feeling this will be our lucky night."

"Yes, sir," Archibald said as he retrieved his hat and disappeared through the door.

Rumpsley was far from what I had imagined him to be. He was a sturdy fellow with a generous nose, an infectious smile and an unruly growth of hair, largely devoted to luxuriant eyebrows and a moustache of massive proportions. From a distance he might have been mistaken for a German Schnauzer dog with a mouthful of straw.

The ranger turned to me and extended his hand. "Mr. Merrill, is it? I'm Boris Mickeilweisky. That's pronounced Mickelewski. Call me Borski, or just plain Ski. Everybody does, it's much simpler. I'm temporarily in charge of the campground here. Ranger Rumpsley was called out on a four-month emergency assignment to a wildlife class in Vermont. I've taken over for him until he gets back."

Expecting a bone-crushing handshake I extended my hand, preparing an extra firm grip of my own. I was pleasantly surprised to find that Mickeilweisky's shake was unremarkable. This fellow wasn't a starched, straight arrow type at all. He seemed quite the opposite — my kind of guy.

"Thanks for coming," he said. "Just step into the office here and have a seat. He opened a little swinging half-door alongside the counter and indicated a chair. There seemed to be a faint accent in his voice — Polish or Bulgarian, perhaps — which might account for the magnificent east European mustache. The ranger had a relaxed manner, obviously not overwhelmed by his own importance. My apprehension about the visit began to ease.

"I hope our letter didn't mystify you too much. This noise incident happened before I came on board here, so I only know about it secondhand. Ron Rumpsley just had time, as he was leaving, to mention that you were coming, so I'm a bit hazy on the facts, but I'm sure we can get this cleared up quickly. Ronnie left a bunch of notes here."

The ranger opened a folder containing official-looking papers and copious handwritten notes. "He believed in doing things thoroughly," said Mickeilweisky with a note of apology in his voice. "It looks like he has everything neatly arranged. First, here's the tape recorder with your name on it." He produced the recorder from the bottom drawer of his desk. "Now let's see what Rumpsley has written."

The ranger began reading from the form. "Re: Exhibit A. It seems clear," he writes, "that this recorder was not the instrument that was the cause of the noise problem on the night in question. I've played the tape in the recorder. What is on it appears to be a mélange of excited talk in a foreign tongue — nothing resembling what Mr. Roperstein described in his noise complaint. This may be what is known as rap music, but I could be mistaken. I don't profess to be an expert on modern music."

The ranger put aside the report and picked up another. "This one reports the theft of a boom box recorder from a camper's car on the night in question. It's Exhibit B. According to Ronald, an Earthtremblor Boom box 34XPT 18, reported stolen from campsite #17 on July 19. Found in campsite #48. Complainant Roperstein states that the instrument in question is easily capable of 150 decibels. In fact, says R. (his words) 'those things can blow the balls off an aluminum alligator. They are frequently used in Asia to keep elephants out of rice paddies.' As mentioned in his previous report, complainant Roperstein is a retired audio engineer, and his opinion in this matter must be regarded as accurate. The tape in the machine (Exhibit C) is entitled 'Stuffin' All Da Chicks' by Big Daddy Badass."

Ranger Mickeilweisky smiled. "At the end of the report Ronnie says he tried to listen to the tape but he thinks it was in Japanese." He chuckled, "It's not like Ronnie to use humor in his reports, but maybe that last bit wasn't meant to be funny. It's hard to know."

"Anyway," said Ranger Borski, thumbing through more papers, "this whole thing looks like a tempest in a teapot to me. No harm done, a few campers inconvenienced, what's the big deal?" Then he asked, almost as an afterthought, "You any idea how your tape recorder got mixed up in this whole thing?"

This was the question I had prepared for, and I was not caught off guard. "I spent a night in the campground several weeks ago," I lied, "left the recorder on the table. Next morning it was gone."

Ranger Mickeilweisky seemed like such a regular guy it pained me to have to lie to him. On the other hand, I imagined it would have been a pleasure to lie to Ranger Ronald Rumpsley. I had actually been looking forward to it.

"Nowadays that seems to be the fate of anything left untended around here," said the ranger, with a sigh. "We have one hell of a theft problem. Lots of small stuff like cell phones, battery chargers, and video games, not to mention bigger things like 'Earthquake boom boxes'. We can't seem to catch the kids involved." The ranger was massaging his right hand. Apparently I had overdone the handshake. I considered apologizing and then thought better of it.

"How do you know it's kids?" I asked.

Ranger Borski didn't answer my question. He was intently studying another document. "Here's something interesting," he said. "It's another report from Ronald. In this one he is questioning the Ropersteins about the noisy party. Asks them who it was that was making all the noise. Listen to this: 'Mrs. Bertha Roperstein, age 82, spouse of complainant A.J. Roperstein, age 83, describes the noisemakers as being animalistic young people of both sexes behaving like primitive people at a tribal orgy'. They used coarse language that she could not understand, and most of them seemed to be large, hairy and ugly. All of them were intoxicated, she said. Testimony of Mr. R. suggests that since Mrs. R has poor eyesight and is hard-of-hearing, her recollection may be less than accurate. Also, according to Mr. R it was very dark and the disturbance was at the edge of the campground some distance away. Mr. R likened the incident to fraternity parties he remembers from his college days 'when many of the boys wore raccoon coats and sang loud bawdy songs'. Mr. R agreed with Mrs. R on one point saying he was certain that the partygoers 'were all drunker than hell' (his words). He stated that the decibel level of the noise unquestionably surpassed 150 decibels."

Things started to come into focus. It was hardly a surprise to me that my tape recorder, which had been loaned to Macduff Shakesbear, was found on the ground the morning after rangers had received complaints about a noisy party of furry participants. Clearly Duffy and his crowd of irresponsible, hormone-enhanced bear friends were pushing the limits of propriety. No longer just garbage can nuisances, they had crossed the line into a potential inter-species conflict that could end only one way. I knew my responsibility was to head off this disaster before it went any further.

"Are you sure it's kids doing this stuff?" I asked again, hoping to get a line on what the staff in the park was thinking.

"It's hard to imagine adults doing it," said the ranger. "Why not check to see what's on your tape there. Maybe we can get a clue off it. Ronald probably didn't listen to the whole thing."

I hesitated, not sure of what we might hear, but decided that I could bluff my way out of whatever it might be. If it was Duffy on the tape it seemed unlikely that he would be speaking English. Just then we heard heavy steps on the porch. Young Wilmer Archibald the park aide, was stomping dirt from his shoes.

"Okay, it's all set. We'll catch him for sure tonight, Ski," he said, hanging his hat on the peg.

I gave the ranger a questioning look.

"Bear trap," he said. "We've got some problem bears around here. Been trying to catch them and relocate them. What did you use for bait, Archie?"

"We're all out of that 'Essence of Bear Must' stuff. A camper down by the bridge gave me some stale donuts. Should do the trick; bears are very fond of donuts. If we had a six-pack of beer I'd put that in there too. Then I know we'd catch the crafty buggers."

"This bear likes beer?" I asked innocently, my interest suddenly aroused. "Never saw anything like him," said Borski. "Once we saw him run through the campground on three legs with a carton of donuts under one arm and a six-pack of beer hanging from his mouth. Scared the hell out of everybody in the campground. Ran right over the top of a state senator who happened to be visiting the park that day. 'Course we didn't have our dart guns ready, so he got clean away."

"Old Ronnie Rumpsley was beside himself; I thought he'd have a stroke. The big bosses at park headquarters caught hell from a lot of upset campers. Don't know whether it's true or not, but two campers reported that the senator wet himself during all the excitement. Naturally the big shots have been putting the pressure on Ronnie ever since to get the bear problem under control. He's been nervous as a bullfrog in a hatbox; gets freaked out real easy. That's why they sent him to wildlife school back in Vermont. They've got a class in bear trapping back there. 'Controlling the Nuisance Bear' they call it."

"How do you know it's the same bear doing all this stuff?"

"Easy," said young Archibald. "He's a half-grown male bear with a faded white splash on his chest. If such a thing is possible, he always seems to have a smirk on his face. I call it a smirk, anyway. He's cocky. Acts like he knows exactly what people are thinking."

The ranger had brewed up a pot of coffee. He and his aide seemed quite relaxed as we sat around the little office discussing bear matters. I thought I should add a few thoughts of my own to keep the conversation going.

"You know," I said, trying not to be boastful or pretentious, "I've done quite a bit of reading on the subject, and from what I have discovered, bears are smart — a whole lot smarter than dogs, and in some ways they're a lot like people. You may have your hands full catching your beer-loving bruin."

94

"Well, I don't know whether I'd go quite that far," said the ranger. "We had him in the barrel trap a couple of weeks ago but he got loose somehow in the night. When we caught him, Ronald was euphoric. He was already writing out his report about how he planned to dart the bear first thing in the morning, tattoo him and put a radio on him. He was going to throw him on the back of a mule and transport him over Hayden pass, and leave him out in the middle of nowhere. Had the report all done, but when he and his helpers went out in the morning with the equipment the trap was empty. Poor fellow went ballistic. Accused all of us of letting the bear out. Even threatened to fire young Archie, here. Of course, he looked incompetent to the big shots at headquarters. They had him on the carpet — blamed everything on him. That senator was raising hell, too. You know how things go when a politician gets involved, somebody's got to take the rap. We never figured out how the bear got out of the barrel, but it sure wasn't one of us who let him out."

I certainly had no intention of telling the rangers how Duffy had escaped from the trap, for there was not the slightest doubt that it was Duffy they were talking about. But I figured it wouldn't do any harm if I gave them some oblique clues.

"There's one story I remember reading about," I said, "where two orphan bear cubs were being raised by a guy up in New England. He discovered that they cooperated in making a hole in the cage, so they could get out and go roaming around at night. He couldn't figure out how they did it until he caught 'em in the act. There was a weak place in the fence — a loose staple maybe, and he saw one of the cubs holding the wire open so the other one could go through. They took turns at it. These were just young bears, too,

95

and adult bears are much smarter than cubs. Maybe another bear let your miscreant out of the trap."

"Well, I agree they're crafty," said Borski, "but it would be a stretch for me to imagine that one bear could let another out of a barrel trap that has a hasp and one of those harness snaps holding the door shut. Bears aren't that dexterous."

I came close to telling my companions that I once knew a bear that could run a laptop computer, but I was pretty sure that I would lose my audience if I did. "Well, gentlemen," I said, arising from my chair, "time is passing. I better be getting on home before it gets too late. I wish you success in catching your bear. I'll be interested in knowing how it goes. Will it be in the paper if you catch him?"

"I doubt it," replied Borski. "We don't report that kind of thing. It gets the animal rights people all stirred up, and we really don't need the publicity. Before you go let's check what's on your tape. Maybe Ronald missed something."

I had been hoping that the ranger had forgotten about his earlier request. I wasn't keen on listening to the tape in front of them. If Duffy **was** speaking English I might have a problem explaining what it was all about. As I switched the tape on I quickly realized that I needn't have worried. The whole thing was bear jabber with a lot of snorting, tooth clacking and guttural blather. None of it seemed to be Duffy's voice, so I suspected that it was the tape that he promised to make of Ralph's COB meeting. Voices were raised in a loud argument, and I heard what sounded like a scuffle followed by several high-pitched yelps.

"Sounds like Saturday night in a Hungarian night club," said Borski with a chuckle.

"Or maybe the belt sander races at the Model T tavern in Hoodsport," offered young Archibald.

"Thanks for coming up, Pete," said Ranger Mickeilweisky. "Like I said, that noise matter was a tempest in a teapot. It's a closed issue as far as I'm concerned. Ronald Rumpsley is a fuss-budget about stuff like that. Thinks everything has to be recorded. He's got a ton of those kinds of reports in the file. Well, at least, you got your recorder back. If you ever get back this way, look us up."

"I'll do that. Thanks for everything, Ski. Say, Archie, if you run into Stork, your old professor, say hello for me. He probably won't remember who I am. Just tell him I'm the old guy he had the conversation with over the ant log up above the South Shore road a couple of years ago. Remind him we shared a doobie together. You might also tell him I've given the stuff up. Come to think of it, he probably won't remember the incident at all, considering the shape he was in."

I drove slowly out of the campground trying to decide what I should do. I wasn't sure how Duffy felt about stale donuts, but I was apprehensive about the determination of the ranger staff to catch the 'rogue' bear that we had spent so much time discussing. I had my cell phone with me and decided to give my friends a call. Perhaps by some miracle I could contact either Duffy or Ralph and warn them of the danger. Stopping by the bridge over the end of the lake I checked to see if I had enough signal to call Ralph, and then dug his phone number out of the dark recesses of my wallet. Just as I started the car to drive to a less conspicuous spot before making the call, a park service pickup drove up with Wilmer Archibald at the wheel. He rolled down his window.

"We got to thinking about those stale donuts," he said. "Ski isn't sure that bears go for stale stuff. He's sending me down to see if I can find some Krispy Kremes. He read somewhere that black bears can't resist Krispy Kremes. We'll see. Take care," he shouted as he accelerated down the dusty road.

Hmmm, I thought, what has Ranger Mickeilweisky been reading that I haven't? I drove across the bridge and found a reasonably secluded spot where the occasional hiker or fisherman wouldn't be listening to my conversation. I dialed up the number. The phone rang four times and then I heard Ralph's guttural voice. He was speaking in bear.

"Hey, Ralph, it's me. Speak English."

"Yeah, what do you want?"

"Is Duffy there?" I found myself shouting.

"Quit shouting, I'm not deaf," grumbled the old bear. "I'm busy. I've got a meeting going on. Duffy's not here. He's off playing house with his girlfriends. Call him at his own phone number — 496-BEAR — that's 496-2327.   If you get a hold of him, tell him to get his ass back over here. He's supposed to be at this meeting." The line went dead.

Oh my God, I thought, now they've each got a phone. What next, conference calls?

I called Duffy and got an answer on the second ring. Except for a lot of female giggling he came in loud and clear. It sounded like he was right next door, which turned out to be exactly the case. He was just above the Elk Creek road, about a half–mile away, playing hopscotch with his children, or so he said. I gave him the gist of what I had learned at the ranger's cabin and told him about the

98

donut bait in the barrel. "I'll let old Bartley have the stale ones," he said, "but if they put Krispy Kremes in there I may have to go for them myself. I'll get my buddy Bigbutt Beasley to hold the door up while I snatch the loot. Then we'll share the Krispys."

"Bear cooperation," I said, half to myself. I felt sorry for Ski and Archie.

I gave him Ralph's message. "Yeah, it's a sub-committee meeting to make rules about how close bears can go to the campground. Just a lot of hot air. I'll get there when I can."

I asked Duffy to come down and get the tape recorder, which he promptly did. He came racing down the hillside breathing heavily. As far as I could see he didn't even check to see if there were other people around before he charged down onto the road. Getting a bit careless I thought.

I noticed that Duffy still had his makeshift fanny pack. I gave the recorder to him and, as I suspected, he said that he had put the complete proceedings of one of Ralph's COB meetings on the tape.

"Listen, Duffy," I pleaded, "be more careful where you leave the recorder, and try to get that thing translated into English so I can understand it. Write it in your notebook and call me when you're done. I'll come up and get it."

"No problem, dude. No sooner said than done. I got to get back to the game. The girls are waiting," he said, bolting from sight.

"How's the book coming?" I shouted.

"What book?" I heard as his voice faded away in the distance.

CHAPTER EIGHT
Bear Alert!

Now that all those bears — the ones I knew at least — had their own telephones, I stopped worrying about making long-range meeting dates. Trying to set dates two months in advance for days when it might not be raining was not a very satisfactory arrangement. I decided if they wanted to talk to me they could just call me on a cell phone, so I went about my business, which consisted of a lot of resting and puttering, and a minimum of thinking about bears.

When a month had gone by and I hadn't heard anything from either one of them, I began to think that maybe Ranger Mickeilweisky and his sidekick, Park aide Archibald, had actually succeeded in trapping Duffy, and made him a resident of the Olympic Mountain high country, somewhere up near Badger Valley, perhaps. Gradually I began to think that this wouldn't be such a bad state-of-affairs. Duffy was becoming a nuisance bear by every definition of the word; not just in the matter of raiding garbage cans, but in much more imaginative pursuits, such as holding raucous parties in the campgrounds, breaking and entering automobiles, stealing food out of bear traps, and racing through campsites upsetting local politicians. Duffy had clearly become too "humanized". It was about time he got back among his own kind and learned to become a bear again.

I think Ralph had given up on Duffy ever reforming himself, and was resigned to the notion that his delinquent grandson would end his days in a zoo, or as a wall decoration in a rustic cabin somewhere. He had told Duffy more than once that in the world of relations between bears and human beans, the bears would always "suck hind tit", as he put it. He often told me that it didn't do any good to remind humans about who was here first. We bears, he would say, are second-class citizens.

I remember hearing Ralph give Duffy a fatherly lecture during one of our meetings up by the berry patch when he was just a cub. Ralph gave the youngster a short history of bear-people relationships and explained the official policy of human law-making agencies regarding bears.

"People are very strange," said the old bear. (Ralph often started his sentences this way.) "They build their houses right in the middle of where bears have been living since the first sun came up. They haven't the foggiest idea how to live off the land, so they have all these places they call stores, full of fancy foodstuffs. They buy their grub there, then take it home and cook up great big meals, only half of which they eat. What they don't eat they call 'garbage', and they put it in cans on their back porches. There was a time when this garbage was taken by trucks to a central location, and dumped in big piles where it was eaten with relish by appreciative bears, seagulls and other animals."

"Finally," said Ralph, in what was about the first time I'd ever heard him say anything good about people, "the human beans had actually found a perfect solution to a vexing problem: too many hungry bears and too much unwanted garbage. At a single stroke, with the creation of these outdoor dumps, they kept the bears well-fed while getting rid of their garbage at the same time. The relationship between people and bears entered a period of *Pax Ursana* — mutual goodwill. For years bears and people were friendly. Garbage truck drivers were even on a first-name basis with the local bears."

Ralph said he could remember his father telling yarns about a special driver named Clarence, who brought the refuse from the penitentiary where they wasted a lot of food. He'd always let the bears know where the best stuff was. He said they never had it so good, but he knew that those days couldn't last. He was right, of course, because when the environmental movement came along garbage dumps were suddenly declared toxic. They were closed up and covered over with inedible dirt. All the hungry bears in search of an easy meal were forced to return to the back porches to eat out of the cans like before. And just like that people had "nuisance" bears again and wondered why.

"Human beans," Ralph had said, "are forever shooting themselves in the foot."

At the time I listened to Ralph without comment as he discussed the merits of garbage in a bear's diet. I thought it best not to bring up the questionable nutrient value of tin cans and other inedibles. Ralph didn't always take kindly to having his theories questioned.

As fall approached I decided to drive up to the campground on Labor Day just to see what happened there on a busy three-day holiday. I could check our secret hiding place in the stump hole on the chance that Duffy might be done with his tape translation. The several phone calls I had made to his cell phone number had not been answered, and it occurred to me that the people who owned the stolen phones had probably caught onto the fact that they were being bilked when they got their bills at the end of the month. Ralph and Duffy had probably had their cell phone service cut off by now.

The weather was sunny and warm as I drove into the mountains in early September, and since it was the middle day of the holiday weekend the traffic was not heavy. As expected, the campground was overflowing with fun-seekers of every description. A sign at the entrance alerted latecomers that the park was full, with nary a campsite vacancy. Attached to a tree alongside this sign was another that immediately caught my eye. **BEAR ALERT!** the notice said, followed by additional words that were too small for me to read.

That the Staircase campground was full on Labor Day was not a surprise, but a bear alert was another matter altogether. As a matter of fact it surely must be a first. No self-respecting bear with any regard for his safety would be hanging around this campground on the busiest day of the year. Then it occurred to me, reluctantly, that this would be exactly the kind of day when an enterprising bear like Macduff Shakesbear **would** be hanging around the place. The very idea made me uneasy.

I drove slowly through the grounds observing America at play, from the toddlers in their plastic playpens to the gray-haired geriatrics taking their ease in their plastic lawn chairs under the plastic awnings of their thirty-two foot long air-conditioned Winnebagos. Scantily clad young men and women in summertime

103

dress watched programs on small plastic TV sets, and drank from plastic bottles and cups. Occasionally music could be heard issuing from automobiles, which were made primarily of fiberglass, a form of plastic. America, it must be said, was largely a plastic society.

As I cruised through the place, with very little on my mind, I observed Park aide Wilmer Archibald, a clipboard in hand, talking to an elderly visitor beside a middle-sized RV. I waited until he was finished, and then drove slowly up beside him. "Hey, Archie," I called, "how's it going?"

"Come up to the office and I'll tell you. I'll be there in ten minutes." He headed down the road to another campsite.

I worked my way through the grounds and parked next to the little ranger cabin. Noticing one of the Bear Alert signs stapled to the bulletin board outside the cabin, I got out of the car to read the small print.

BEAR ALERT!
NOTICE TO CAMPGROUND VISITORS
Due to an increase in bear sightings in and near the campgrounds, visitors should be extra vigilant.
KEEP YOUR FOODSTUFFS COVERED
OR STORED INSIDE YOUR VEHICLE
Under no circumstances should campers feed bears
No matter how cute or tame they seem to be,
BEARS ARE NOT PETS!

Underneath this admonition there was a familiar list of "dos and don'ts" in the event of a "bear encounter", and at the bottom of the notice:

REPORT ALL BEAR SIGHTINGS
TO PARK RANGERS PROMPTLY!

True to his word, Archie arrived in just ten minutes, writing as he walked. We shook hands. He looked harried.

"What's new, Archie?" I asked in my usual light-hearted way. "You keeping things under control around here?"

"It's touch-and-go," he replied. "Some days are better than others." He held up his clipboard, which appeared to hold a sizeable stack of forms. He pointed to the "report all sightings" on the Bear Alert sign. "Bears were on the prowl again last night apparently. Got half a dozen more reports this morning. Listen to this one," said Archie, thumbing through his forms. "This guy says he saw a bear playing golf down on the Cushman course just at dusk last night. Said he had a golf bag over his shoulder and everything; swears the bear had on one of those little flat hats, too. My God, what's next?"

"I suppose a bear could play golf," I said, "if he had the right kind of clubs."

"Yeah, sure, and pigs could fly if they had wings." Archie seemed out-of-sorts. My levity was not helping matters. I needed to remember to ask Duffy, if I ever saw him again, if he had "found" a set of golf clubs.

"Still got bear problems, eh?" I asked. "Haven't had any luck with the trap?"

"Oh, we catch bears alright, but it's always the same bear. We've caught him so many times that we're on a first name basis. We've relocated him three times but he always comes back. Some of the big shots at headquarters want to euthanize him, but Ski and I aren't going to do it. Old Dumbo — that's what we call him — isn't a threat to anybody. He's just not very smart."

"Bears are a lot like people," I said. "You've got your dumb ones, and you've got your smart ones."

"And you've got your devious, clever ones, too," said Archie, with a sigh of resignation. "You should read some of these things," he said, flipping through the papers on his clipboard. "If half of everything on these reports is true we got a bear that ought to be running for some kind of public office. He's smarter than most of the politicians we got now."

There wasn't a doubt in my mind who Archie was talking about. It had to be Duffy, still refining his nuisance skills.

"How'd the Krispy Kremes work in the trap?" I asked.

"Well, now that you mention it," said Archie, "the Krispy Kreme deal illustrates exactly what I'm talking about. First, I had to go clear to Tacoma to get the damned things. We ate some of them ourselves and baited the trap with the rest. Next morning the trap was sprung and the Krispys were all gone. There's no way a bear could get those things out of there without springing the gate — unless he had help that is. That night we baited the trap again with the old stale donuts, and the next morning Old Dumbo was sitting in there with crumbs all over his chin. I had to drive him up into the hills again. Took him all the way to the Wynoochie this time. He hasn't come back. Not yet, anyway."

"Is Ski still on the job here?" I inquired.

"Yeah, Ski's down at the other end of the campground taking down bear reports. He'll be back pretty soon." Archie was studying his papers. "Just listen to some of these things: A Mrs. Alberts of

Kansas City said she came back from the river and saw a bear trying to open the back of her car; Mr. Orweiler of Pocatello watched from behind a tree while a young bear stole a deck of cards and his dark glasses from the picnic table; Ms. Gordon, no address given, just finished cooking a pot of beans when a bear walked up and stole the whole thing, pot and all. She's put in a claim to the park service to get her pot back. Here's one from last week: Bear inside RV watching television. Owners called 911 on cell phone, nobody responded. Complaint registered with rangers. Complainant intends to sue government for anguish and suffering. I could go on and on," said Archie wearily.

"Does this bear ever threaten anybody?" I asked.

"Not so far. He seems like he's polite and well-mannered, but you know about bears. You never know when one might turn nasty, especially if you corner it."

"It doesn't sound like you're ever going to corner this one. He seems to have unusual skills. You know, Archie, I think this creature has entertainment value. Maybe you could train him to put on shows in the evening. Maybe he'd work for meals, think of the publicity."

Archie looked at me like some of my screws had come loose. Apparently Wilmer Archibald had never heard of old Pixley Poomer who, according to Ralph, had a part time job in the park, just showing up once in a while to entertain the tourists. In return the park service supplied him with enough dog kibbles to keep him well-fed and contented. Of course, Pixley was defanged and declawed, and too old to harm anyone. Readers of the book *Ralph, Conversations With A Bear* will remember that the reason Ralph

107

wanted to move to the park in the first place was the prospect of getting an easy job like Poomer's.

I knew Archie wasn't going to believe any of this even if I had the energy to explain it to him. In any case there was no possibility that Duffy was going to submit to defanging and declawing under any circumstances.

"Hey, listen to this. Here's another one," said Archie, reading from the next report. "'Buster (Heavyfoot) Upchurch says his helmet and leather gloves were stole (sic) from his Harley bike while he was asleep in his bed roll on the night of September 1. Value $550. Wants restitution. Threatens legal action. Helmet was won in a fair-and-square bar fight in Sturgis S.D. last year. Has sentimental value.' Come on up to the office, I've got to sort these things out," said Archie. "I'll put on some coffee."

The telephone was ringing as we entered the ranger's office. Archie answered.

"Staircase Campground, Archibald speaking. How can we help you? Hi, Gluey, what's up? Yeah, I think Ski took the report...okay. I'll tell him when he comes in...sure, you bet. One of us will pick it up. Thanks for the help. Yeah, I know, there's a lot of weird stuff going on...we're working on it. I'll let you know if we hear anything. Thanks, Glue, keep in touch." Archie hung up the phone and went about the business of making coffee.

"That was Elmer LePage, the groundskeeper down at the golf course. Everyone calls him Glue or Gluey. Name he got when he was in grade school. You know, Elmer's glue, Lepage's glue. What else could you call him? Anyway, he says they found a set of golf clubs down there, bag and all. Probably the one Ski took the report

108

about the other morning." Archie was leafing through his pile of incident reports.

"Yeah, here it is. Guy in campsite #16, 24 foot Holiday Palace. Name's Warren A. Warsherbarger. Reported golf clubs and bag missing from his rig two days ago. Claims they were stolen right out of the storage locker on the side of his RV. Had the initials W.A.W. stitched on the side of the bag. Hard to miss according to the report."

"Did Glue mention anything about a little plaid hat?" I asked.

"God damn bear still has the little hat," said Archie. "Mark my words, the next time that bear runs through the campground he'll have that little hat on."

"Or maybe a motorcycle helmet," I said.

Archie poured each of us a cup of coffee. "Cream? Sugar?"

"Black is fine. You know, Archie, with as many incident reports as you've got there I don't see how all of those things could be done by one bear. When would he sleep?"

"Well, they weren't all done in one night, you know, but I think we're clearly dealing with a hyperactive animal. I don't think he sleeps much. These aren't all the reports, either. Ski probably has just as many. He's still getting more from the other end of the campground."

"You'd think with all this wild animal stuff going on," I observed, "you'd have a lot of people leaving the park. Those bear alert signs all over the place can't be very reassuring to timid campers."

"The funny thing is," said Archie, "this critter is so crafty that most of the people don't associate what's going on with a bear. Most of them think it's vandals, you know, delinquent kids. For all we know, maybe it is. The folks who claim they've actually seen this bear mention that he hasn't threatened them at all. Some have said he even seemed polite, except for the lady with the bean pot. She was really pissed off. As soon as she made her report she left in a huff. Said she'd be getting in touch with her congressman. The guy with the bear in his RV didn't seem much amused either, now that I think of it."

"Where is it all going to end, Archie? You guys got any plan?" I thought if I could get a clue about what the park authorities had in mind I might warn Duffy in time to save his hide.

Archie was looking out the window. "Here comes Ski. He's the one to ask. I think all the big shots are planning a meeting. He'll know about it."

Ranger Milky Whiskey, as he was sometimes known by his colleagues, removed his Mounty hat as he came through the door, threw his clipboard on the counter and moped his brow with his red bandana.

"These three day holidays are going to be the death of me," he said with feeling. He turned to me with his hand outstretched. "Hi, Pete, good to see you again. What brings you up here?"

"Came to see if you had any vacancies. Thought you might be hiring rangers," I said facetiously.

"Right at the moment I would say that anybody who wants to be a park ranger has got to have holes in his head. Has Archie told you about our latest problems?"

"Bear problems, he tells me."

"Bear problems big time."

"Did you get anything interesting down at the south end?" asked Archie.

"Mostly petty stuff," replied Ski. "Bear sitting in car singing along with radio; bear in dark glasses looking in tent; bear stealing books; bear stealing almost brand-new guitar. Here's one that's a bit different reported by Barney Barnstable of Cedar Rapids, IA down in #20. He lost a whole basket of picnic lunches snatched off his table by a bear galloping through his campsite. It seems the older bear had a cub with him. The cub got a six-pack of diet coke. This is the first time there's been more than one bear. Don't know what to make of that," said Ski.

"I would say you have an unusual bear in more ways than one, Ski," I offered. "Male bears seldom hang around with cubs. You sure Mr. Barnstable wasn't hallucinating?"

"Dammit, man. I'm not sure of anything anymore. I wish Ronnie Rumpsley would get home so I can give him back his damn campground. I want a transfer to the typing pool." Ski picked up a form from his desk and his eyebrows knitted as he poured over an announcement of job vacancies. "Here's one, engineering equipment officer — that's a forklift driver. I could handle that. I'd be a forklift driver with a PhD in forest conservation."

"The tourist season is about over, Ski, and it won't be long before the bears go into hibernation. Hang in there, there's better days a comin'," I said, using one of my favorite expressions.

"Not soon enough," grumped the ranger. "Had any calls from

headquarters, Archie?"

"Nothing this morning."

Ski looked at me solemnly. "There's a big shot coming from Yellowstone to tell us how to handle our bear problem, so we've got to assemble all the local experts. I know what they're going to say already: 'dart the bear and then put him to sleep'. That's standard procedure. Of course, it's too dangerous to shoot the bear around the campground. You might accidentally pick off a stray tourist, so we'd have to dart him first, although there is still a danger of putting a camper to sleep if your aim isn't good. Before you do anything, of course, you have to deal with all the forms that have to be filled out, and all the agencies that have to be notified. Man, you wouldn't believe the paperwork. I suspect they'd need to do several more studies, but by then the bears will be hibernating. Next spring they'd have to start all over again. Well, when they wake up I'll be somewhere else and it'll be Ronnie's problem. I sure hate to think that they might actually euthanize our clever ursine friend. I've gotten sort of fond of him."

"I wonder what the bear plans to do with the guitar?" I asked.

"Probably start an act and go on the road. With all those claws he won't need a guitar pick."

"Maybe, I'll go with him," mumbled Ski. "I can sing a few Hungarian country songs." The ranger moved behind his desk. "Well, I hate to break up this little seminar but I've got to get started transcribing all this stuff and send it down to the office."

"I'll be moving along then, gentlemen," I said, as I headed for the door. "I wish you well on your project. I have a feeling you'll get it worked out."

They will if I get the word to Duffy, I thought as I returned to my car.

After leaving the park I drove to our rendezvous spot on the deserted road near the Big Creek Park. As was my custom, I drove slowly into the little road not knowing what I might find. After all, this was the spot where I was once watched by a hungry cougar while waiting for my bear friends. All was quiet and deserted. I turned the machine around and got it headed back out the way I'd come in, just in case I needed to make a quick getaway. I don't know why I was being so cautious, although I was a bit tense after listening to the tales of bear depredations in the campground. The information I was gathering about the determination of the park people to rid themselves of their bear problems once and forever had certainly been depressing.

I stopped the car near the old stump where Duffy had excavated the hiding place. I hoped, without much confidence, that there might be some kind of note in the hole telling me how I might contact the bears again, since all my efforts to reach them by phone had been unsuccessful. A lot of new vegetation had grown up in the area and it took some time to find the place. Busy ants scurried in and out of the entrance to the hole, but otherwise it seemed undisturbed. It took courage to reach into that dark place. There could be snakes, badgers, gophers, or porcupines back in there for all I knew. In my uneasy state I even imagined a troll having moved in since I was last there.

I had worried needlessly. The hole was empty except for what I had hoped would be there — Duffy's notebook, dry and intact. Bless his larcenous little heart, I thought, he had carried out my instructions, and had transcribed the tape into what appeared, at first glance, to be reasonably legible English.

I quickly became so engrossed in reading the beginning of his translation that I failed to notice the slow approach of another automobile down the narrow road. Not just any automobile, but the plainly marked car of a deputy sheriff. I wanted to kick myself for not parking my vehicle farther off the highway where it wouldn't be visible. Now I needed to do some desperately fast thinking. Instinct told me that this deputy would be none other than my old nemesis, Fred Edd, Mason County's super sleuth. I had once had what I had come to call a "contrariously multifarious" relationship with him back when I was trying to spirit my two bear friends out of their previous habitat.

Deputy Edd and I were always at odds about things, seemingly without ever quite knowing why, although it more than likely had to do with what he considered to be my illegal cohabitation with wild animals. I suspected that he really didn't understand the law, and that I was probably taking it too seriously. I often thought that after everything was all over, and I had gotten my bear friends settled, we could have sat down over a beer somewhere and easily gotten our differences sorted out. Unfortunately this was not the time. We didn't have any beer, and I was already busy making up a big lie to talk myself out of an embarrassing situation, as I once again tried to protect a couple of errant bears who really didn't appreciate my efforts.

Deputy Edd sat in his cruiser behind his big black glasses talking on his radio. "Running my numbers," I think they call it. He alighted from his car and approached. The sheriff was wearing his short sleeve summer uniform, his belt weighted down with a plethora of the tools of his trade. Things were hanging there that I didn't remember seeing before, undoubtedly more suppressive chemicals and explosive devices. As he approached, Edd seemed to be checking to see if my license plate was bolted on straight. I remained seated in an awkward position near the stump, doing my best to concentrate on the notebook in my lap.

"Well, Mr. Merrill, we seem to run into each other in strange places," he said evenly. "What brings you to this remote spot?" Edd didn't sound contrary or accusatory, just nosy, which I had to agree he had a right to be. It was certainly within the normal duties of a deputy sheriff to investigate a senior citizen sitting in tall weeds in the desolate backwoods. Nevertheless I was already on the defensive.

It had been a couple of years since Edd and I had last spoken. Being a normally law-abiding citizen, I had scant contact with members of law enforcement other than in a casual way at crowded civic events, the scene of an accident, or on the rare occasion when I might have exceeded the speed limit slightly and been cautioned to "keep it down a little". For reasons never clear to me, Deputy Fred Edd brought out the worst of my latent hostility toward authority figures. I imagined that it probably had something to do with those big black glasses he wore, or the unbecoming swagger in his walk. To me Fred Edd was the personification of the schoolyard bully.

I could hardly have found myself in a more awkward position, but with a practiced air of nonchalance and *savoir-faire* I hoped to convince the deputy that sitting in the bushes near a remote mountain road was nothing more than a part of my daily routine. My little brain was in overdrive, feverishly fabricating lies, an unfortunate habit I resort to in these situations.

"Greetings, Deputy Edd," I said, doing my best to sound sincere, but suspecting that I was speaking too rapidly. "How nice to see you again. I'll bet you're wondering what I'm up to. Well, I'm here on a treasure hunt. I belong to the Northwest Poetry Club, and every year we have our progressive poetry treasure hunt. We have to guess where each successive verse of our poem is hidden, then write a new verse with another clue in it to show where to go next, and so on and on. The poet who gets back to the start first wins the contest. The prize this year is a brand new volume of the sonnets of Yeats and Keats." I was running out of breath.

I couldn't believe what I was saying! What if the deputy was a poet? Did Keats and Yeats write sonnets? Damned if I knew.

"Really," said the sheriff. Though I couldn't see them through his impenetrable lenses, I knew his eyes were roving about searching for evidence. "Not studying bugs anymore? Seems like the last time we ran into each other you were studying ants, weren't you?"

Damn, why hadn't I thought of that? Ants would have been a whole lot easier to explain than poetry. Well, it was too late now. I'd have to bluff my way through.

"Oh, no," I said, "I still have an abiding interest in entomology, but I'm also passionate about poetry. It's fairly easy to combine the two. Listen to this, I recently wrote a heroic couplet to the common American piss ant." (Fortunately I had this little number committed to memory. It was an epic I had composed once while sitting on my deck on a hot summer day, clearly influenced by a dram too much of the grape.)

Tiny busy feet aflutter, hurrying to uncertain fate

116

You don't know where you're going, just try to estimate.
You'll sometimes find your way in circles
But you'll get there quicker going straight.

The deputy just stood there by the front of his car, uncertain about what to do, and apparently at a loss for words. I suspected that he was mentally reviewing county statutes trying to remember whether reading bad poetry in public could at least be a misdemeanor.

"Now, here's the verse that led me here," I said. "This was a tough one. See if you can figure it out, Fred. Listen to this." I ad-libbed furiously. "It's called...

THE SILENT STUMP
Just up the lane, not far at all
Bare passed the campground there.
You'll find the stump
Long dead and damply still.
Look,
Look there for signs of excavation
At about the point of bifurcation
Where the cache will be
That holds your holy grail.
Down among the sightless creatures
With less than pleasant earthy features.
You must search with groping hands,
Fumble, fumble blindly, friend,
Succeed, you must not fail."

117

"That's a little bit of free verse there, Fred," I said, nervously.

"It would have to be free," he replied. "I don't think anybody would pay you for it."

Even though I couldn't really tell what was going on behind those fearsome black glasses, I had the feeling that Deputy Edd was looking at me like I was some sort of wounded animal that ought to be put out of its misery.

And to tell the truth that's exactly what I felt like. I plunged bravely on, barely concealing my growing hysteria, and digging myself ever deeper into a labyrinthine quagmire from which I might never emerge.

"Now here's the clue to the next station, Fred. See if you can figure out where I should go next....

DUMPSTER AT THE 'T'
Well sought and won
Good comrade thee,
You've found your clue
'Neath this old tree
Now move you nether
To streets all asphalt
Hard as leather,
Beneath a dumpster
On a busy corner
Where next you'll find
A clue we've called
Clue number nind."

"Well, that's not going to be much of a challenge," said the sheriff. "You just drive down to the Model T tavern and look under the dumpster. You know where that is don't you?"

"You're a quick study, Fred. Maybe you should join our club. I'll bet you'd be good at it." It never hurts to use compliments to defuse a sticky situation, I always say.

I thought I detected a weak smile. "May I make a suggestion, Mr. Merrill?"

"Just call me Pete, Fred. Sure, you think of a better poem?"

"No, Pete, my suggestion is that you give up all this bullshit. I read your book, you know."

Oh, my god! **FRED EDD HAD READ MY BOOK ABOUT RALPH!** Why hadn't I thought of that possibility? Now I had gone from a merely sticky situation into the deep doo-doo. I had said some less than complimentary things about Fred Edd in that book. I had made him into a complete clod, easily outwitting him at every turn.

I could feel my face burning with embarrassment. "Heh, heh, Fred," I fumbled. "I took quite a bit of literary license in that story, you know. There was no malice intended." I began to thumb nervously through the pages in Duffy's notebook.

When I looked up I was startled to see that Fred had removed his glasses. For the first time since I had met him I could see his eyes. Fred Edd had real eyes and eyebrows! I shaded my face from the glare of the sun to get a better look at him. I could see that his eyes were large and pale blue, not beady and suspicious as I had always imagined. It unnerved me to see a decidedly pleasant expression on his face, and it occurred to me that Fred probably kept those black glasses on to give himself a more authoritative appearance. I realized

119

there must be a lot of cops in the world with gentle blue eyes, but I guessed it would be lots easier to put the cuffs on a bad guy if he didn't know you really had a nice friendly look about you. Disconcerted, I nearly made an inappropriate remark that would only have made my embarrassment worse. This just might be my opportunity to make amends with my old antagonist, and I needed to make the most of it. Unfortunately, what I did say probably wasn't exactly the message I wanted to convey.

"By George, Fred, without those glasses on you look like a real..." I found myself backtracking again. "What I mean is...ah, you look like somebody I know..." This wasn't true at all.

"You mean like a real person, maybe? I've been told that before. Just last week, as a matter of fact, in the courtroom of a visiting judge from Olympia."

I felt a little better. Fred was making things easier for me and I was grateful.

"By the way," he asked, "did you ever get that postcard I left for you down there on your statue of Ralph?"

For a second I was puzzled by his question, and then it occurred to me that he was referring to the postcard that Duffy had sent, and which I had always assumed that Fred had delivered.

"So it **was** you who brought the card down to my place. How did you happen to get a hold of it?" It had been so long ago that I had nearly forgotten it.

"Ronnie Rumpsley found it and gave it to me. I had an idea it might be for you. It was just a wild guess."

Deputy Edd leaned back against his patrol car, his arms folded across his chest. "By the way, Pete, if it's any interest to you, I never had any objection to you hauling bears around the countryside in that flimsy little truck. I like bears. It breaks my heart when I have to shoot one that's been hit by a car. Did you really get them up to the park like in your story?"

"Yep, it happened just like I wrote it. Except for the talking part, of course. Bears can't really talk, you know." I had already told so many lies today, one more wouldn't matter much.

"Oh, really," said Fred, feigning mock surprise. "I'm glad you told me. By the way, I'm hearing rumors they've got some bear problems up in the park. I hope your friends aren't involved. I guess there's a big high-level meeting coming up. They've got bear experts coming from back east. Borski wishes Ronnie would get back, heaven forbid. He's not happy."

"Fred, do you know if Ski has read my book?" I asked, as casually as I could.

"He hasn't mentioned it to me," said the sheriff. "You want me to lend him my copy?"

"I'd just as soon you didn't. He might get some wrong ideas. You'd be surprised how many people believe all the stuff in that book."

I could hear the patrol car radio crackle. The sheriff moved quickly to the car. He put his dark glasses back on as he answered the call.

"Roger, copy. Got it. I'm on my way." He looked at me. "Wreck down on 101," he said, slamming the door. "I'll catch you later." Fred fastened his seatbelt and quickly backed away, crushing the thick underbrush.

"Don't forget to look under the Model T dumpster," Fred

shouted as he gunned the car, braked quickly and backed up to where I was still squatting in the grass. "By the way, Keats wrote mostly odes, I think. Remember the Nightingale and the Grecian Urn? All about the pictures on a Greek wine jug. Weird stuff."

Fred smiled, waved, and disappeared toward the highway in a flurry of dust.

CHAPTER NINE
The Council of Bears

DUFFY GETS THE COB PROCEEDINGS ON TAPE

As soon as I arrived home, I went right to work transcribing the seventy-eight pages of disorderly scrawl in Duffy's notebook. He had used both sides of each page, writing in a variety of media — ballpoint pen, pencil, felt pen, crayon, even fountain pen. I tackled the job with a mixture of apprehension and anticipation. It wasn't easy; it took me two weeks.

I have transcribed the document as faithfully as possible. Duffy thoughtfully provided me with a list of the bears that are members of COB, and I have included caricatures of some of them that he has approved as being fair likenesses. Duffy's descriptive commentary is typed in bold italics, and I have entered some comments of my own for clarity. These are identified with the notation, "Ed" (author's editorial). I have also fixed Duffy's

123

atrocious spelling and have attempted to doctor up his tangled syntax.

THE MONTHLY MEETING OF THE COUNCIL OF BEARS, (COB) SOUTH OLYMPIC CHAPTER HELD AT BEAR PRAIRIE CONFERENCE GROUNDS, RALPH B. SHAKESBEAR PRESIDING. RECORDED AND TRANSCRIBED FROM THE BEAR LANGUAGE INTO ENGLISH BY MACDUFF SHAKESBEAR, HIS GRANDSON.

This was the monthly meeting of COB, whose members are all elders of the various bear clans from the south and east side of the Olympic Mountains. As elders they are assumed to be wiser than young bears, (This is a common false assumption made by the older generation of all species.)

There's the usual babble of voices as members arrive, which I will not attempt to transcribe. In fact throughout the meeting there is always the babble of voices. COB meetings lack structure. Bears, by nature, do not embrace regimentation, which is one reason why Ralph has had so much difficulty organizing the park bears. I have done my best to isolate legible conversation where possible. Where not possible, I have taken a few small liberties.

Here is Duffy's list of the bears that are members of COB — which I have included as a sort of *Dramatis Personae.* Ed.

RALPH BEAUREGARD SHAKESBEAR — Self-appointed Big Squeeze. Officially, the "dominant bear" of the south end park bears. He says he is no longer sexually active (which is the main function of a dominant bear) having lost some of his vigor to

RALPH

advancing age. He is the unquestioned elder statesman of the clan and is still able to show other bears who's boss when it suits him. He prefers to rest a lot.

MRS. ELIZA JANE POOMER — Widow of Pixley Poomer who was the dominant bear in the park before Ralph. She serves as secretary of COB. She is a special friend of Ralph's and spends a lot of time resting with him at his palatial cave above the Skok valley.

"LIMPY" THE HIBERNATOR — Lost part of his left hind foot in a bear trap many years ago. Called The Hibernator because he's the first one to bed in the fall and the last one up in the spring. He's the COB expert on foreign affairs. (Meaning bear matters on the other side of the summit, since he was once "relocated" over there.)

"WINES" LONGFOOT — Has developed a process for fermenting berries into a popular drink much in demand by clans west of the mountains. Wines is almost deaf and suffers from some memory loss.

GRACIE "WINNIE THE POOH" LONGFOOT — Ralph considered her a bear of "very small brain", hence the nickname, Winnie the P. She is treasurer of COB. Gracie was an orphan who pretty much raised herself. She sucks her thumb when agitated.

LIZA JANE

EMMERLINE — Companion of "Flatso" (Old Mr. Flatulence) former member of COB and a bear whose unsavory personal habits have caused Ralph to ask for his resignation. Emmerline is considered about as smart as bears come. She is the COB parliamentarian.

GRUMPY — A very old bear who has an addiction to bear grass. Will go miles out of his way to graze in the grass. He is opposed to almost everything except mad cow disease. He is very deaf and can't see too well.

BARTLEY "DUMBO" NUMNUTS — Has been captured by park ranger's barrel trap many times. Absent from today's meeting because he has been relocated to the backcountry once more. He is the COB authority on park regulations; especially those involving nuisance bears, and has a thorough knowledge of modern

WINES

technology like radio collars and transmitters. Ralph thinks Bartley will eventually return. He always does.

"WEARY" WESTERLY — The sole representative to COB from "over the hill" as he calls it. Weary is seriously overweight; he is the only member who has his own "stomach hole", a depression in the earth that he excavates for his stomach, allowing him to sleep more comfortably during the meetings. Weary mumbles a lot and is hard to understand.

"TWITCHY" BROWN — COB Sergeant at Arms. Has a highly sensitive nose. It is his job to warn members of the approach of danger — cougars, rangers, tourists, etc. Claims he can detect 10,000 different scents. His name comes from the color of his coat. He hears fairly well but can't see worth a damn.

FLOSSIE SHORTCLAW — Can document over 100 different

family descendents in the Olympic Park. Says she is an "expert on everything". If there is such a thing as a dominant female bear, Flossie is it. Most of the younger male bears seek her out for advice.

MOTHER DUCKABUSH – She represents the northern regions all the way to Quilcene. Doesn't make many meetings because of the distances involved. She is a grandmother many times over. She seems homespun and matronly, but

TWITCHY

has a salty core. Ralph considers her way too soft and too liberal, but he doesn't tell her so.

SKOKOMISH SALLY – Matron of the Skok drainage area. Knows everybody worth knowing. Is the best forager and cook in the COB organization. Her gopher casserole is a particular favorite.

SECOND GROWTH SAM – Sam doesn't live in the park. He represents the fringes of bear territory in the national forest and on the edges of "civilization". Considered the expert on people matters, especially breaking and entering techniques. Sam is always on the run from the authorities. He is on the permanent state and federal list of nuisance bears. Has been darted at least once. Says it's no fun. Sam is outspoken on most issues. Is critical of some of the "old fogies" in COB. His hearing is marginal.

There is a widespread belief among Homo sapiens that bears never gather in social groups, especially in mixed groups of sex and age. This is not true. In Ralph's fatherly discussion with me regarding garbage dumps in the "good old days", he recounted how the easy access to food attracted bears of all kinds in large peaceable gatherings at the dumps. Bears have gotten a reputation for solitary behavior mostly because of the difficulty they have in finding food. A foraging range of five square miles for an adult bear is barely enough in some cases. The members of COB bring their own food to their meetings when they can find it. These potluck–type gatherings are very popular and many more bears would attend if membership in COB was not restricted to elders.

ENGLISH TRANSLATION OF THE COB MEETING

RALPH: (*forcefully, rapping gavel*) Let's have this meeting come to order. Will the secretary tell us the minutes of the last meeting?

MRS. POOMER: (*Mrs. Poomer is easily flustered and often loses her way*) Only six members were at the last meeting because of the lateness of the rut. (*I don't know whether rut has one "T" or two.*) Most of the meeting was devoted to housekeeping matters. The President thought that some of the food brought to the last meeting was inappropriate. Rabbits should be dead at least a week and deer haunches kept since the spring thaw, unless properly prepared, are not suitable fare. The President states that if there is any doubt about what is appropriate he should be consulted. In fact he seemed to insist upon it. Second Growth Sam took issue. Said it was none of the President's business what he ate. It was noted by the President that Bartley was in trouble with the park authorities because he has been seen hanging around the campground again. He's skating on thin ice, whatever that means.

MOTHER: I think Finns are nice, too. My third daughter lived with one up by Nine Stream. She had triplets just after Christmas that year. They're named Olaf, Bjorg and Wekko.

FLOSSIE: If I have a choice between a Finn and a Swede, I'll take the Finn anytime...

MRS. POOMER: *(Plunging on gamely)* President Ralph cautioned the members about approaching too close to the campground. His sources say there have been reports of vandalism and the rangers are blaming it on bears. There is a new ranger in the campground. His name is Milkiwiski, or something like that.

FLOSSIE

We don't know much about him yet. That's all I can remember about the last meeting.

WINES: *(offended)* You're not going to find any milk in my whiskey, my stuff is certified pure. Guaranteed 100% organic. Last year a bear walked clear from Quilcene just to get a jug from me.

WEARY: You gotta be kidding, Wines. Nobody would walk all that distance just to get a hug from you. From Flossie maybe, but not you.

RALPH: *(impatiently)* Can we please have order here? Are there any omissions or corrections to the previous minutes? Do we have a move to accept the secretary's report?

TWITCHY: I'll do a movement on that.

EMMERLINE: For god's sake, Twitchy, excuse yourself from the meeting before you do that. What sort of a place do you think is?

RALPH: Is there any old business?

LIMPY: Seems like everything we do is old business. I haven't heard anything new since I joined. What's the purpose of this meeting anyway? What's all this movement business?

RALPH: Do we have a treasurer's report Madam Treasurer?

GRACIE: There has been no movement in the treasury since we have no money in the treasury.

RALPH: Can we have a move to accept the treasurer's report?

EMMERLINE: I move we accept no movement in the treasury.

EMMERLINE

RALPH: We've had a move. Do I hear a second?

WEARY: I say we don't move until we get some money.

RALPH: Oh, hell, I'll second it myself.

EMMERLINE: That's illegal.

TWITCHY: I don't see no eagle. If there were an eagle around here I'd have smelled him by now. Speaking of smells, that damned old Weary is farting in his sleep again. Give him a kick, Limpy.

EMMERLINE: *(annoyed)* Mr. President, as parliamentarian I wish to raise a point of order.

RALPH: Point of order, Emmer?

EMMERLINE: How come you booted Flatso out of COB for doing the same thing Weary is doing right now? I don't think Miss Manners, herself, could smell the difference between the two of 'em. If Flatso's out, Weary needs to go. This is abjectly unfair.

SAM: What is "abjectly" unfair? Quit using them big words, Emmer. A thing is either unfair or it ain't, and it ain't fair to have to smell old Weary all the time.

RALPH: Flatsy has other bad habits, too. What's the next order of business, Emmer?

EMMERLINE: I think new business is next, if we haven't done it already. I've kind of lost track.

RALPH: Is there any new business to come before this body?

GRUMPY: Roddy? Yeah, I saw Roddy just the other day over near Milk Lake meadow. Poor old guy's all crippled up with lumbago. You ought to invite him to a meeting some time, Ralph. He can tell us some good cougar yarns.

RALPH: *(loudly)* Roddy stretches the truth, Grumpy.

GRUMPY: If telling the truth is a qualification to belong to this outfit we're all out-of-order.

RALPH: *(testily)* How did Roddy get into this discussion in the first place?

GRUMPY: You brought him up, not me.

RALPH: Is there any other business?

WEARY: (**raising himself to a sitting position**) I brought a report from the Northside COB chapter. They want you to know that the big shots at park headquarters are all worked up about bears in the high country, pooping on the trails and spooking the pack trains and getting the horses all nervous. They're talking about sending posses up there to run the bears off. They want to make all the trails bear-free zones.

WEARY

RALPH: Keep your eye on this matter for us, Weary. If

anything develops, let us know.

WINES: Who said it was going to snow? Anyway, I say it won't snow until real late this year. And I know we're going to have a good berry crop, too. I can tell by all the blossoms.

GRUMPY: There're a lot of possums up around my place, too. They're not bad eatin' either, if you serve 'em right. When it's in bloom, I add a leaf of skunk cabbage for color.

MOTHER: *(surprised)* Who'd have thought that Grumpy would know anything about cooking? And speaking of cooking, I think we should move to thank Sally for the very nice fresh shrew and mouse dish she brought to the meeting.

LIMPY

SAM: Fresh shrew ain't near as good as old shrew. Two weeks ain't too long to age shrew for best flavor.

MOTHER: *(offended)* I don't see you ever bringing anything to eat at our meetings, Sam. I move and second.

EMMERLINE: I don't think she can do that. You can't move your own second, Mother.

MOTHER: *(puffing up her cheeks)* Tell it to the marines, fatso.

RALPH: *(impatiently)* I wonder if we can get this meeting back to order. Can we have the report of the foreign relations committee? Limpy, do you have a report for us?

LIMPY: No.

RALPH: Try to think of something, Limpy. All meetings have to have committee reports.

LIMPY: Well, let's see, I heard last month that one of those

West Slope bears came over from the Hoh River and was trying to have foreign relations with Shorty Shortleg's sister Mamie. Mamie had already mated with Big Ben Hardback, so this Hoh River dude was out of luck. She sent him packing. Bit him on the butt, or so I'm told.

RALPH: Is this apt to cause any kind of border tension, Limpy?

LIMPY: I hardly think so, Chief. Even those dumb West Slopers know the rules about relations.

FLOSSIE: *(incensed)* Mr. President, Weary is making personal smells again. Can you get him to stop?

RALPH: Give him a kick, Limpy. Wake him up.

FLOSSIE: Mr. President, I move we vote Weary out of membership. He's offensive. I second it too.

RALPH: By-laws say you have to have two-thirds vote to kick somebody out. You got two-thirds, Flossie?

FLOSSIE: What's two-thirds?

WINES: Hell, I ain't seen any blue birds around here for years. You seen any blue birds lately, Weary? *(Weary is asleep again)*

RALPH: *(flustered)* Motion fails for lack of two-thirds, dammit. Now let's get this meeting back on track. Sam, you were put in charge of the cougar committee. You got anything to report?

SAM: Human person reported cougar down near the transfer station. Sheriff put up a whole bunch of cougar alert signs. Since Ralph's grandson ran Big Bubba off up to Mt. Ellinor, I ain't heard of no cougars around here. I got a report on goats if you want it, Ralph.

RALPH: Sure, Sam. Everybody in favor of Sam's report on goats, please say "aye". *(silence)* The "ayes" have it. Go ahead, Sam.

SAM: The park people say there're too many goats in the park and they want to shoot 'em. The Greens say the goats are foreign imports to the park and they are eating native grass and they want to shoot 'em too.

MOTHER DUCK

GRUMPY: *(popping his jaws)* I say if they're eating bear grass they ought to shoot 'em.

TWITCHY: Goats stink somthin' awful. Shoot 'em I say.

LIMPY: I don't like boats either. They're too noisy, but I don't see how you can shoot 'em. Some of 'em are way out on the water.

SAM: Goats, Limpy. Goats, goats, not boats. Sheesh.

MOTHER: *(offended)* Goats have just as much right to live in the park as anyone else. Stop talking about shooting goats.

WEARY: *(rousing himself)* Those green types aren't native to the park, either; let's shoot them, too.

RALPH: You want a motion of some kind, Sam?

SAM: Beats me, I don't care. Do what you want. I don't know what you're talking about.

RALPH: All opposed to goats please say "aye". *(There's a hubbub of ayes)* All in favor of goats say "aye".

MOTHER and GRACIE: *(with feeling)* Aye.

RALPH: The "ayes" have it. The movement is adopted.

LIMPY: I hate the noisy damn things. Shoot 'em all I say.

RALPH: I think our time is about up. It's time for the President's report. Let me have everybody's attention. *(Emmerline and Flossie continue with their private conversation, oblivious that Ralph is trying to speak)* Would it be too much to ask that we have quiet?

GRUMPY: Limpy still thinks we're talking about boats. Who ever heard of boats up in the mountains? I wonder if they make hearing aids for bears?

RALPH: *(raising his voice)* I have important information that concerns all the bears in the park, old and young. I think you should pay close attention. *(Wines kicks Weary who has fallen asleep again)* Sources say that there is something going on with the park managers about bears...

MRS. POOMER: What is "sources say"? What does that mean, "sources say"?

TWITCHY: That's what reporters say when they don't know what they're talking about.

RALPH: My sources are real and I know what I'm talking about and it's about bears and you better pay attention especially if you have children or grandchildren that you care about because pretty soon there is going to be big trouble about young bears in the park. There is a park bulletin out that says there's going to be a meeting about

SECOND GROWTH SAM

vandalism in the campgrounds. Some of the rangers think it's bears — young bears — who are causing the problems. And if it is our young bears that are guilty it behooves us...

SAM: Behooves? What's behooves?

GRACIE

RALPH: Means we should do something about it, Sam.

SAM: About what? Dammit, Ralph, I wish you wouldn't mumble.

RALPH: *(ignoring Sam)* If you know about any young bears that are causing mischief in the campground tell them to stop. Since I took over the management of the bears in this end of the park, things have been going pretty smooth and I hope they stay that way. If any of you know about any of this vandalism, let me know.

WINES: I still say it's way too early for snow.

GRACIE: Who brought the pot of beans?

RALPH: My grandson Macduff made the beans.

GRACIE: Be sure to tell him thanks for us. They were very tasty.

RALPH: Thank you Gracie, I intend to talk to him about the beans.

EMMERLINE: *(who hasn't been paying much attention to Ralph)* We haven't had Whine Time yet.

"Whine Time" was first called the COB "Pain and Gain Moment", an activity thought up by Ralph as a way of keeping track of the health of the older park bears. All members of COB, at the end of each meeting, are asked to report on any personal problems or successes. The recording secretary calls the roll, and then each member tells what he has done during the past month. Since all of the reports seemed to be complaints, it wasn't long before the pain and gain time became "whine time".

136

RALPH: Mrs. Poomer, call the roll please.

MRS. POOMER: Limpy.

LIMPY: Haven't done nothin' for the last month except rest. Damned old wound hurts all the time. Hope we get early snow so I can get some sleep.

WINES: I just told you it ain't going to snow for a long time yet.

MRS. POOMER: I saw three youngsters doing unspeakable things over behind Big Cedar.

RALPH: Vandalism-type things, Mrs. Poomer?

MRS. POOMER: I can't say. They were unspeakable things. Wines, you're next.

WINES: A skunk sprayed me over at Dry Creek.

GRACIE: What did you do?

WINES: I ate him.

GRACIE: How gross.

WINES: Skunk is not bad, but it's an acquired taste, Gracie. You should try one sometime. You might like it.

GRACIE: I'm a vegetarian and you know it, you old fool.

RALPH: Emmer, how have you been?

EMMERLINE: I've been fine but Flatty has an upset stomach. He got into some bad dog food down in town. He thinks somebody put poison in it. He's had the runs something terrible.

RALPH: We've all been warned to stay out of the fake dog food. Your Mr. Flatso is a slow learner. *(That's Ralph's way of saying that old farty Flatso is stupid)* That's one of the reasons he's not a member here anymore. I'll tell you all once more. Some of the merchants downtown are tired of bears in their garbage. They're

137

trying to poison us. Use caution. That's fake dog food in those bags. The dogs know it, but some of our people are going to find out too late. Spread the word. Weary, you got anything to say? Wines, wake Weary up. *(Wines kicks him)*

GRUMPY

RALPH: Weary, do you know anything about the dog food downtown?

WEARY: Yeah, it tastes awful. I got the runs from it.

GRUMPY: I'd run from it too, if I were you. I've heard it's poison. Stick to bear grass and you'll be all right. Bear grass has a natural laxative effect. It's gentle on the stomach. Recommended by nine out of ten physicians.

RALPH: And if any of you are interested in my health, I'll tell you I've got a hellish case of the lumbago in my back hips.

FLOSSIE: I hear there is a very good bone doctor downtown, Ralph. Maybe he can fix your back hips. I've heard he's very good at hips.

SAM: He don't take bears. I know that for a fact. He ran me off with a shotgun once. Even if he did take bears I doubt he does back hips. He's a human bean doctor. Human beans don't have back hips. Just middle hips.

TWITCHY: I don't think what you got is lumbago, Ralph. You got what they call arthuritis. Lots of old folks get arthuritis. You're old. Your joints seize up when you get old. I got a touch of it myself. Can't sleep good.

FLOSSIE: I guess Weary doesn't have any arthuritis. Weary

sleeps way too good. Wake up, Weary, we're talking about you.

SALLY: What you've got to do, Ralph, is get Second Growth Sam to get you some of that pain medicine next time he breaks into the drugstore. They got whole shelves of the stuff — all kinds. Next time you get a chance to watch television you listen, they tell you which one is best. Some of those human beans are so bad off with arthuritis they get grumpy, just like Ralph. Then they take a little bit of that

SKOK SALLY

medicine, come home from the store, dance around the kitchen and take their wives out to dinner. It's like a miracle. A wonder drug.

SAM: I'm not going into that store again. Last time I almost got caught. Got my head stuck in the window screen. Human beans say going into a store like that is a very serious thing. They call it a felony, I think. I heard the police tell the store guy he could shoot me for doing a felony, which I am trying to avoid.

GRUMPY: I went into a farmer's woodshed once and it fell on me. He planned to shoot me too, but I was too quick. I was younger then.

RALPH: I would like to know how many bears here have arthuritis, or think they have. Raise your paws please. *(Everybody except Sam, Grumpy and Weary raised a paw. Weary is asleep).* SAM, DO YOU THINK YOU HAVE ARTHURITIS? *(Ralph is shouting)*

GRUMPY: What's that?

RALPH: Never mind, I think I know a way to get this wonder drug without getting Sam shot, or having the drugstore fall on him.

Leave it to me. I think maybe by next meeting we'll all be dancing in the kitchen. I move the meeting be adjourned. Do I hear a second?

TWITCHY: *(standing on his back legs, his nose twitching)* You better adjourn it, I can smell cougar over near Dry Creek, a coyote down by the pump house and a park ranger comin' up the road in a pickup truck. Chevy, I think. Smells like it needs an oil change.

RALPH: Meeting adjourned.

This was the end of the formal meeting. There was a lot of noise as the old bears wandered off in various directions. Grumpy and Sam got into an argument about goats, and they squared off as though they were going to fight but as usual, when old bears act this way, they were only bluffing. They puff out their cheeks and do a lot of snorting and clacking, which doesn't mean anything. In a few minutes they were all gone except Weary who had decided to stay and take a nap.

At the end of the translation Duffy had written a message to me: "I was pretty sure it was me that Ralph was talking about at the meeting when he mentioned the bean pot. I wanted to get out of there as quick as I could, but the old fool caught me before I could get away. He's always lecturing me about bad stuff he thinks I do around the campground. There're a lot of other bears that do worse things than I do, but he doesn't believe it. Hope you could read the translation. It was a lot of work and I'm not going to another COB meeting. They're too boring. Anyway, Ralph wants to see you about getting some of that arthuritis miracle drug. Call me about a meeting. I have a new telephone number — 476-4009."

"P.S. Do you know anyplace where we could get some ear trumpets? Duffy"

I tried the number Duffy gave me for several days with no luck. I also tried Ralph's old number with the same result. Once again we seemed to be out-of-touch. Weeks passed, then a small terse item on page three of our weekly paper spurred me into action:

BEAR PROBLEMS IN PARK
Officials at Olympic National Park Headquarters report an increasing number of bear depredations in local campgrounds. Originally believed to be the work of juvenile vandals, the problems are now thought to be caused by a growing population of nuisance bears in the park. Rangers are studying the issue.

If it was true that the park authorities were studying the problem, it meant that I should have plenty of time to act before they reached a decision. Nevertheless, the next morning I drove to the supermarket and bought a generous supply of all the popular arthritis remedies I could lay hands on, and headed up country to our rendezvous spot. I checked the stump hole and found a folded piece of used park stationary with a message from Duffy. There was no date on it, and it looked like it had been there for some time. A creature had been nibbling on the edges of the paper.

The note read: "Ralph is anxious. Meet me on the high road above the campground. I'll take you to him."

Duffy had included a crudely drawn map which showed the

141

causeway across the end of the lake, and what I assumed was the Elk Creek road that went up the cliff above the river on the west side of the campground — that narrow little logging road that I had sworn never to traverse again. On the map, at a spot that appeared to be far beyond where I had met Duffy early last spring, was an "X". I assumed this was the place where Duffy wanted me to meet him.

I sat there in my car considering the many reasons why this was a dumb idea. First, after driving for miles up this treacherous road, how would I know that Duffy would be there? Second, was there a place where I could turn my car around? Backing my car in the Safeway parking lot was challenge enough; a one-way road involving a precipitous cliff was out of the question. Third, why couldn't Ralph come down and meet **me**? In bear years he wasn't any older than I was, but then maybe that was exactly the reason why he couldn't get down to meet me.

I was looking for my pen to write a reply to Duffy, telling him that the idea wouldn't work, when the young bear himself came galloping out of the underbrush, gasping for breath, all covered with dust and brambles.

"I saw you from up on the hill. Come on, let's get going." He was trying to open the rear door, which was locked.

"Hey, hold on there, Duffy. Calm down. We've got to talk this thing over. Where do you think you're going?"

"We've got to go up and see Ralph. He's sick."

"Take it easy, Duffy. What's he sick of?" I asked.

"He can't walk," said Duffy, breathlessly. "It's his back hips, like he said at the meeting. The arthuritis thing. Did you bring the medicine?" He was still trying to get in the car.

"I brought some pills," I said, "but I don't think they'll help much if he can't walk. You could take them up to him. I don't want to drive all the way up there on that dangerous road, just to deliver some pills that probably won't help him anyway."

"You've got to go. He wants to see you." I thought I could see tears forming in his eyes. "I'll drive if you want."

"Man," I said, "that's an even dumber idea than anything you've thought of yet." I quickly got back into the driver's seat before he could try something stupid.

"Duffy, can you guarantee me that there is a place up there where I can turn around without having to back up?"

"Sure, man, there's a great big meadow up there just half a mile from Ralph's place," said Duffy, eagerly. "You could turn a house trailer around up there, man. It's where the loggers used to work."

"So, it's not in the park then?" I asked suspiciously.

"No, it's just outside the park in the forest. Ralph lives in the park, right on the boundary, just before you get to Four Stream. It's easy, let's go. Ralph is real sick. He thinks he's going to die."

I wondered if I should take some pills myself — stupidity pills — but Duffy's sincere pleading convinced me I should make the trip, even though I was certain Ralph was in no danger of dying from bad hips. Duffy climbed in the front seat and away we went.

CHAPTER TEN

Temporary Relief for Moderate Pain

It wasn't until we had crept past the steep cliff on the first half-mile of the narrow little road that I felt relaxed enough to stop and let Duffy climb into the front seat. He had been riding in the back in his usual awkward position, out of sight, lest an alert motorist spot him, or worse yet, a passing park ranger. We negotiated the steep "road from hell" section of the track, and entered the second growth forest where I had met Duffy last spring. The road widened and I began to breathe a little easier. This was the place where snow had been several feet deep in April. Now the woods were dry as dust and the grass in the occasional meadows was parched and brown.

All the way up Duffy had been reading the labels on the boxes of pain killers trying to decided which was the best. "All these boxes say 'for temporary relief of minor pain'. I think Ralph wants something for permanent cure of major pain. He's not going to be happy."

"Listen, Duffy, according to what you wrote in the COB minutes, Ralph saw an ad on TV that said if he takes enough of the stuff he'll be dancing in the kitchen by tomorrow morning."

"That's something I want to see," said Duffy, skeptically. "The old fool doesn't even have a kitchen."

The road leveled out. It wasn't any wider, but the going got easier. "How much farther, Duffy? This car is built for streets, not mountain roads."

"It's not much farther. Just on the other side of those big trees. You'll see a clearing there," he said pointing. "That's where you want to park. You really ought to get a jeep if you're going to drive these back roads." He had his head out of the window sniffing the air.

"In case you have forgotten, my furry friend, it was never my intention to be driving mountain roads in any sort of vehicle. I'm up here very reluctantly, at your request, on some ill-defined mission of mercy. I would rather be elsewhere, almost anywhere else, in fact." Duffy ignored me. I should have remembered that this kind of sarcasm is usually lost on bears. Duffy's indifference pissed me off.

"By the way, Duffy, the rangers told me a bear stole a lady's bean pot in the campground. Was that the bean pot they had at the COB meeting?"

"Ralph already chewed me out about the bean pot. No need for you to go on about the stupid bean pot. I took it back to the campground, and I almost got caught by Wilberforce or whatever his name is."

"Wilmer Archibald is his name. That should be an item for the good news section of the local paper. 'Bear caught returning bean pot he stole; nothing is gained by being a good Samaritan, says bear.'"

"Not funny," muttered Duffy. "Here's the place," he said, pointing. "Park over behind those bushes."

We had arrived at a clearing just as promised. I couldn't see anything that resembled a bear's lair, or even the suggestion of one. Duffy jumped from the car stuffing pillboxes into the plastic bag as he went.

"Follow me," he said. He loped to the edge of the clearing before I could untangle myself from my seatbelt.

"Hold up, dammit," I shouted. "I don't move as fast as you do." Duffy waited impatiently as I caught up. "How far is it, man?"

"Just over the edge here," he said, indicating a faint path through the underbrush. I didn't like the sound of that "over the edge" business. We traversed the brow of a fairly steep hill and descended on a trail that was barely visible, but not too difficult. About five minutes of walking brought us to a shelf obscured by small trees that partially hid the entrance of a cavern.

I assumed we had arrived at the "lair of the bear", the headquarters of Ralph, chief honcho of the south end black bears. I suspected that I should be awed by his exalted presence, but I still thought of him as just an older version of the lonely young bear in my back woods who had befriended me, an aging member of an alien species with whom he had formed an unlikely kinship.

"Hey, Ralph, I brought the old man," Duffy shouted as he peered into the gloomy interior of the cave. "Come on out!" I could hear stirrings accompanied by grunts and groans. "It takes him awhile to get up. I'll go help him. Just stay here." Duffy disappeared into the darkness.

I waited uneasily, and soon old Ralph shuffled laboriously into view, followed by Duffy who was rolling a short length of log that he up-ended in the sunshine at the entrance of the cavern. Ralph

146

continued on toward me blinking in the light, squinting closely as though he wasn't sure who I was. His nose twitched as he sniffed the air. Suddenly his eyes brightened, and his face lit up with that familiar little grin I remembered so well.

"Que pasa, old buddy? Did you bring the pills?" he inquired, in exactly the same way he used to ask me if I had brought the long-necked beer bottles he always expected.

"Howdy, old friend," I replied. "Duffy has the pills in the bag." Ralph moved slowly and in obvious pain. Although I had seen him barely three months earlier he had clearly aged in the interval.

He sat down heavily on the stump provided by Duffy, and attempted to cross his legs as he had during our conversations in years past. After several failures he gave up the effort, and just sat quietly on the log. "Open up some of those pill bottles for me, Duffy."

Duffy dumped the bottles on the ground. "Which kind do you want? I got naproxen, ibuprofen, silicon dioxide, acetaminophin, celecoxib, tramadol indomethacin, ketoprophen hydroxypropyl, and I bought some aspirin for myself. I found it in the campground."

"Gimme some of the 'dancing in the kitchen stuff,'" said Ralph wearily.

"I don't know which one that is," replied Duffy.

"Then just gimme a handful of each."

"Ralph," I said, "you've got to have some water to wash that stuff down. It'll get stuck in your throat, and it tastes awful. Not even a bear can handle that."

"Did you bring some beer?" he asked, with the first sign of hopefulness I had seen.

"I'm afraid not, old fellow, I honestly forgot."

"A pity! Duffy, run down to the creek and get a bucket of water."

"Right, gramps." Duffy disappeared into the cave and returned almost immediately carrying a galvanized bucket with "Nat. Park Service" stenciled on the side. He took off on the run down the hill with the bucket hanging from his lower jaw.

"I'm not sure that stuff will fix your pain, Ralph. You're probably going to need something stronger, and you've got to have a prescription for that."

"I have a friend who can get prescriptions," Ralph said. "I just need to know what to get. I'll get the names off these bottles."

"How do you get water up here when Duffy isn't around?" I asked him.

"I got other friends. Liza Jane comes up every day, brings me newspapers and magazines. My COB friends help out."

"Lisa Jane?" I asked, forgetting that she was a COB member. Eliza Jane Poomer was the widow of Pixley Poomer, the dominant bear before Ralph arrived on the scene.

"She's a good friend. I can't depend on Duffy much any more. He's like a cockroach on roller skates, always busy, always into something illegal, or at least unethical. You've got to talk to the kid. I know the rangers are setting a trap for him. I keep hearing rumors. They've got all the high mucky mucks working on a scheme to catch him. If they do there aren't going to be any second chances. The least they'll do is put him in a zoo somewhere; most likely they'll 'put him down', as they so euphemistically phrase it. The rangers have run out of patience." Ralph sounded weary, as though he, too, had nearly reached the limits of forbearance.

"Duffy might enjoy being in a zoo," I said flippantly, knowing full well that the young bear would waste away with boredom. Duffy was a bear that could not be contained in a cage, even though he'd be a great crowd pleaser; he had enough tricks up his sleeve to keep zoo audiences endlessly entertained. "I'll do what I can, Ralph, but I think you have more influence with him that I do. He respects your opinions, even though it may not seem like it."

"Listen, you have friends in the ranger station down at the campground," said the old bear without looking at me. "Keep your ear to the ground. They've got some knavery planned. See if you can find out what they're up to. Maybe we can warn the young fool early enough so he can outwit them before he's hoist on his own petard."

It caught me by surprise to hear Ralph quote Shakespeare. It was like old times. I was pleased, and sought to encourage him. "From whence comes your quotations, old squire?"

"Hamlet, of course," he said, with a hint of sparkle in his eye. "Don't get much chance to impress anybody anymore. I start talking like the Bard around here they just think another one of my screws has come loose. Damn, I wish you had remembered to bring a six-pack. We could spend the rest of the day talking about the good old days."

"Well, I'll tell you what, Ralph, if I ever get back up here I'll bring two six-packs. Beer's a good restorative for bad hips, and does wonders to bring back old memories, but this is one hell of a long trip, and it's not easy for an old coot like me. Tall cliffs and narrow roads are for the kids. I don't even have a four-wheel drive machine, you know. Shows you how backward I am."

"Calling a car a **machine** shows how backward you are too. Hell, old man, that went out when you were six years old." Ralph seemed to have found rejuvenation in needling me. It was like old times, even without the stimulation of a six-pack.

"Can't you find yourself a cave somewhere down the mountain that's easier to get to?" I asked. "I could visit you now and then."

"No, this is the best spot in the park. That's how come I've got it. We have to find you a four-wheel drive rig, maybe teach Duffy to drive. We could have meetings just like the old days. With your influence and my savvy we could run this place." Ralph was becoming energized.

I suddenly formed a mental image of a little open Jeep speeding up an impossibly steep mountain road driven by a wild-eyed, half-grown black bear accompanied by a terrified old man who was clinging to the vehicle with a white knuckled death grip, while being fired upon by a squad of park rangers with high-powered rifles. The image chilled my blood.

"Perish the thought," was all I could think to say.

"Maybe get one of those Hummer things. They say they can go anywhere."

"A Hummer wouldn't even fit on that road," I said.

Duffy reappeared carrying the park service bucket. It was about half full of water.

"Okay, gramps, here's your water. You know that crick down there is nearly dry."

"Open the bottles, Duffy. I'm ready to dance."

The childproof containers baffled the best efforts of the young bear, and he was about ready to smash the bottles with a rock when

I came to his assistance. "Easy, Duffy," I said, "those things will confound the cleverest of creatures. Let me have a go at them." Eventually I succeeded in getting one of each kind open and then we were faced with making a decision about which brand was the one he needed.

"I don't think any of these are the right kind. I don't remember what it was." Ralph looked earnestly at me. "You remember which one is the kitchen stuff?"

"Not a chance, Ralph. I never pay attention to TV ads. You're on your own, man."

"Alright, then, I'll take some of each." He poured a handful from each bottle into a paw, and began lapping them up, followed by draughts of water from the bucket.

"Easy, Ralph," I said. "Some of that stuff is pretty potent. You could overdose, man. Take it easy." I gathered up the bottles. "You better sleep on that before you take any more."

"They didn't say how many to take on the TV. If one is good, lots must be better." Ralph was trying to get me to give him the bottles.

"Not necessarily so, old boy. See how you feel in the morning." It seemed to me that he was already looking a trifle stressed.

Ralph belched, stuck his head in the bucket and finished off the remainder of the water. "You need to get me some more water, Duffy. Try not to spill so much this time."

"Yes, your majesty." The young bear disappeared down the hill again.

"Duffy's a good kid. I'm going to miss him when he's gone." Ralph shifted uneasily on his stump.

"Where's he going?" I asked.

"That will depend on what the rangers decide to do with him after they catch him," said Ralph sadly. "They will catch him, you know, and here's something else I heard from my sources. You know that ranger they sent back east to bear school?"

"The one they call 'Right-Angle' Ronnie?"

"Yeah, that's the one. He's coming back pretty soon, and he's learned all the sneaky new tricks for outwitting bears," said Ralph. "Did you know that they can tell what bears are thinking? It's bear psychology they study. As old Lady Macbeth would have it, 'something wicked comes this way leading on to bloody events'. That crazy old broad knew whereof she spoke."

"I doubt even the latest in bear psychology can figure out what Duffy is thinking," I said. "That lad seems to break new ground every day."

We sat silently for a time, each with our own thoughts.

"Wanna see the inside of my cave?" Ralph asked.

"Sure, but how am I going to see? It looks pretty dark in there."

"Look right over there by the entrance," he said, pointing. "There's a mirror. Bring it here and I'll show you." I gave the piece of broken glass to Ralph. "Now, I'll reflect the sun inside and you go in and look around. I don't usually need the reflector in the mornings. The sun shines right in there — when the sun's shining, anyway."

The inside of Ralph's home was interesting to say the least. Its most obvious asset was the large bed in the back corner. Made up of generous amounts of grass, boughs, dried ferns and other natural growth, it struck me as being completely comfortable, even luxurious, as would befit the headman of the clan. I spotted the "throne" that Duffy had described to me — a large log with a backrest where Ralph held court. There were a number of furnishings not usually found in a bear habitation, things obviously obtained by one means or another from park campgrounds, including a number of colorful towels, caps, sunglasses, and eyeshades, a golf club, folding chairs, and buckets and plastic utensils of a wide variety. It looked like Ralph had wearing apparel suitable for any occasion. In a back corner was a guitar, which had to be the one that I had heard about from the rangers. I was overwhelmed to say the least. "Human beans" weren't the only species with a penchant for material goods, I thought.

"What are those things in the corner?" I asked, pointing to a pile of small barrel-like canisters.

"Those are the very latest in bear-proof food containers," said Ralph. "The rangers give them out to back woods hikers to keep their food in so bears can't smell it. They're all full. Duffy steals them, so there must be some pretty hungry campers up in the backcountry. We haven't figured out how to get into them yet, but Duffy's working on it. He says they put stuff like noodles alfredo and beef stroganoff in 'em. This is the kind of behavior that gives us bears a bad reputation." Ralph's makeshift searchlight went out before I could continue my inventory of the contents of the cave.

As I returned from the gloom of Ralph's abode I saw that Duffy was back, this time with a nearly full bucket of water, and Ralph was gulping down large quantities, threatening to empty it before Duffy had even caught his breath. I didn't know what this great thirst portended, but I hoped it meant he was diluting his overdose of chemicals to a manageable level. I intended to suggest to Duffy that he stay the night with Ralph to cope with any sort of emergency that might come up. I was fearful of what mischief this overmedication could produce. Even though the stuff was fairly innocuous, and made for human consumption, Ralph had ingested huge quantities of it. Then I remembered all the tales about the junk bears ate out of garbage cans and decided to relax. Since bears apparently had stomachs of cast iron this bit of overkill might be just what he needed. By morning his "back hips" would probably be in the pink, and Ralph would be waltzing in the cafeteria.

But just in case I thought maybe I should stay in touch.

"Duffy, do any of your many telephones actually work?"

"Sorry, dude, the latest model malfunctioned just the other day. Exhaustion of the battery, I suspect."

"I'll tell you what I'm going to do," I said, "having reluctantly come to the conclusion that our present hodge-podge communication is hopelessly inadequate. When I get back to town I'm going straight to the store and sign up for a brand new telephone system with unlimited mileage, guaranteed reception, our very own charging gadgets, and a unit for each of us. Then there will be no more thefts of telephones, or dead battery problems. Hang the expense."

"Why don't you buy a Hummer while you're at it," asked Ralph, dryly, "and hang the expense? I hear you can pick one up for about sixty grand." Ralph was beginning to sound like his old sardonic self. Maybe the pills were working.

"Duffy," I asked, "do you still have your fanny pack?"

"Sorry again, dude. I snagged it on a blackberry vine when I was fleeing the wrath of young Ranger Wilberforce. Lost the whole assembly, including the logger's suspenders."

"I'll get you a new one. Hang the expense."

"Extra large size, forty-six inch waist. Best quality, please. Get my name embroidered on it maybe?"

"No use getting one of those things for me," said Ralph, wearily. "I'm not going to get out of this cave any more. My time is up."

"Nonsense, Ralph, you've got lots of time left." I tried to sound positive. "Who ever heard of a bear dying of sore hips?"

"I have," said Ralph. "Old Bignose Sixridge. His hips got so bad Bubba the cougar ambushed him up by Sundown Pass. Bignose didn't have a chance. He kept bubba's whole family fed for a month. Don't tell me about bad hips," grumbled Ralph.

"Well, on that uplifting note," I said, "I'm going to hit the trail and get out of here while the getting is good. Duffy, you stay with your gramps tonight. Watch for signs of distress and check the stump hole. I'll put the supplies in there as soon as I can. Better bring some more water up, too, in case he gets thirsty. And for God's sake, Duffy, do me a favor and stay away from the campgrounds. There's trouble brewing down there. You might consider leaving those food canisters alone, too. They don't do you any good if you can't get into them."

"You want to take all the fun out of life, man. I keep the rangers on their toes. They're trying to invent a new model of theft-proof bear canister right now. The only trouble is it's too heavy to carry. Takes three hikers to move it."

Duffy led me back up the short trail to my car. As I buckled myself in I cautioned him not to let Ralph get into any more of the medicine. "If you have any emergency messages before we get the telephones, leave them under the stump," I suggested as I turned to leave.

Duffy watched without comment as I headed for home.

Knowing the route and the terrain down the mountain made the trip fairly easy. There was no traffic and no need for backing up. I decided that before I lost my resolve to "spare no expense" on this screwy telephone idea, I had better head straight on down the highway to the humongous big box superstore at the county seat to see what my options were. It was sure to have all the latest communication gadgets. In fact, the store's ads claimed that they had at least one of everything ever produced, with the possible exception of hay balers and steamrollers, and I was inclined to believe it. The biggest problem in a super center was finding what you wanted without being run over by reckless shopping cart operators who paid scant attention to the in-store rules of the road, or to driving courtesy either.

On the way to town I considered the possibility that a walkie-talkie set might fill the bill, saving me considerable expense on membership charges and all the other incidentals one finds in the small print when signing up for a cell phone. As I entered the store a kindly associate guided me to the telephone department, where I quickly discovered that consumer model walkie-talkies only had a range of "up to" five miles, which wouldn't do the job. The bright young fellow peddling the cell phones assured me that he had exactly what I needed, but as I viewed his wares I realized I had another problem. All of his instruments were so small Ralph could easily swallow one of them without realizing it. And we really didn't need a color screen, movies, digital pictures, video games or a choice of 2500 popular tunes either.

Without revealing the fact that the telephones were for use by a couple of large black bears, I finally managed to convince the young salesman that I needed something bigger and more substantial. (Actually I told him the phones were for my twin sons who were both loggers who stood seven feet tall and had extremely big hands.) Eventually he admitted that he might have some older, and larger, models in the storeroom and headed off to look for them. You'd have thought that this guy would be glad to peddle a set of obsolete telephones out of the basement, but as I left the store he was still chattering about the virtues of the microscopic models that slip right into shirt pockets and feature ten different versions of solitaire to ward off boredom.

And as I started home I remembered to buy Duffy the latest model in extra large fanny pack — without embroidery

CHAPTER ELEVEN
Confessions of a "Bear Expert"

Ranger Boris Mickeilweisky was busy filling out forms in the back room of the tiny ranger's cabin at the upper edge of the campground. The last big holiday of the summer was over and barely a third of the campsites were occupied. Boris welcomed the relief from the constant pressure of tending to the needs of the never-ending stream of tourists. Even the drudgery of paperwork provided a sense of relaxation when it could be done without constant interruption. Requisitions for repairs and new supplies,

 along with reports on campground use, overtime requests and the dozens of other details, all of which required papers to be filled and filed, sorted and stacked, had kept the ranger at his desk since early morning.

He had just reached the small pile of incident reports, which were normally complaints of a minor nature made by campers involving such things as campground disputes, noise complaints, overflowing garbage cans, and empty toilet paper holders. These matters, not serious enough to require the attention of the ranger or his aides, were routinely referred to the maintenance staff on the correct forms, and then dispatched to the proper destination according to well-established channels. During its one hundred years of operation the National Park Service had come up with forms for everything. Today Boris was finding it soothing just to check little boxes and fill in blanks. Hardly any thought was required, and the only writing necessary was the scribbling of his name in the allotted space.

About four forms down in the pile, an incident report of special interest caught his eye. It had been taken by Wilmer Archibald, his summer park aide, and was dated five days earlier. Boris wondered why Archie hadn't mentioned it to him. It concerned an issue that had plagued the campground all summer long, and one that was now attracting the serious attention of the park big shots at headquarters in Port Angeles. The problem was bears, and this innocent little complaint was from a camper who reported what sounded to her like a bear snorting outside her tent in the middle of the night. She also mentioned a book found on her camp stove in the morning that hadn't been there when she retired. Although it seemed like an innocuous report, the ranger was concerned. There hadn't been any bear sightings in the campground for several weeks, and Boris was beginning to think that maybe his problems were finally over. He reminded himself to quiz Archie about the complaint when he returned from headquarters where he had gone to get the mail. Ranger Borski poured himself another cup of coffee and went on with the business of checking forms and signing his name, but bears were still in the back of his mind.

Down in Hoodsport, shaggy-haired Wilmer Archibald enjoyed a leisurely donut and cup of coffee at the café while he waited for the sorting of the morning mail over at the park offices. The mail was late that morning, so Archie had a bit of time on his hands, and while he waited, he finished the last chapter of the book a camper had given him several days earlier. Titled *Ralph, Conversations With A Bear*, it was a story about a couple of black bears that had been befriended by a resident down in the flat country who had transported them to the outer reaches of the Olympic Park to remove them from the dangers of encroaching civilization. While the tender ending to the story touched Archie, something about the animals disturbed him, and he had the uneasy feeling that he might actually know the two bears. He resolved to discuss the book with Borski when he got back to the campground.

Arriving home I put the new phones on the charger so as to have them ready to go the next day when I intended to deliver them to the hole under the stump. I checked my answering machine and discovered, to my surprise, a message from Ranger Boris Mickeilweisky at the Staircase campground. What now, I wondered as I dialed his number.

"Park aide, Archibald," a voice said after a couple of rings. "How can..." I interrupted the remainder of his salutation.

"Archie this is Pete. Is Ski there? I had a message to call him."

"Yeah, just a second, Pete, he's right here."

"Hey, thanks for calling," came the voice of the ranger. "Is this the author of the book about Ralph the bear?"

My heart sank. "I'm the guilty party, Ski." Even though I knew that this was going to happen sooner or later, I had never had a clear plan about how to explain myself when it finally did.

"Archie and I both read it. It's quite a story. He wants you to bring him a copy and sign it for him. Why don't you come up and we'll have a little seminar? We've told you about our bear problems and you seem to know a lot about the animal. We need some help."

"I think I did read something in the paper. Don't remember what it was," I lied.

"When can you get up?" the ranger asked, in a way that sounded more like a command than a mere suggestion.

"Well, Ski, it just so happens that I was coming up tomorrow to see a friend in Hoodsport. I guess I could run on up to the park then." That wasn't exactly true either, but it was close enough. "I'll see you about ten-thirty."

"Sounds good. We'll be watching for you."

Come morning my obsolete batteries were charged. I made a couple of test calls and everything worked. I repacked the phones and charger into the box, which I wrapped carefully in plastic to protect it from the elements. After tying it with twine to make it easier for Duffy to carry, I set off for the trip that was becoming more familiar to me than I wished. At exactly ten-thirty, having first stopped to deposit the package, I arrived at the little ranger shack and was greeted by Archie and Ranger Borski.

The ranger was filling out a backcountry permit for a tourist. Archie motioned me into the office and directed me to a seat. "Did you bring me a copy of your book?" he asked eagerly.

"Right here, my boy, personalized, signed and certified." I noticed a rather battered copy of the same book on the desk. I decided it must be the one given to Archie by the camper who had heard the snorting bear outside her tent. Ski arrived from the outer office.

"Thanks for getting up here so promptly, Pete." He picked up the book and got right to the point. "The description of your young bear, Duffy, has attracted my attention. He sounds exactly like the bear that's been raising hell around our campground all summer. How much of this stuff is true?"

I suddenly realized that I was going to have to start talking like a politician — beat around the bush, be evasive and employ 'don't let 'em corner you' tactics.

"Well, Ski, if you can accept the fact that I talk to bears I guess it's all true."

"And what does that mean?"

"I guess it means whatever you want it to mean. You're going to have to take some things on faith. You've heard of literary license, haven't you?"

"Let me put it to you straight, Pete. Can you talk bear?" (Quite surprisingly, this wasn't the first time I'd been asked this question.)

"That depends on what you mean by 'talk'. There are all kinds of ways of talking, some easier than others. You remember Dr. Doolittle, don't you?"

"Yeah, the book was fiction, if I'm not mistaken," Ski replied.

"Do you ever talk to your dog, Ski?"

"Sure, but my dog doesn't talk to me."

"Are you sure? What's the use of talking to him if he's not going to talk back to you?"

Ranger Borski was showing small signs of frustration. "Damned if I know, now that you mention it. I think he understands me, I guess. You can tell by his expression."

"Maybe you can talk 'dog' then, Ski. Congratulations," I said.

"Maybe I can talk 'bear', too, but I'm damned if I'm going to get close enough to try."

"You read the book, Ski, remember the part where I first met Ralph?" I asked. "I came very close to, forgive my language, crapping my pants. There was this full-grown black bear about ten feet away from me, talking to me. I thought I was a goner, but in half an hour we were good friends, or as close to good friends as a bear can ever be to a human bean." I inadvertently used Ralph's term.

Ski sensed that he wasn't getting any place, and changed his line of questioning. "Is Ralph up here in the park, too?" he asked.

"I'm not sure I can answer that," I said evasively. "Bears roam around a lot from what I've heard."

"Come on, Pete. I'm on your side in this thing. We've got a lot of work to do if we're going to save that young bear from an untimely end. It's very lucky we found your book, old man. If that bear is really your friend Duffy, and if we play our cards just right, it may be the key to keeping him from becoming cougar bait. I don't want to be indelicate here, but when we have to dispose of the carcass of a nuisance bear we simply leave it out in the woods for the cougars and, dare I say it, for other bears to clean up."

"Look here, Ski, right at the end," said Archie excitedly, as he paged through the book, "he leaves the bears up on Elk Creek road. If Duffy is here it's a good bet Ralph is too."

"Just for the sake of the conversation," I said, in my best story telling voice, "let's pretend the bears are around here somewhere, and that I know them, and that I can talk to them, and that they will listen to me, and that they will follow my suggestions to stop being bear-like, and behave like people, and follow the park rules. What happens next?"

163

Borski reached across his desk and picked up an official-looking document. I could see that it was typed on the letterhead of the National Park Service.

"What I've got here is an interoffice memo which started its journey up in Port Angeles at park headquarters. It's been initialed by everybody along its path, and surprisingly, hasn't been marked 'for eyes-only'. Either somebody at headquarters has slipped up or they are being uncharacteristically loose-lipped about this matter. I guess I'm not breaking any government rules by reading it to you."

Borski leaned back in his swivel chair. I tensed up, preparing for a bureaucratic broadside. Archie went out to the desk to wait on a tourist.

"I'm not going to read this whole thing to you," said Borski. "There's a lot of tedious inter-agency busywork, but here's the memo: 'On a date to be determined by mutual agreement, a meeting is to be called among certain park officials and outside agencies, including civilian experts in the field, to discuss new regulations and procedures needed to cope with an increasing number of bear incursions into local campgrounds'. The Staircase campground is mentioned specifically as being a problem," said the ranger as he continued. "The meeting will be conducted by Ranger Ronald Rumpsley who has recently completed a comprehensive course on wildlife management dealing specifically with bear issues.' It also mentions a bunch of other biologists and wildlife types who may attend, schedules permitting."

"Right at the end of the memo it says that a number of state officials have expressed concern about the safety of visitors to campgrounds due to wildlife (specifically bear) depredations."

Borski paused and looked at me. "That last bit comes from the state senator who was bowled over by a young bear in broad daylight in the middle of the campground a couple of months ago. The letter goes on to say that strict rules may be required to cope with the bear incursions which, as the letter says, have been 'growing in boldness, audacity and impudence,'" Borski paused. "That last bit sounds like it was written by Ronnie Rumpsley."

"Then there's a lot of stuff about routing and who gets copies in D.C. I don't see the President mentioned here, so I guess the memo didn't go quite that far, but you can be sure we're being watched by the 'fathers' in Washington." The ranger put the paper back on his desk and looked at me.

"I want you to attend this meeting."

I did my best to maintain my composure, but inside I was in turmoil. Oh my god, what now?

"Why me, Ski?"

"You're an expert. You've written a book about bears — the very kind of bears we're going to talk about at this meeting."

"That book was fiction, Ski. It's whimsy. Nobody takes me seriously; at least I hope they don't. How could I possibly contribute to solving your bear problems?"

"I suspect you know the answer to that question as well as I do," answered Borski. "If nothing else you could provide a little comic relief to proceedings that promise to be as dull as all the other meetings we have around here."

Archie had returned to our conversation. "I hope you schedule this thing before I have to go back to school," he said. "I don't want to miss it."

"You needn't worry, Archie," said Borski. "You're going to be on the agenda too."

I suddenly felt a great need to get out of there and get on the telephone to my ursine friends. I suspected that we might soon need a strategy session of our own.

"When do you expect your meeting will be?" I asked.

"Next week. We've scheduled an open meeting at the library in Hoodsport on Thursday at one o'clock. There seems to be a lot of public interest. Rumpsley has invited everybody who has registered a bear complaint in the campground, along with any townspeople who have had bears in their garbage cans. The press is invited too, and anybody else who has nothing else to do. It'll probably be a three-ring circus." Borski looked at me owlishly. "Maybe Ralph and Duffy would like to come."

"Why don't you send them an invitation?" I asked, facetiously.

"You give me their address and I will," said the ranger. "Better yet, why don't you invite them?"

"Good joke, Ski."

"You have no doubt heard that the park service is very sensitive about its public image, and I want to warn you right now that Ron Rumpsley is a stickler about transparency. He wants to make sure everybody knows just what's going on in his bailiwick. He loves presiding over public meetings."

"Transparency?" I inquired.

"New bureaucratic term that means 'nothing hidden; everything out in the open'. Congress uses it a lot nowadays. It's a very slippery concept, of course."

"What's likely to happen at the meeting?" I asked.

"This will be what Rumpsley likes to call an 'informational, fact finding' session. There'll be a lot of public comment, anecdotes, personal opinion and so on. He's probably already made up his mind about what he's going to do about the bear problems, but he's got to go by the book, and ask for public input, you know. Everything has to conform to regulations, and everything needs to be documented."

"What do you think he's going to do?" I asked.

"Get official permission to shoot all the bears within three miles of the campground," said Borski sadly. "No more bears; no more complaints from disturbed campers. Blessed peace and tranquility prevails."

"Can Rumpsley do that?" I asked him.

"Ranger Rumpsley has more influence than I like to think about. He's got an uncle back in Washington who's an assistant secretary of something or other, so I wouldn't underestimate him. And now that he's a graduate of the Bear Control Institute, or whatever they call it, he's automatically an expert on the subject. Ronnie has never had a 'teddy bear' mentality when it comes to his opinion of the species. He is incapable of recognizing that some bears are smarter than he is, which, I might add, they clearly are."

Oh, man, I thought. There go Ralph, Duffy, little Lucy and Dromio, all their friends and relations and the whole COB organization. I tried not to panic. I needed to spread the alarm on behalf of the bears, and I hadn't much time. The big meeting was only a bit over a week away. My mind raced. It might be well to alert the animal rights people, I thought, and maybe even Oddware Stumple, Professor of Social Protest down at The Evergreen State

College. I'd get Archie to contact him. Get him to round up his troops and awaken the masses. They'd need to start making signs, and get out the bullhorns. There was no time to lose.

"I can't let this happen, Ski."

"That's why I want you at the meeting, my friend. You just might have to come up with something dramatic if things get real sticky."

"Like what?" I asked.

"Oh, I don't know. I was thinking along the lines of a tame bear on a leash, something like that. It's worth considering. No harm in thinking outside the box, you know," said Borski, blithely.

"I think you can put that idea right back **in** the box, Ski. I don't have that much influence."

"It was just a thought."

CHAPTER TWELVE
A Meeting or a Circus?

Our meeting ended with me promising to attend the big function at the library, and to make every effort to get people who might have an interest in supporting the bear side of the issue to be there too. Before I left the campground I spoke to Archie about contacting Oddware Stumple down at TESC, and he said he would take care of it. Archie also suggested I get hold of the PAWS folks and the Animal Liberation Army, or whatever it was called. I nixed the latter idea out of fear that they might burn down the library with all of us inside.

I quizzed Archie about Borski's sentiments on the bear issue. I had never actually heard Ski express an opinion on the matter, and God knows, Duffy and his friends had caused enough mischief in the park during the summer to give the average park ranger fits.

Boris Mickeilweisky had a special affection for bears, Archie assured me, saying that he had once told him that before his family came to America his father had trained animals in a Bulgarian circus. He had bears that rode bicycles and could balance beach balls on their noses. Borski was a staunch friend of bears, according to Archie, even the ones who weren't as benevolent as Duffy, and he was of the strong opinion that in the contest between bears and people, the bears should have the right of way. "They were here first", he would say, "we're just visitors". Anyway, according to Archie, Ski enjoyed the intellectual challenge of dueling with the young bear; in the battle of wits between them they seemed to be fairly evenly matched.

I left the campground confident that if I had to take a stand on the issue at the big meeting, I would have moral support from some of the park people, at least.

For five miles or so outside the boundaries of the park the road was unpaved, and as I headed home I was reminded again of just how dry everything was. Great clouds of dust followed each car. The trees and vegetation on the sides of the road, most of the year a glossy green, were an unattractive dirt brown. To be sure it was the usual end-of-the-summer drought, but this year it was uncommonly dry, there having been no rainfall for over three months. Under such conditions the forest and park people begin to put restrictions on how the trails and campgrounds can be used; wildfires become a constant threat. Signs posted along the road warned of the danger.

On the remote possibility that Duffy had visited our under-the-stump cache while I was up talking to the rangers, I turned onto the lonely little road to check it out. Much to my surprise I found the hole empty; the telephones were gone. Duffy was certainly keeping very close track of my movements. As I groped around under the stump I realized that it was exceptionally dry there, too. Even the carpenter ants had gone elsewhere.

I put in a call to Duffy as soon as I arrived home. He answered promptly and his voice came through strong and clear. Apparently our obsolete phones were of good quality. My first question was about Ralph's health.

"The old boy slept for two days after you left," said Duffy. "I wasn't sure he was ever going to wake up. I was about to go out looking for some pallbearers. Then yesterday he came to, pretty groggy, but feeling better. He knew that you'd brought the pills, but he couldn't remember much about your visit. The acetominophen extended release stuff is best, but he has to take a quadruple dose, and he's going to run out real quick. He says his back hips are better, but he's a bit light-headed. He goes around humming and popping his lips a lot, which is unbearlike — especially unRalph-like. Anyway, as you might guess, he wants you to bring some more medicine before he runs out."

"You tell your grandpa that I'm not coming back up there until somebody gives me a ride, and I don't know who that would be." I said. "Tell him to get old what's-his-name — the COB guy who breaks into drugstores — to get him some more pills. Incidentally, Duffy, you can buy that stuff right off the shelf in the grocery store, you know. Why don't you get some of those clothes you've got stashed in Ralph's cave and fix yourself a disguise, like maybe a long skirt, a colorful blouse and big dark glasses? Or, put on that little golf cap and waltz right into the store and buy all of the acetaminophen stuff you want. They'll never recognize you."

"What little golf cap is that?" asked Duffy.

"Let's not beat around the bush, my friend, the little golf cap you swiped out of Mr. Washerbarger's motor home a couple of months ago."

"Washerbarger? That's a funny name."

"Better yet, get a big hat that covers your ears. The clerk in the store might get suspicious if she sees those big hairy ears of yours."

"I don't remember taking a golf cap out of a motor home," said Duffy, guilelessly.

171

"Alright, now listen carefully, Duffy," I said. "While we're on the subject of swiping and stealing and other transgressions, listen to this. I've just come from a meeting with the rangers in the campground, and you were the main topic of conversation."

"Moi?" asked Duffy, in an imitation of Miss Piggy. "Of what dost thou speak?"

I gave the young bear a complete summary of what the rangers and I had talked about, along with a chilling description of the dangers that he and his friends would face based on decisions that were sure to be made at the library meeting.

"Come to think of it, Duffy, forget all the stuff I just said about going into the grocery store in a disguise. The best thing you can do is lie low for a while. Stay away from Staircase until things quiet down, assuming they ever do. If Rumpsley has his way, any bear within three miles of the campground is going to be fair game for his assassin squads."

"Would that be Ranger 'Right-Angle' Rumpsley, recent graduate of the New England Institute of Bear Control?"

"The very same," I said. "He's back and he intends to solve the 'bear problem' within his jurisdiction promptly and 'humanely'. And it's in your best interests to stay the hell out of his way, and please tell Ralph to do the same."

"Ralph is beyond the three-mile limit. I doubt he could walk that far anyway," said Duffy, "and I can outwit Ronnie Rumpsley any day of the week."

"You have been warned, my boy. Don't come whining to me if you get in trouble. Is Ralph there?" I asked.

"Sunning himself right outside the cave. You want to talk to him?"

"Yeah, put him on." I heard the usual static and clatter before Ralph cleared his throat and mumbled a greeting.

"You know what's going on down here, Ralph?" I asked.

"Not exactly," came the reply. "Nothing good, I suppose."

Holding a conversation with Ralph on the phone was sort of like talking on a short-wave radio. There was always a pause while he shifted the receiver from his mouth to his ear. Then I would have to wait a bit, never sure whether he was about to talk or about to listen. Sometimes both of us talked at the same time and occasionally we both just listened in silence. We stumbled along as best we could.

I explained, briefly, about the upcoming meeting.

"That's what I told you was going to happen. I've got my sources down there, you know." He coughed several times and changed the subject. "You going to bring me some more extended-range stuff for the arthuritis pain? I don't dance in the kitchen yet, but at least I can walk around some. The back hips are better." Was the old bear breathing harder than usual I wondered?

"I'm not going to get up there for a while, Ralph. I got too much going on down here. I'll get some medicine and leave it under the stump as soon as I can. I'll put in something for that cough, too. Have Duffy pick it up, but for God's sake, tell him to be careful."

"You know what I've always told you," said Ralph. "A bear won't be seen if he doesn't want to be seen. The kid is a master of stealth. It's just that sometimes he doesn't use good judgment."

"Guess what, Ralph?" I needed to ask the question before I forgot it.

173

"What?"

"I was up on the old trail today. You remember the old trail don't you? Up behind the shop?"

"Sure, I remember the old trail behind the shop. Remember it well."

"I saw bear scat up there. Can you believe that?"

"I believe it. Probably a Toonerville bear. We used to call them the vacuum bears. Anytime smart bears left a territory, the dumb Toonerville bears moved in. Filled the vacuum, as it were. I wouldn't mess with him if I were you. No use talking to them, they don't know English, anyway. And they're not very civil." Ralph sounded disinterested.

"Maybe it was cougar or a big dog," I ventured.

"Could be," said Ralph. "The only way to be sure is to taste the scat. Bear scat is sweet."

"Forget I brought it up, Ralph. Put Duffy back on."

"Duffy is gone. He said he had to make some contacts. Probably spreading the word about the big meeting. Either that, or he's down at the campground getting something to eat out of somebody's cooler."

"What do you think about this hot weather, Ralph?" I asked. "You handle it alright?"

"Oh, yeah, it's good for the joints. It gets too hot I go in the cave. Woods are mighty dry and that creek where Duffy gets the water has already dried up." There was a long pause. "A lightning storm could raise hell up here. Or some dumb camper with a campfire."

"Park people got signs up everywhere," I said. "No fires in the back country."

"A lot of campers can't read," mumbled Ralph.

"By the way, do you get the local paper up there?" I asked.

"Lisa Jane brings it up when she can find it. It's usually about a week old."

"Well, you watch for news about the big park meeting. It'll be in the paper. I'm going to be there."

"That'll be a waste of your time. Rumpsley will make a lot of speeches. He's a windbag; full of hot air. It's going to be boring as hell, you know."

"You got anything I should tell 'em if I get a chance?"

"Yeah, tell 'em hands off the bears. We were here first."

"That's exactly what Ranger Borski said to me."

"Ranger Borski? Who's he?" Ralph asked.

"Ranger Boris Mickeilweisky," I replied, "is the guy who took Rumpley's job at Staircase."

"Oh, you mean Milky Whiskey. Yeah, he's a reasonable guy. I suppose you know that he's got orders to trap Duffy. If he can't trap him, then he has permission to shoot him."

"Who told you that, Ralph?"

"Sources."

"He's on our side, Ralph," I said. "I don't think he'd do that."

"Orders from headquarters, man. Good soldiers follow orders, you'll see." Ralph coughed several times.

"What do you think of me getting the animal rights people to the meeting – PAWS, PETA, and all the others? By the way did you know there's an Animal Legal Defense Fund? Some lawyers on your side might help."

"Are you planning a meeting or a circus? You get those outfits to your confab and you automatically get the TV cameras, too," commented Ralph. "You're probably going to need a bigger hall."

"Hey, Ralph, do you remember Oddware Stumple, the environmentalist guy we met up in the woods? Back when Duffy was just a little cub?"

"The 'Free Tibet' guy with the VW bus?"

"That's the one. I'm told he organizes protest marches and things. I might get him to come. What do you think about that?"

"Suit yourself," mumbled Ralph. "Just make sure he understands which side of the issue you want him to be on. Those guys get mixed up real easy."

"Here's something else you don't know, Ralph. You remember Fred Edd, the deputy sheriff?"

"Old snoopy? Yeah, sure, he used to hassle us down at the old place. He's one of the reasons I moved out of your neighborhood."

"Well, I found out not long ago that he's on our side too," I said. "We had him figured all wrong. I'm going to see if he'll come."

"You better get him to bring the rest of the department with him. You'll need 'em for crowd control," observed Ralph. "You going to have a brass band there? Maybe some cheerleaders? It seems to me you're getting carried away, man. Rumpsley's gonna do what he wants no matter what you do."

"We'll see, Ralph. A little publicity on this deal won't hurt. But you've got to make sure Duffy doesn't show up anywhere near the library while the meeting is going on. That would be a disaster."

Ralph coughed. "By now you must know how much influence I have over Duffy. He's going to do his best to get Ronnie Rumpsley's goat, and it makes no difference what I think. If he decides he wants to go, he'll be there." There was a pause. "Here he comes now. You want to talk to him?"

"Put him on, Ralph, and take care of that cough," I said.

"Duffy here, what's up?"

"Just remember what I said. Under no circumstances are you to show up at that meeting. The whole sheriff's department is going to be there. Rumpsley would like nothing better than to be able to shoot a nuisance bear skulking around the middle of town. It would prove his point. Do you understand?"

"Understand, dude. I get the message. Over and out." Somehow, I wasn't totally convinced.

CHAPTER THIRTEEN

Soft Soap For Ranger Rumpsley

A small news item in the local paper gave the time and place of a public meeting to be held at the Hoodsport library to get public comment on the bear problem at the park. "*As a result of the increasingly aggressive behavior of bears in the local campgrounds,*" it said, "*new policies are being considered to cope with the situation. It is hoped all interested parties will attend, especially those who have had encounters with bears during the past summer, both visitors and local people alike.*"

It was clear to me that Rumpsley was trying to stack the deck, both from the location of the article — it being on an inside page of the second section of the paper — and from it's low-key message. It sounded to me like he didn't want to arouse the attention of the animal rights people who would surely upset his apple cart if they got wind of what he was up to. He probably hoped nobody would attend the meeting except the 'shoot the bears' crowd.

I decided it was my job to alert the 'other side' to protect my friend Duffy from a messy end. My efforts yielded the following results:

- Wilmer Archibald reported that Oddware Stumple promised to give his Advanced Social Protest 201 class a mandatory assignment to attend the meeting with bullhorns, megaphones and signs. Stumple promised to appear in person if he could.

- I reached several animal rights groups (there were far more of them than I realized, including Feminists for Animal Rights and the Animal Legal Defense Fund). All of them showed interest, and promised to do what they could to help.

- Deputy Fred Edd said he had already been assigned to the meeting by the department, but wasn't sure if he could testify on behalf of the bears since he had evidence that Duffy had been mixed up in some thefts in his younger years up in the woods behind my house. He said he would be lending moral support, if nothing else.

- Ranger Borski was clearly torn between the two camps. His job required that he support the park position, but his personal sentiments were clearly with the bears. Borski had developed a fondness for Duffy's creative ways of questioning authority. If asked to testify he promised to support the position of leniency and moderation as best he could.

- I contacted the local press to make sure they knew the importance of the issue to be decided at the meeting. I explained that the choice would be between a park entirely devoid of any semblance of a "wilderness experience", including traditional wildlife and any number of other interesting creatures, or a place where a real outdoor experience might still be had, with the exciting prospect of meeting real live wildlife face-to-face. (I may have laid it on a bit too thick here. I suspected most people would just as soon **not** meet a bear face-to-face anywhere.)

I had done my part. Now I would simply wait for the meeting, which was just four days away. Wait and fidget.

While fidgeting in my shop the next morning the thought occurred to me that I didn't know whether Ronald Rumpsley had read the Ralph book, and if so had he discussed it with Borski. I wondered if it would it be wise to get a copy to him if he hadn't seen it. I had no idea.

I called Borski for the answer. "Rest easy on that score," he said. "Ronald Rumpsley doesn't read anything but government manuals. The Revised Code of Park Regulations is his bible. Whimsical fiction isn't even on his literary radar screen." Then Borski let me in on some disquieting news.

"It hasn't reached the newspapers yet, but it looks like a bear may have broken into the drugstore in Hoodsport Saturday night. Some drugs were stolen — mostly pain killers and cough medicine."

"What makes you think it was a bear?" I asked.

"Chunks of fur caught in the window screen," said Borski. "They're going to do DNA tests."

Damn, I thought, that's the modus operandi of old Second Growth Sam, the COB member with the special talent for breaking and entering. I suddenly realized that I had gotten so caught up in making certain that the interests of my bear friends were protected at the meeting, that I had completely forgotten that Ralph needed more painkillers. He must be getting desperate. My only consolation was that it wasn't Duffy who had gotten into the drugstore. Or was it? I thanked Ski for the information and dialed Duffy's number.

"Macduff Shakesbear here, at your service." Duffy was cutting up a bit. He knew it had to be me. I was the only one who knew his number.

"Duffy, what's this I hear about the drugstore being robbed?" I asked without preamble.

"True story, dude. You didn't come through with the goods down at the stump. Ralph was in great pain so I sent for old S.G. Sam who took care of the problem. He was happy to help."

"Tell Ralph I'm sorry I forgot. I've got too much on my mind. Damn, this sure isn't going to do our cause any good at the meeting. How's Ralph doing, Duffy?"

"Not good, man. He's all doped up. He can't get out of bed. Coughing a lot too. Maybe he took too much of the medicine. And I'm not sure but what he may have swallowed his telephone. It seems to be missing."

"You watch him now, Duffy. Don't let him take more than four pills a day," I advised, taking a wild guess about the dosages. If one pill was recommended for people, four seemed about right for a bear. "Don't worry about the telephone. If he did swallow it, it'll show up sooner or later."

A car came to a stop in front of the shop. It looked like there was a couple sitting in the front seat. "Gotta go, Duffy, I've got visitors. Keep me informed."

As I went outside I realized that it wasn't a couple in the

usual sense, but Phineas and his faithful canine co-pilot, Maximo. I hadn't seen them for several months. Max seemed irritated and I wondered if he and his master had been arguing.

Phineas removed the key from the ignition and climbed out of the car. He turned back and spoke sharply to the dog. "And don't touch any of the controls," he snapped.

"Max is out-of-sorts. He wants to go home to watch the reruns of Lassie on the TV, even though he's already seen 'em all fawteen times each." This was followed by my friend's customarily abrupt greeting. "Osarmer blow any more buildings up today?"

"Dang, Phineas, I haven't seen you for months. Where you been?"

"Went back to Maine to visit my old high school girlfriend, Betsy Lou. She wants me to move back theah. She's got a big house, chickens, pigs, lots a potatas. Needs help takin' ceah the place. Guess we'll go, me and Max. Gonna sell out heah. Leavin' next week."

"Be sorry to see you go, Phin. Get's pretty cold back there, doesn't it?"

"Saw it down to sixty below once. Just gotts ta keep bundled up. Ya get used to it, ain't so bad. Whataya think of that bunch runnin' for President? Gonna have to winnow 'em out some. Say, I finished that book about the beahs. Some of that true, is it?"

"Quite a bit of it, Phineas. All but the talking part."

"I'm going to take that book to Betsy Lou. She'll get a kick out of it. She knows a lot about beahs. Got 'em right in her back yard almost. Don't none of 'em talk though."

"Yeah, you don't run into talking bears very often," I said. "You just have to be lucky."

"Or mebby unlucky," said Phineas. "Say Max and I ran into a beah up on the hill just the other day. Looked real scrawny. He saw Max and took off runnin'. Acted more scared than anything."

That would be the Toonerville bear for sure, I thought. "I'm not looking for any more bears, Phin. Bears can be a big pain in the neck. Take my word for it."

"Yeah, I think everybody knows that," said Phineas. "Did I ever tell you about the time the bear ate Betsy Lou's chickens?"

"Was that the time the bear was trying to have his way with Maximo?"

"No, that was a different bear. This was the time a big old beah got into Betsy's chicken yaad. He was sittin' in theah eatin' pullets to his ha'ts content. All the rest of the chickens was settin' up on the roost in the top of the cage squawkin' and hollerin'. Betsy Lou called old Ira Perkins, the sheriff. Ira was up for re-election at the time. Claimed there weren't nothin' he didn't know about beahs. He came out with his shotgun and pulled down on the beast and let go with both barrels. Trouble was his aim was a tad high. Killed all them chickens on the roost and clean missed the beah. Old beah went gallopin' back into the woods with two of them hens hangin' outta his mouth."

"County had to buy twenty new chickens for Betsy. Ira lost the election to Asa Shortshank. Asa told the story to anybody who'd listen, and then claimed **he** was a straight shootah — had it on all his campaign signs. Moral is 'if your goin' to shoot chickens afta they're hatched, make sure your aim is good'." Reuben slapped his knee and laughed heartily. Max barked from outside, demanding attention.

"Old dog's gettin' restless. Best be headin' out," said Phineas, moving to the door. "You ever get back to Maine, you be sure to look us up. We're way up there at the top of the country by the Canada borda. Gonna be easy to go right across the line and get my medicine. Lots cheapa over theah. We get to vote first on Election Day, too. You'll be readin' about us in the papahs."

Phineas and I shook hands solemnly. I could hear him scolding Maximo as he drove away.

George Morlanby finally finished packing his small camping trailer, which was parked in the driveway of his modest home outside Beaverton, Oregon. He had spent the last week carefully considering the supplies he would need for a four-day trip around the Olympic Loop in western Washington. George and his wife Amy had been planning this short outing since spring, waiting for a time when they could both get away from work long enough to make their first trip in the new trailer that George had bought last winter at the outdoor show in Portland. They knew it was pretty late in the season to be planning a camping trip in their part of the country, but they had been watching the weather reports carefully and things looked promising. The summer had been exceptionally long and dry and the extended forecast showed continued fair and warm weather for the coming week.

George and Amy, both novice campers, were guilty of the mistake that most rookie campers make. They were packing far more stuff than they needed, but George, an accountant, being the methodical type, enjoyed checking and double-checking the list of essentials that he had been preparing for several weeks. The final item to be stowed away was the bag of toys just handed to him by his four year old daughter Meghan who had also been careful to pack far more things than she would ever have time to play with during the trip.

"Albert is going to ride with me in the car, daddy. He said he doesn't want to ride in the trailer." Albert was Meghan's little brown teddy bear, her constant companion and confidant.

"That will be fine, dear," said George absently. "Is mommy about finished?"

"She's packing the lunches. I'll go tell her we're ready."

George glanced at his watch. Good, he thought. If we get going within a half-hour we can make the campground by early afternoon. We're running right on schedule. This is a promising start.

Phineas's short visit had served to divert my attention from upcoming events, but for the rest of the afternoon there was little to ease my mind about what I faced the next day. Shortly after noon I received a call from Borski at the park.

"Rumpsley's frothing at the mouth, Pete. He's threatening to call off the meeting and just start shooting bears. Says he's already got enough authority under park regulations to shoot nuisance bears, and as far as he's concerned they're all nuisances. That break-in at the store pushed him over the edge."

"That's not his business," I said. "That didn't happen in the park. How can he do that?"

"He says he knows which bear did it and that that bear lives in the park," said Borski. "He's already got the sheriff sending extra people up here to help Fred in case the bear comes out of the park. All of us rangers are now packing side arms and we have been told to have our rifles loaded and in our trucks ready to go."

I was almost afraid to ask Borski what bear Rumpsley had in mind.

"One guess, old man. The bear with the splash across his chest."

"Well, dammit, Ski. He's got the wrong bear."

"It hardly matters to him. Bears are bears."

"Ski," I said, "give me Rumpsley's telephone number. I think its time to explain the facts of life to your Mr. Big up there." Borski gave me the number and signed off by wishing me luck. He sounded discouraged.

I had had one previous conversation with Ranger Ronald Rumpsley to set up an appointment back during the tape recorder incident, but when I had gone to meet him at the campground he had already been reassigned to the bear control school back east. I doubted he would remember the conversation, so I decided not to mention it when he answered his phone.

Rumpsley obviously had carefully honed his people skills, and he was polite and deferential, until I brought up the matter of bears. Then his voice immediately went from being pleasantly convivial to defensively cold. Rumpsley was suddenly all business.

Not knowing whether Borski's information about Rumpsley's threat to call off the meeting was general knowledge or not, I didn't bring it up lest I compromise his trust in me. I figured I'd have to beat around the bush a bit, something that I had become proficient at since I wrote that nonsense about talking bears. I was as good at obfuscation as some of our best diplomats.

I congratulated Ranger Rumpsley on his decision to hold an open forum on the bear issue, and said that as a citizen interested in the welfare of animals, I had a concern about their recent behavior in the park, just as he did. I threw in some soft soap about his good judgment in bringing the issue before the public to allow both sides of the controversy an opportunity to express themselves in an open and forthright manner. Bears can be difficult, I told him, but with the correct approach they were as amenable to reformation as any wayward child. It was simply a matter of employing the right methods. Sometimes, I said, the corrective techniques do not work and then, reluctantly, more direct steps must be taken.

When I was through with my rambling dissertation Rumpsley couldn't possibly have known which side of the issue I was on. He assured me that the meeting would go on as scheduled, and asked me to be sure to come up and introduce myself.

By the time our conversation ended I was pretty sure he hadn't read the Ralph book, but I couldn't decide whether that was good or bad. I put in a call to Ralph thinking he might have some final words of wisdom or common sense about bears, which I could interject into the next day's proceedings, hoping for something that might help their cause.

Duffy answered the phone. "Where's Ralph, Duffy?"

"Ralph is in bed, dude. He's pretty sick. He's having trouble breathing. Coughing a lot too."

"How long has that been going on?" I asked in some alarm, remembering that he had been coughing when I talked to him a couple of days earlier. "What are you doing for him?"

"Liza Jane brought up some sassafras yesterday and that helped a little. I gave him the cough medicine that Sam got from the drugstore, and I'm going up the river this afternoon and look for some goochiweed. That's sure to fix him up."

"Goochiweed? What's that?" I asked.

"It's the main ingredient of goochiweed soup, a powerful bear medicine. It fixes most everything. I don't know why I didn't think of it sooner. I remember my grandma used to make it."

"Does this stuff have any other name? I've never heard of goochiweed. How does it work?"

"Goochiweed can be fixed in a lot of different ways, but it's best if you mix it with a little pulverized pigweed and just a dash of bog orchid. When you mash it all up real good, and wash it down with some of Wines Longfoot's fermented blackberry juice, it acts a lot like what you human beans call the salts," said Duffy. "It's a purgative. Shakespeare talks about it in one of his books. I'm darned if I can remember which one. Maybe it was Chaucer. I'm getting a little rusty. Well, anyway, goochiweed goes through a bear like a dose of salts. Cleans out all the bad stuff. Ralph should be up and around in no time once I find the goochiweed."

"How far do you have to go to get it?" I asked.

"There used to be a good patch of it up river a couple of miles," said Duffy, "so I'd better get going. I've got to get some more water when I'm down there, too. After Ralph takes the goochiweed it's going to take a lot of water to keep this place cleaned up."

"I'll call you again in the morning, Duffy, before I head off to the meeting."

"That'll be cool, man. Wish me luck."

George Morlanby paid his fee at the park entrance and found room for his car and his small trailer in the parking lot near the ranger's cabin. They had arrived almost exactly on the schedule he had calculated before they left home that morning. It was just three o'clock, which allowed plenty of time to find a good campsite, get the trailer unfolded and the supplies all unpacked before dinnertime.

Once again George congratulated himself on his careful

planning. He noted their arrival time in his notebook, along with the day's mileage and the weather outlook. Since Meghan was asleep in the back of the car George was careful not to slam the door as he got out. She had been whiny all afternoon, and had only been asleep for a half–hour. She would be crabby if she woke up now. Amy stayed in the car while George entered the ranger station to get directions about finding a campsite.

Park aide Wilmer Archibald, in his last week of duty before school started, greeted George with a smile as he came through the door. "Welcome," said Archie. "Looks like you brought some nice weather up from Oregon. What can we do for you?"

"We'd like to camp for a couple of days, if you've got room for us," said George.

"Plenty of room," replied Archie, producing a map of the grounds. "The big summer rush is over. There are lots of good spots." He began a detailed description of the facilities, and gave an explanation of procedures, including the standard precautions about fires and animals.

"Please notice the signs about the campfire restrictions, and be sure to keep all your foodstuffs locked tightly in containers so they won't be a temptation to any wandering critters who might be around." As per orders from headquarters, Archie deliberately avoided actually saying the word "bear". Rumpsley considered bears to be detrimental to good public relations. He then pointed out the restrooms, garbage bins and laundry facilities on the map. "Just go ahead and find your own campsite, and we'll be around before dark to collect the fee."

"Can you show me where the trails are?" asked George. "We

want to take a hike tomorrow, but we don't want anything too strenuous. Two or three miles is probably our limit. We have our four year old daughter with us."

Archie pointed out the trails that went up both sides of the river, and commented on scenic spots and points of interest. "There's nothing strenuous for the first couple of miles, but beyond that you'll have to do some climbing. This side of the river takes you up to the old burn where we had a wildfire a few years ago." Archie traced the area on the map with his finger. "It shows what can happen when people get careless with campfires. You should have a good day for a hike. It looks like we're going to have real nice weather while you're here."

George gathered up the maps and brochures and returned to the car, making two circuits of the campground before he and Amy decided on a spot close to the river. "We'll be lulled to sleep by the water," he said. "This is neat."

Amy helped George position the car. He was no good at backing a trailer, but eventually succeeded in getting things the way he wanted them. He was excited about raising the roof and extending the sides of his rig for his first night of wilderness adventure.

Meghan continued to sleep soundly in back seat.

CHAPTER FOURTEEN

Street Theater and Goochiweed Soup

There had been an item in the county newspaper describing the issues to be discussed at the meeting. It was clear that the reporter had only interviewed Ranger Rumpsley when he wrote his story, since there was nothing at all in the tone of the article that could be thought of as being pro-bear. I didn't know what I expected. As usual the animals would not be represented, except perhaps by the "rights" groups that might show up at the meeting, and I held out little hope that they would have much influence on the proceedings.

The day of the meeting dawned cloudy and warm. There had been a bit of drizzle during the night, but the long-range forecast called for a continuation of our prolonged drought. As I drove into town everything seemed quiet. I could see nothing to indicate that anything unusual was going on, and it wasn't until I turned up the road to the library that things began to change. The first hint was the presence of a sheriff's car parked at the intersection. The deputy, who was unknown to me, waved me to a stop. "You need to park along the road here. There are a bunch of protesters in the library parking lot, and there's no more room up there."

"Is Fred Edd here somewhere?" I asked.

"Yeah, he's up there trying to quiet down the crazies behind the library. You'll have to park down here and walk up if you want to see him. He's pretty busy."

I did as directed, picking up my cell phone as I locked the car. I planned to call Duffy before the meeting began. The closer I got to the library, the noisier it got. TESC's Social Protest 201 class, called SoPro 201 by the students, was already on the job.

Deputy Fred Edd was standing astride the entrance to the library parking lot. He looked at me owlishly and asked, "Are you the guy who sent these people up here?" I shrugged and tried to look innocent.

"They're pushing the limits of the First Amendment right along with the limits of my patience. Where did you find these characters? There's a kid up here with a bullhorn who's even got his directions all wrong. He seems to think he's at a world trade meeting. Wants to stamp out child labor in the coffee fields."

"He must be making up credits for a riot he missed last year," I said. "I'll see if I can find out who's in charge." I was peering over the heads of the crowd trying to catch sight of my old friend, Professor Oddware Stumple, which was no easy feat since there were huge puppets representing everybody from Donald Rumsfeld to Catholic priests boogying to the sound of drums and bugles. Several of the students, who actually had the message right, were chanting 'SPARE THE BEARS, DON'T RUIN THE BRUINS' over and over again in unison, their ponytails bouncing in awkward cadence. I noticed a bemused gentleman in a dark suit carrying a briefcase standing next to an unsmiling lady in sensible shoes near the door to the library. Animal rights attorneys, I decided.

Then I spotted Oddware, 'The Owl' Stumple, short pants, big boots and all, in earnest conservation with Archie Archibald, his shirt pockets crammed with papers, pens and pencils, just as I remembered him from years' past. While he did appear to have a new pair of glasses he was wearing the same baseball cap he had when I last saw him, still cluttered with stickers and pins. Right in the front, and prominent in its place of honor, was a 'SAVE THE BEARS!' button with a picture of a grizzly on it. As I worked my way through the rapidly growing crush of people to greet Archie, Oddware squinted at me in a puzzled manner, trying to remember where he had seen me before.

I introduced myself. "Of course I remember you," he said, pumping my hand vigorously. "We had a splendid little meeting at your camp above the canal. You were policing the forest grounds, and I was on my mission to map and record illegal dumpsites. It was a rewarding afternoon." We had to raise our voices to be heard over the din of the protesters. Oddware was clearly invigorated by the activity going on around us. "Oh this does warm the blood, don't you think?"

I smiled weakly and turned my attention to Wilmer Archibald. "You're out of uniform, Archie," I said. "How come?"

"The job is done, man, summer's over. I'll be going back to school next week. You know what?"

"What?" I asked.

"I'm going into wildlife management. I expect I'll be doing my masters thesis on black bears. Maybe I'll need some help from you later on."

"You do a masters thesis on black bears based on information you get from me, Archie, you'll set wildlife management back a hundred years. Nevertheless, I'm flattered. Where's Ski?"

"Ski's inside the library getting things set up. We're going to have a slide show and everything."

194

Oh, bully, I thought, there's nothing like a slide show to put everybody to sleep.

"I hear there may be some surprises in the program," said Archie, in a lowered voice. "You don't want to miss it."

"Is Rumpsley here yet?"

"Rumpsley's in there at the 'prosecutors' table, getting his notes in order, sorting out the evidence, and setting traps for the dissenters."

"By the way, Archie," I asked, "have you seen any animal rights types?"

"Yeah, there's a carload of them now," he replied, pointing to a double-wide, tandem-seat stroller containing six small children, which was being pushed by two determined middle-aged ladies. Each of the tykes was wearing a homemade paper hat with the initials CUTSBA written across the front, and each clutched a teddy bear.

"What's a CUTSBA, I asked?"

"That stands for 'Children United To Stop Bear Abuse,'" said Archie. "That's Mrs. Kelly's daycare group doing their part for the cause. She told me last week that she was going to be here. Mrs. Kelly is outraged by the idea of the park people shooting bears."

"Dang," I said, "I hope some photographers show up. That should melt the heart of the most rabid bear hater. Archie, try to get Mrs. Kelly to take her charges into the library, and push 'em past old Rumpsley a couple of times. See if she can melt his heart."

Archie spoke briefly to Mrs. Kelly and returned with the news that the extra-wide stroller wouldn't fit through the library doors. It was naptime, anyway, and she would have to return her charges to the center. Just as the little group turned to leave I was pleased to see a reporter from the Weekly Bugle taking a picture of the daycare group. We'll get that on the front page for sure I thought.

Surveying the growing crowd I spotted a group of raffish-looking fellows standing off in one corner of the parking lot drinking beer. One of them, a tattooed citizen named Toad, held a homemade sign, which read: GOV'T HANDS OFF BEARS! SPORTSMEN COME FIRST!!! He and his companions were all dressed in the garb favored by loggers — wool shirts, suspenders, big boots and cut-off trousers. Two of them wore hard hats. Noting that one of them was without his suspenders made me wonder if he had once had a confrontation with Duffy out in the woods.

From the size of the growing crowd I thought it best to reserve myself a seat in the library before they were all taken. As I looked around the room for a vacant chair I noticed a starched ranger studying papers at a large desk in the front of the room and decided he had to be Ranger Ronald Rumpsley. It was my first view of the man who seemed bent on removing the fun-loving Macduff Shakesbear and his friends from what we had once thought would be a safe sanctuary for the rest of their days.

Ranger Borski was checking his projector equipment at the other end of the room. Three others in park service uniforms, a man and two young women, who I assumed to be "gophers" in support of Rumpsley's mission, busied themselves setting up an easel for the flowcharts. I wasn't surprised to see the large volume of park regulations prominently displayed on Rumpsley's desk. The hefty book had to be "Rumpsley's Bible", as I had once heard Wilmer Archibald refer to it.

I greeted Borski. "Hi, Ski, your show about ready to start?" I had come alarmingly close to calling the meeting a circus, but thought better of it a split-second before I spoke.

"Thirty minutes," replied Borski, looking at his watch. "I've still got to set up the flowcharts, recorders and VCRs." He was working to untangle a snarl of electrical cables. "How's it going with you, Pete?"

"I thought I'd better get myself a seat before they're all filled up. Where's a good place to sit?"

"Right over there by the window," he said. "You'll get a good view of everything, and if things get out-of-hand you can just dive through it and save yourself. Just leave something in your chair to reserve it, and then come on over here. I want you to meet Rumpsley."

Borski did the honors, referring to me as a man who "had done quite a bit of research on bears, even written a book on them." As Borski had suggested, it was obvious that Rumpsley had not come across the Ralph book, or I was sure his reaction would have been much different. As we shook hands I made some innocuous remark about how much attention his meeting was creating. His handshake was surprisingly limp, coming from a stiff-necked type nicknamed "Right-Angle" Ronnie, but that was a name given to him by Ralph and Duffy, neither of whom had never shaken his hand, or anybody else's, for that matter.

"This bear issue can't be ignored any longer. It simply must be addressed," said Rumpsley seriously. It was clear that he was a man born to be stuffy. "We can't go on like we have been or our campgrounds will become wastelands. People and bears just don't mix. We have a serious safety concern here." He was paging through his book of regulations.

"Martin, I've misplaced my list of regs pertinent to nuisance bear depredations. See if you can locate it in our papers here." He was speaking to his assistant. "If you don't find it, you'll need to make another list before the meeting starts."

"Yes, sir," replied Martin, without enthusiasm. "Bear depredations."

"Boris, I hope you're going to keep those noisy creatures out of the library once the meeting starts. Talk to the sheriff about it. This is going to be an orderly meeting, or I will cancel the whole thing. Serious work cannot be conducted in a circus atmosphere."

"I'll do my best, sir, but we must be aware of the First Amendment."

"The First Amendment does **not** guarantee circuses at public meetings. Peaceable meetings, yes, Boris — the First Amendment says peaceable. Shouting through bullhorns is not peaceable. Find that sheriff and send him in here." Rumpsley's face was beginning to turn an unattractive shade of purple.

"Yes, sir," replied Boris, as we turned and scurried from the building, he to find the sheriff and me to watch the circus.

The Morlanby family had a restful night. In fact, they all slept so soundly that none of them were awakened to see or hear the bear that put his nose through the mosquito net curtains at 3:30 A.M. The bear was disappointed. George Morlanby had taken such care in covering his foodstuffs that the he could smell nothing enticing enough in the trailer to hold his interest. He wasn't even tempted by the cellular telephone lying next to the sleeping lady's head, since he already had a brand new one in his fanny pack. Feeling a trifle letdown the bear went on about his nightly routine of checking campsites.

As they awoke the Morlanbys were pleased to note that it had rained a bit during the night. The dust had settled, and the forest had a pleasantly fresh fragrance. By nine o'clock, with their breakfast complete and the dishes cleaned up, George began to lay plans for the day's activities.

"Why don't we make the hike up the river today?" he suggested to Amy. "We'll take the trail up the west side of the river for a couple of miles. Let's pack a lunch and find a place to eat by the stream. What do you think of that idea, Meghan? Ask Albert if he wants to go."

"I know Albert wants to go," replied Meghan, excitedly. "He's going to ride in my backpack. I'll fix him a lunch too."

Chattering amongst themselves about what fun camping was, the family set about getting things together for their excursion, and by eleven o'clock they were ready to depart. George, in shorts and hiking boots, led the party, carrying the backpack with the lunches. Amy brought up the rear, and Meghan hiked along in the middle of the group with little Albert riding backward in her pack, alertly peering out at the passing scenery. Both George and Amy knew that before their trip was over they were likely to be taking turns carrying Meghan, who would surely be a very tired little girl. At the trailhead George registered their names on the hiker registration form indicating that they were planning a day hike to Beaver Flats.

As they started up the trail the sun appeared through the overcast and George broke into song. "We're off to see the Wizard, the wonderful Wizard of Oz", he sang as the others joined in. It was a happy little group.

As I stepped from the library I saw that there were new protesters in the crowd, which had become noticeably larger. Most prominent was a man on stilts who was wearing a homemade bear suit, and carrying a recycled sign that had once said, "GIVE PEACE A CHANCE". The word "peace" had been crossed out and replaced with "bears". Pasted to his back was the all too familiar plea, "FREE TIBET". This was clearly a make–do operation. Another protester walked by carrying a banner that read, "SAVE THE UNIVERSE", which I thought went a bit beyond our mission. Borski hurried by in search of Deputy Edd, carrying the orders from Rumpsley, as I walked around to the "quiet" side of the library and put in a call to Duffy.

"This is Macduff Shakesbear, speaking. How may I direct your call?" Duffy was cutting up again.

I decided to go along with the gag. "I'd like to speak to the president of the COB organization," I said.

"The president is out of his office this morning. May I take a message?"

"Okay, Duffy, let's cut out the comedy," I said. "What's going on up there? How's Ralph?"

"I'm pleased to report that the restorative powers of the

goochiweed have once again worked their magic." Duffy was clearly elated. "Ralph is on the mend. The fever has broken, the heartbeat is strong and respiration normal. The old fellow is sitting up and taking nourishment — specifically, some of the elixir of fermented elderberry brought to the sick room last evening by Wines Longfoot when he heard that Ralph was ailing."

"Damn, Duffy, that's good news! Put him on, let me talk to him."

"Can't just now, dude, I'm down at the river getting more water. I haven't cleaned up the mess in the cave yet. That goochiweed soup is powerful medicine let me tell you, man. And listen, I remember where I heard of this stuff before. It was grandma's name for the ingredients in the witches' brew in Macbeth — 'pilot's thumb, lizard's leg, liver of blaspheming Jew' — Shakespeare's play, you remember? Goochiweed was grandma's name for 'gall of goat'. Pigweed was 'root of hemlock' and 'bog of orchid' is what Shakespeare called 'fillet of swamp snake'. It's funny how that kind of thing comes back to you."

"Would that stuff work on human beans? We might be able to go into business. We could make millions."

"The dose I gave Ralph would probably kill any six human beans instantly. Don't even think about it. This was a dose of last resort; I knew only heroic methods would do. Ralph was in bad shape. I was sure he was going to check out. I didn't think he would make it until morning."

"By the way, about the telephone. Ralph had swallowed two of them, not just one. They were those little bitty ones I got down in the campground. Fortunately they came out, along with everything else, so there's no harm done. He's up now and moving about, complaining as usual. I'm not sure he knows how close he was to shuffling off this mortal coil."

Duffy quickly changed the subject. "We both want to know what's going on down at the summit meeting."

"They're just getting set up," I said. "Rumpsley thinks he's got enough evidence to permanently remove all you *Ursis americani* from this end of the park, and I mean permanently. He's very serious about it. You and Ralph better start looking for new territory."

"Yeah, we'll see about that," said Duffy. "Dang, I wish I could be down there. I could mix with Oddball's rabble-rousers. They'd think I was just another guy in a fake bear suit. I could sneak a whoopee cushion into Rumpsley's chair. He's the kind of guy who could use some ego-modification."

"You stay right where you are and take care of Ralph. We'll handle things down here. Now I've got to get back, the meeting should be about to start. I'll let you know what happens."

Spectators were filing into the library when I returned. Deputy Edd seemed to have succeeded in quieting SoPro 201. The students were grouped around their leader near their vintage bus, which was decorated with signs and slogans, several obviously left over from previous campaigns. They appeared to cover every issue imaginable, including the need for more portable potties on asparagus farms.

It was standing room only when I entered the building, but the front row chair I had reserved for myself was still vacant. Ranger Rumpsley had just seated himself, and was preparing to start the meeting. It was precisely one o'clock.

He straightened his tie, cleared his throat and addressed the crowd in his pompous manner, reading far too quickly from a prepared statement. He spoke in a monotone.

"Ladies and gentlemen. Thank you all for coming today to help the park service solve a problem of vexing importance. For those of you not familiar with the administration of our section of the park, my name is Ronald Rumpsley, Supervising Ranger, charged with maintaining the safety and integrity of the southern divisions of our glorious treasure, the Olympic National Park. It is my...uh... responsibility to preserve a safe environment for those who visit us here, and to see that all who come will enjoy a memorable experience free from harm in...uh...a worry-free environment. Within the past five months we have been troubled by the presence of an increasing...uh...number of problem bears in our division of the park. These bears...uh...have become emboldened in their audacity and increasingly cunning in their methods, not only within the park itself but outside the...uh...park as well, as I am sure some of you here know full well."

Those in the audience who had heard Rumpsley speak before were already beginning to doze off.

"All of you know that black bears are...uh...crafty and unreliable beasts. Their reputation for untrustworthiness is...uh... legendary and once they think they have the upper hand in their relations with humans they...uh...will exploit it to the fullest. There is danger that this is now happening in the park. Serious depredations have occurred here all summer, not only in the park...uh...but here in town as well. As you know we had another store break-in just last week, and...uh...we are sure we know the identity of the responsible bear."

In spite of the tightly closed doors of the library we could still hear the chants of the protesters in the parking lot. It sounded like they were singing, "all we are saying is give bears a chance."

Rumpsley continued, "Park regulations already in force give us the authority to trap and relocate nuisance bears. Unfortunately... uh...the activities of the problem bears in our campground this past summer do not strictly meet the park service definition of nuisance bears. This is because the bears we are seeing now do not...uh... come into the campground to steal food and threaten campers so much as they engage in...uh...serious property crime — stealing, vandalizing and disturbing the peace. For some time we have thought that these activities were the work of...uh...juveniles, but the careful detective work of my staff has convinced us that these depredations are the activities of a group of extremely clever juvenile bears. I have submitted this information to park headquarters in the east and...uh...they are studying the problem, and expect to have new guidelines ready for us by next year. The information we gather at this meeting, and others like it, will help them reach their decisions."

"The misguided protest groups you hear out in the parking lot demand that animals, like humans, be given the full and equal protection of the law. Although we would like to comply with this humane consideration we are forced by the seriousness of the problem to take a stronger course of action...uh...of action. We are fully aware that property crimes...uh...are not capital crimes, and as such do not warrant the summary execution of the perpetrators. If we were able to capture these bears and relocate them to the backcountry, our problem would be solved. Unfortunately we find we are dealing with a group of bears with...uh...unusual cunning and stealth."

"All of our efforts to capture them have failed. In some cases they have clearly worked in cooperation with each other to circumvent our own best efforts. It is almost as though they listen in on our meetings. Our traditional methods are not working and therefore it is my...uh...reluctant decision to undertake a program of direct action, beginning immediately. All bears, young and old, must be considered nuisance bears who have already used up their one period of grace. Accordingly they are to be exterminated – shot on sight." There were gasps from the crowd.

"My rangers have been given authority by me to carry out this plan, with the...uh...tourist season now over and our...uh...public areas less crowded, there is little likelihood that gunfire will be of any great danger. All of my...uh...people are certified sharpshooters, and they have been instructed to use utmost caution. Because these bears are clever and unusually smart it shouldn't...uh...take more than the elimination of two or three of them to convince the rest that they should leave the area. We can no longer delay in this matter. We must take action before the...uh...hibernation and the birthing of a new generation of bears, even more devious than the previous one."

There was the sound of shifting chairs and some uneasy muttering from the audience. Someone in the back of the room shouted, "You don't have authority to make that decision."

"What's that you say?" asked Rumpsley, sounding surprised.

The man in the suit got to his feet. "Edison Shufflewait, General Counsel, Legal Rights For Animals League, Northwest Division.

The killing of animals is an abominable practice under any circumstances. Killing them outside of already established statutes is unlawful. You are depriving these bears of their constitutional right to due process of law."

Ranger Rumpsley's face reddened ominously. "These bears have deprived my park guests of their right to a stress-free camping experience. I am exercising my authority to protect the citizenry within my jurisdiction, and I would appreciate you allowing me to continue with my presentation. You can raise your concerns at the proper time."

"You can bet on it," said the speaker.

"I would now like to present a series of slides taken by my staff during the past summer, which will graphically illustrate the sort of bear behavior I have been describing. These photos are not of the highest quality. They were primarily taken in poor light, because it is in the nature of bears to be active in the dark, but I think they will be sufficient to illustrate the problem we have in the park. Martin, lower the lights, please."

"The first picture we have is of one of the animals we are concerned about. I'm sure that many of you are familiar with him."

The ranger pushed the lever on the projector, and up popped a shot of a voluptuous blonde in a bikini swimsuit, which barely covered her essential parts. Rumpsley, sputtering in embarrassment, quickly thrust a new slide into view. It showed two bears copulating, the top bear smiling broadly for the camera while the bottom bear displayed a look of complete boredom. The snickering in the audience became general laughter as the ranger struggled to remove the picture from the screen. Taken after dark the next slide appeared to show Duffy, who was grinning broadly into the camera, and holding up his middle finger. Everybody was wide-awake now. Rumpsley, sensing that he was about to lose control of the meeting, sputtered with anger and shouted at Martin to stop the projector and turn on the lights.

"Some of those people outside have clearly been tampering with my equipment," Rumpsley said, through clenched teeth. "We'll have a short delay while we correct the problem."

Turning to Boris he whispered hoarsely, "What's happening here? What's the meaning of this outrage? Are those people outside responsible? Get that sheriff in here and have him find their leader."

There was general pandemonium in the room. Rumpsley had completely lost his cool. "That was a picture of the bear that is causing all the trouble in the campground. How did it get into the projector? Boris, dammit, I demand an explanation! Who's responsible for this outrage?" He snatched the carousel from the projector and vanished into the library office. I noticed Borski looking at me, his eyebrows arched in frustration, his forehead furrowed. With a shake of his head he too disappeared, following Rumpsley.

On a hunch I went in search of Wilmer Archibald.

CHAPTER FIFTEEN
Crisis in the Valley

"Albert's hungry, mommy," said Meghan.

"Yes, dear," said Amy Morlanby, "we'll stop in a few minutes. Daddy's looking for a good place for a picnic."

They were just a mile north of where the old bridge had been before it washed out in a violent flood several years earlier, and not far from the still visible scars of the old Beaver Burn, the last large wildfire in the southern end of the park, which had occurred fifteen years earlier. George had hoped to find a place to eat near the water, but it looked like the river was getting farther away instead of closer. The first flat spot was going to have to do. George was getting a bit hungry himself. They would have their lunch, and then start back. He saw trees ahead; there should be a shady spot there close to the dry creek bed.

"Albert wants to know what we're having, mommy."

"Tell Albert we're going to have hot dogs and buns and mustard and lemonade."

"Oh good. Albert loves hot dogs. We're going to have hot dogs, Albert." Albert concentrated on the trail behind him and said nothing.

High on the rim of the canyon Macduff Shakesbear sat sprawled on the ground outside the entrance to his grandfather's cave. With his back resting against a young maple tree he observed the movement of the small hiking party on the trail far below. The sun was pleasantly warm; his mind was in neutral, completely at ease. Except for small regrets that he couldn't be down at the library participating in the civic excitement, Duffy was at peace with the world. Ralph was well again, at that very moment snoring loudly on his bed inside the cave. The berry crop had been excellent, and all his friends were well-fed and ready for their winter naps. Peaches had informed him recently that he was going to be a daddy again, and although her news was only of passing interest to him, it did mean that he had succeeded where others had failed. In a year or two he might well run into his offspring someplace, and if Peaches wasn't with them he was unlikely to ever know that they were even related. That's just the way things were among bears. And it also meant that he was one step closer to one day becoming the clan's Alpha bear. Contented, Duffy dozed off, enjoying the soft afternoon breeze, which was blowing up the canyon.

George had finally found what he considered to be a suitable place for their picnic lunch. There were rocks to sit on in the shade, out of the increasing heat, and even though the little creek was dry, the spot would do for the short time they would be there. Meghan perched her small teddy bear next to the trail where he could observe lunch preparations.

George fumbled around in the backpack. "Amy, I thought you were going to pack sandwiches. Where are they?" he asked, as he put the plastic container of lemonade on the ground.

"There wasn't enough bread, George, so I put in the hot dogs and buns instead. They'll do just as well. There's mustard and relish and ketchup if you want it."

"There's just one problem, Amy. We're going to have to eat them cold," said George, with a note of disappointment in his voice.

"We can find some long sticks and roast them over a fire just like we do at home," said Amy, brightly. "Meghan, see if you can find three long straight sticks. Daddy can sharpen them."

"I'll get four," Meghan said, with excitement. "Albert needs one, too." She skipped off happily, looking for sticks in the undergrowth alongside the trail.

"Don't you remember the signs, Amy? Fires are outlawed."

"Oh, George, we don't need a big fire. A little one in the old dry creek bed couldn't hurt anything. There's nothing in there that will burn. We can't eat our hot dogs cold."

"That's not a good idea. We'll just have to have buns and lemonade," said George, testily. "The signs don't say anything about the difference between big fires and little fires. They just say **no** fires. We've got to follow the rules, Amy." George was a stickler about rules, even when he thought they were unnecessary and stupid.

Meghan ran back carrying an armload of sticks, most of which were short. All of them were crooked. "I got the sticks, daddy."

"Alright dear, just put them there on the ground."

"Daddy says we can't roast our hot dogs, Meghan. He says we can't have a fire."

Meghan's face clouded up. "Albert doesn't like cold hot dogs," she said, pouting. "He won't eat them. It's going to spoil our picnic. Please, daddy."

If there was one thing that could make George Morlanby change his mind about something, it was seeing his daughter unhappy.

When Meghan was unhappy, Albert was unhappy, too, and when they both ganged up on him it was just a matter of time before they would get their way. Amy was on Meghan's side, too, which settled the matter. George made a short futile effort to dissuade them, but soon found himself constructing a little fire pit in the dry stream bed, where he scooped the gravel down to a sand base and carefully placed a ring of stones to act as a barrier for the small fire he planned to make. Meghan, pleased with her persuasive powers, hurried off to gather some small dry twigs to get the fire started.

George, a man who normally followed rules to the letter, was decidedly uneasy. All those signs back in the campground kept flashing in the back of his mind. They seemed serious and inflexible, and he fretted about them as he tore up a paper bag for fuel to ignite Meghan's kindling. He wished he had a bucket of water; the small container of lemonade hardly seemed adequate as an emergency fire extinguisher. By the time he had a suitable blaze going the fire was a bit larger than he had intended it to be. Just then Amy called to him to bring his pocketknife to help her sharpen the sticks. As his attention was diverted, Meghan threw more twigs into the flames to get a hotter fire.

It didn't take me long to find Archie, who was out in the parking lot mingling with the protestors, many of whom seemed to be friends.

"How's it going in there? Rumpsley put anybody to sleep yet?"

"Archie," I asked, "did you have anything to do with putting Rumpsley's slideshow together?"

"Heck, no. I'm not on the staff any more, remember? I think Ski helped him. I know he was having trouble finding enough photos, and was substituting pictures he got from other places — out of magazines and stuff."

"By the way, Archie, don't you have a new digital camera? Does it work pretty well in dim light?"

"Yeah, and it's amazing what you can do with digital pictures on a computer," he said, trying to appear innocent. "How come you're asking? Something go wrong in there?"

"So far, Rumpsley's slides have been the hit of the program, at least as far as the audience is concerned. Somebody has been substituting slides in his magic lantern show, and the chief ranger seems on the verge of a seizure. Can you imagine that?"

"I can't think of anybody who would do something like that. How cruel," said Archie, with a faint smile.

A small band of noisy protestors lurched by, dressed in black leather clothes and wearing bandanas across their lower faces. Each had carefully coiffed hair of a different color, which they wore in spikes. A man with purple hair was carrying a brick. They all seemed to be doing a tribal dance of some sort, beating on drums and shouting, "Beartown, baby, beartown's where it's at. Let's hear it for the bears. Up with grizzlies, down with the President."

As the wild dancing continued to swirl around him, the man raised his arm to fling the brick against the window of a park service truck, and instantly found himself in a chokehold administered by Deputy Fred Edd, who snapped a pair of handcuffs on the miscreant with practiced ease, and frog-marched him out of the library parking lot. The crowd in black leather followed along, bellowing about the evils of police brutality. "Up with bears, down with pigs," was the cry.

"That dude would get an 'A' in SoPro 201, except I don't think he's enrolled in the class," said Archie, observing the scene. "Those black leather types are protest groupies who've got nothing else to do but follow the SoPro bus around. They usually wear gas masks and carry bicycle chains. They specialize in breaking windows."

By the time I returned to the library, Ranger Rumpsley was into the flip chart phase of his presentation. "Direct your attention," he instructed the crowd, "to the chart showing the increase in bear depredations in the national park system since 1994, along with a breakdown showing where the incident occurred, the type of offense, monetary loss and the action taken, according to category and seriousness. The following chart will show you how the increase in our own park compares with the latest figures from comparable parks in the system."

Rumpsley flung back the next page on his easel with a flourish to reveal what appeared to be a centerfold from Playboy magazine — a full color photo of a busty bimbo, who peeked suggestively at the audience. Many in the crowd were no longer able to contain their glee as the stuffy ranger quickly turned another page and attempted to continue with his lecture. It was clearly a losing battle. His audience, never completely sympathetic with his side in the bear matter anyway, seemed ready to bolt from the meeting, which was headed toward total chaos.

In a desperate attempt to regain control, Rumpsley quickly called for a question and answer period, which he prayed would prevent further disturbance from the unruly element bent on

213

destroying his carefully planned meeting.

As it often does on warm summer afternoons, heated air began its evening trip up from the valleys and canyons of the lower mountains, seeking to find its temperature equilibrium. What had been a quiet, tranquil breeze began to show signs of restlessness, a need to visit other spaces, and to get there quickly. The leaves in the trees began their late afternoon dance.

George Morlanby tended his fire, which instinct told him was burning a bit too aggressively, what with the fuel Meghan had added while he was sharpening the sticks. He knew that it had been a mistake to let himself be talked into building it in the first place, and he was anxious to get the meal over with as soon as possible. Amy laid out the foodstuffs and utensils, and began fixing hotdogs to the sticks. She had the buns propped up on the rocks to toast them as best she could. Meghan had just seen a chipmunk dart behind a tree and she ran off to give Albert a better look at it. He had never seen one before.

From his position outside of Ralph's cave Duffy smelled the smoke long before he could see the fire. His knowledge of the puzzling habits of humans told him immediately that the three hikers down there on the Skok trail were breaking the rules, as tourists so often did. Usually one of the last to place any importance on park rules, which were made for people anyway, not bears, Duffy paid very strict attention to regulations having to do with fire. While it seemed to him that everything that humans did was unnecessarily complicated, he knew that fires were big trouble. He scoffed at the way the park people went about deciding when the fire season should start, what with all their fancy scientific measurements about dew points, humidity and temperature readings, but at least they were trying to deal with a real problem, and not something completely ridiculous, like keeping bears out of garbage cans.

Fires were something that Duffy had actually spent quite a bit of time thinking about. It amused him that humans needed to analyze pages of scientific data to decide when fire season should begin when he could simply smell it, not that the actual date was of any interest to bears. Duffy figured that he could make a fire easily enough, too, not that he'd ever need one. All he had to do was go swipe some matches somewhere, but why bother? It wouldn't occur to a bear, for instance, to roast a hotdog on a pointed stick. Why go to all that trouble when it could just be gobbled up as it was? Duffy's real interest in fire was the same as it was for any other wild animal in the forest, and that was to avoid it.

There were usually just two ways that a bear was ever forced to confront a fire. One was a fire started from a lightning strike, and the other was from stupidity by human beans, like what was going on down there on the trail right now. In either case, the animals almost always had to depend on the "beans" to come put the fire out. It was one of the few things that they were good for, as far as Duffy was concerned.

He briefly considered going down on the trail to scare the Morlanby family away and put the fire out himself, but he wasn't sure he knew how. There was no water in the creek, and all he'd probably do was burn his feet. With growing alarm he watched as the fire began to get much too big. The little girl seemed to realize it too, and she began to run up the trail. Her parents were busy fussing with their pointed sticks as she disappeared from view.

In about ten minutes the wind began to blow in earnest.

I was never sure exactly what it was that finally put the finish on Ranger Rumpsley's carefully crafted attempt to get public support for a solution to the bear problem. It was probably a combination of things, beginning with a general public apathy about the whole matter in the first place. To a lot of local citizens it seemed like a solution looking for a problem. Except for the occasional foray into the downtown area, bears were more of a curiosity than a danger, although maybe the local druggist wouldn't have agreed.

Rumpsley, who was never one of the park department's more popular officials, found himself fighting a losing battle with a variety of unlikely forces. There was the noisy opposition of TESC's SoPro 201, a group practiced in the kind of outdoor theater guaranteed to create havoc in the best-laid bureaucratic plans. There was also the work of certain "moles" inside Rumpsley's own organization (I had strong suspicions about the identity of these individuals but never attempted to prove them), who upset his meticulously prepared audio-visual presentation. Then there was the vocal denunciation of Rumpsley's plan by animal rights groups during the question and answer portion of the meeting, when the U.S. Constitution and the Bill of Rights were loudly invoked in the interest of the civil rights of all of God's creatures whether on, under or above the surface of the planet. Even dung beetles, I was interested to learn, had the right of public assembly.

At one point in the shouting match between a red-faced Rumpsley and the lady in sensible shoes, the ranger threatened to reduce the population of bears in the park by shooting them from helicopters like so many Alaskan wolves. It was during the shocked silence following this pronouncement that my telephone rang. Actually it wasn't a ring at all, but the opening bars of Beethoven's Ninth Symphony. Rumpsley's anger was immediately directed at me.

"Stop that infernal noise! Take that telephone out of here," Rumpsley roared, as I promptly left the room. It was Duffy on the other end, sounding uncharacteristically stressed and excited.

"There's a fire starting up here, dude! You better get those rangers up here quick! This thing is going to travel fast. There are some people in trouble down there on the trail, too. I've gotta go!" It sounded like he dropped the phone.

"Pete? It's Ralph here. Duffy's headed down the canyon. I don't know what he plans to do, but that fire's taking off like a jackrabbit on steroids. It's right on the edge of the old Beaver Burn on the Skok Trail where there's lots of dry underbrush. It looks like the flames are going up both sides of the canyon. I can see three people running up the trail on the north side of the fire — a man and a woman and what looks like a little girl. They can keep ahead of the fire for awhile, but at the rate it's moving it'll catch them."

"Maybe you better get out of there, Ralph. You're going to be overrun with firefighters as soon as I spread the alarm down here. If Rumpsley spots you he'll shoot you on sight. Probably claim you

217

. started the fire."

"I can't see Duffy any more. Damn, I hope he knows what he's doing."

"I gotta go, buddy. I'll call you later."

"If you bring all those rangers up here, you keep 'em away from me, you hear? There's nothing at my place to burn."

I returned to the meeting, which had turned into a shouting match between Rumpsley and the Animal Liberation Front, or whatever group it was that currently occupied the soapbox. As I entered the room Rumpsley glowered at me as though I had just joined the Wild Animal Welfare League legal team. I managed to catch Borski's eye and motioned him to come outside, just as my phone began its symphonic greeting once again. I hurried out the door with Borski and Wilmer Archibald right behind me. It was Ralph again.

"Hold the phone a minute, Ralph." I slipped the phone into my pocket and turned to the rangers.

"Ski, you've got a fire going in the old Beaver Burn. There are people in danger."

"Damn, how do you know?"

"Sources," I said, not willing to tell Borski that it was Duffy who had called me. "Trust me, they're reliable."

Borski gave me a look of skepticism that seemed to bore straight through me. "This better be on the up and up, Pete."

"Swear to God, Ski. This is no joke."

"I'll have to tell Rumpsley and he probably won't believe me. He'll just think the protestors are pulling another fast one." He disappeared back inside the library.

I pulled the phone back out of my pocket "What's going on Ralph? Can you see Duffy?"

"Too much smoke, old man. But there's a natural break along the trail a ways ahead of where the fire is. If Duffy runs like hell he might be able to show those people how to get out of there. It's a man and a woman and a little girl. You got help coming?"

"Yeah, but it's going to take a while. Nobody will get there soon enough to save them if they stay on that trail. Here comes the ranger, Ralph. I gotta go."

Ralph was still talking. "Tell your ranger buddies that if they can get enough people up here with shovels they'll have a good chance of stopping the fire on this side of the river, up by the big rock slide at Five Stream. They'll have to move fast though."

I hung up as Borski arrived with Archie by his side. "I don't think Rumpsley believed me," he said, "but he seemed happy enough to have an excuse to cancel the rest of the meeting just the same. Those lawyers had him backed up to the wall, and they were about to skin him alive. He was mighty glad to get out of there, I tell you. He's heading down to his office now. Says he's going to find out what firefighting equipment is available. He's put me in charge of the fire."

I told Borski what Ralph had said. "Okay, I've already been on the radio. We'll get what equipment we have on the way, but we don't have much manpower. Everybody is off fighting that fire east of the mountains. Find sheriff Edd and get that Oddware guy over here pronto. I've got an idea. It'll likely cost me my job, but I frankly don't give a damn."

219

The protestors were still milling around in the library parking lot, but they were definitely running out of steam. Most of the shouting had stopped, and a lot of the demonstrators had reboarded their bus, apparently deflated from their efforts. A few remained clustered around the entrance to the library enjoying the noisy argument going on inside. The measure of comparative quiet made it possible for Ranger Mickeilweisky to convey his firefighting plan to his unlikely troupe of hastily assembled assistants.

"Oddball, can these kids of yours actually **do** anything? I mean like helping to put out a wildfire?"

Behind his thick spectacles I thought I saw a hurt look in Oddware's eyes, but he spoke right up to reassure the ranger. "Of course, they can Mr. Borski. They are all splendid young people with excellent work habits, especially when they can get college credit for their experiences."

"Good," said Borski briskly, "but more importantly, can you drive that bus up a mountain road?"

"Oh goodness, yes! I've driven this bus in all sorts of terrain, and all the way down to Berkeley."

Deputy Edd, who was standing next to Borski, looked skeptical. "I'll drive the bus, Ski, I know the way."

"No, Fred, I want you to get clearance from your boss to take your car up there. We may need extra transportation, and your radio."

Borski caught sight of the small group of idle loggers now working on their second case of Bud Lites in the corner of the parking lot. "You guys interested in doing a little public service?" he shouted.

"Name your poison, boss, we've got time on our hands," said the man without suspenders.

"You got your saws with you? Got any shovels?"

"In the truck, man. What've you got in mind?"

"We've got a fire started up at Beaver Flat. As of right now you guys are on the federal payroll. Stand by and I'll tell you what I want you to do."

Borski turned to Archie. "I've got two forest service trucks on the way. You can catch them at the old logging camp and ride up with them — show them where to go. We won't have any water, and there are no helicopters that I know of, so whatever we do up there is going to be done the hard way."

"Okay, boss, but just where is the fire exactly? Nobody has told me yet."

Borski looked at me intently, as if he wanted verification of what he was saying. "My source says to stay on the Elk Creek Road and get as close as you can to Five Stream," he said. "It's down in the canyon along the Skok trail. There're three people caught on the trail somewhere north of the fire."

Borski turned to me and he was all business. "Do you mind telling me how you know all this?"

I'd been expecting the question. There was no way to answer it except to reveal my long-kept secret of a relationship with a talking bear — a talking bear with a cell phone, no less. I could only hope that Borski, a man whose family had trained bears in European circuses, would be understanding. I took the plunge, "Ralph," I said, "and a telephone."

Borski's eyes narrowed. "Oh my God, not that again. All right, I haven't time to quibble. You ride with me, Pete, and bring your magic telephone with you. This will sure as hell end my career with the National Park Service. I know there's got to be a rule somewhere that prohibits the transporting of eighty year old, bear-talking civilians up into the mountains to fight wildfires. Nobody's ever going to believe this."

"Eighty-two year old," I said. "Let's get going."

It was a strange procession of conveyances and personnel that set off up the mountain to fight the fire. First up the road were two oversized red pickup trucks, each driven by an intense young professional with the competence that came from the performance of a familiar task. Wilmer Archibald rode shotgun with the first driver. Borski and I followed right behind, with the ranger on the radio trying to marshal more forces, which seemed to be in very short supply. Behind us came Fred Edd in his patrol car, followed by a monstrous four-by-four pickup truck loaded with eight denim-clad men in outdoor garb, who were still working on their second case of Bud. (They had picked up extra supplies and additional manpower from the Model T as they went by.) The "Hands Off The Bears" sign was still waving from the back of the truck.

The weary old Protest bus came next with Oddware Stumple hunched over the wheel in intense concentration, peering nearsightedly at the narrow road, his SoPro 201 students hanging from the windows, somewhat subdued, but sill cheering and waving signs. Finally came the colorful "black leather" groupies riding in an ancient van with "ANARCHY FOREVER" painted on its side. Their machine was making the trip under loud protest, its mechanical ability to reach the top of the grade seriously in doubt. The ranger hadn't specifically invited the men in leather to help with the fire but, as Archie had told me earlier, these people appeared by instinct wherever any sort of unregulated activity was taking place, their sole purpose being to find a way to promote confusion. Actually the whole procession looked more like a gypsy encampment being escorted out of town by the local constabulary, than it did a firefighting brigade.

Borski didn't spend time dwelling on the unconventional nature of his unruly crowd of volunteers. He was all business. "Get your 'source' on the phone," he ordered curtly, "and find out what's

going on up there. See if you can find out about the people caught in the fire." We had just crossed the causeway at the end of the lake, still at least twenty minutes from our destination. "I've been in some strange situations during my career, but this one beats them all. The only way it could be more cockeyed would be to have Rumpsley up here, leading the charge. Thank God for small favors."

I dialed Ralph's number and listened with growing concern as the phone rang twelve times before he answered.

"Ralph, it's me. What's happening?"

"Your guess is as good as mine, man. I saw Duffy for a second about ten minutes ago. He had those tourists with him in the chute, but that fire is going to jump the rocks easy unless the wind quits."

"There's a whole rabble of us coming up, Ralph. We'll be there in less than a half-hour. Where are you?"

"It got too smoky. I've moved up above the road, never mind where. I couldn't see anything from my place, so I left. No use looking for me when you get up here, you won't find me. I'm beginning to think I don't want to live around here anymore. I'm going to start looking for new real estate. You know how I feel about crowds."

"Stay near the phone, Ralph. I'll call you later."

CHAPTER SIXTEEN
On the Line

The untidy caravan labored up the mountain toward the canyon rim above the fire. The two forest service truck drivers and the "incident commander", Ranger Borski, were the only professionals in the throng of hastily assembled volunteers. Approaching Four Stream we were greeted by great billowing clouds of dirty, brown smoke. It certainly didn't look like mere shovels alone would be enough to control this fire. When we passed the spot where Duffy had once led me down to Ralph's cave I knew that the old bear would be somewhere nearby, watching our approach. I didn't reveal any of this to the ranger; it was enough that he knew I was in touch with Ralph, without knowing just where he might be. The road had become little more than a rough trail by the time the pickups came to a stop, and the drivers jumped from their trucks, unloading shovels and other hand tools including the ever-popular Pulaski, the double-sided pickaxe that firefighters preferred for moving earth quickly. Deputy Edd pulled to a stop behind us.

The beer-fueled loggers piled out of their truck a minute later, looking like a modern version of the Keystone Cops. "Give us some tools, boss," shouted Toad, the burly, tattooed leader of the group, "and we'll put this thing out."

"Hold up there a minute, boys," Borski said. He had been talking on his radio. "I've gotten word from headquarters that we've got a chopper on the way. They've managed to redirect one that was just taking off from Tacoma on its way east of the mountains. They're sending it up to us, but it won't get here for twenty minutes or so. It'll pick up water from the lake on the way. You guys watch for it. They'll try to hit the leading edge of the fire. Stay clear when you see them come."

A lanky logger named Swede and his sidekick, with the name "Lugnut" printed across the front of this hardhat, were already halfway down the slope, each with a chainsaw on his shoulder. Archie followed, a Pulaski clutched in one hand, a shovel in the other, all three of them stirring up clouds of dust.

As Oddware's bus groaned to a halt and disgorged its assortment of colorful occupants, Borski began to have second thoughts about deploying them on the fire lines, but he reluctantly waved them on when Archie and the two forestry truck drivers promised to keep a close eye on the students of SoPro 201. Only when Oddware pledged to absolve him of any responsibility, did Borski agree to issue shovels and Pulaskis.

Professor Stumple had been positively eloquent in pleading his case to let his students fight the fire. "This will be a wonderfully valuable opportunity for these splendid young people to prove their mettle," he rhapsodized. "It will bring credit to their spirit and gumption, not to mention the honor they will bring to their university, The Evergreen State College, home of the Fighting Geoducks." Oddware's passion overcame Borski's reluctance and, convinced that manpower of any kind was crucial to checking the fire before it got completely out of control, he gave his begrudging approval to their deployment. He issued the usual warning to be careful not to get caught under the helicopter water drop.

Deputy Edd put aside his radio and left his car to inform Borski that a team of twenty firefighters was en route from park headquarters; they would hike up the Skok trail from the south, but were not likely to make it to the fire in less than two hours at the earliest.

"If we don't stop this thing within two hours, we're out of luck," muttered Borski. "That helicopter is probably our only hope. What do we know about those people caught in the fire, Fred? Any word?"

"Nothing. I haven't heard anything at all. Ask your wildlife expert there," he said pointing at me. "He's the one who seems to get word about these things before the rest of us."

Borski turned to me, "What about it, Pete? What do your sources say?"

"I've heard nothing new," I replied. Borski and the deputy were standing at the crest of the canyon watching the disordered progress of the little volunteer army as it careened down the steep hill. Oddware was galloping at the head of the group, holding an uplifted shovel with a 'FREE TIBET' flag tied to the top.

"Onward, fearless Geoducks! Once more into the fray," he shouted.

While the ranger and the deputy watched him in disbelief, I slipped around behind the protest bus and dialed Ralph's number. For reasons I still didn't clearly understand, I couldn't bring myself to stand right next to my friends and talk to a bear on the telephone. It was a mental hang-up I couldn't seem to shake, even though both the ranger and the deputy had read the book about my adventures with Ralph and Duffy. It just didn't seem right. It was as though I was violating a confidence of some sort.

When he answered the phone Ralph didn't bother with a salutation. "Am I talking to the ringmaster of the circus down on the flat there?"

"There's a shortage of experienced help, Ralph. We're making do with what we've got."

"Do you really believe you'll put out the fire with that gaggle of misfits? Why don't you add a little color — put 'em all in funny hats, maybe some red rubber noses. Might as well have 'em look like clowns. You human beans beat all."

"Ralph, I'm worried about Duffy. Have you heard from him? Has he got his telephone with him?"

"He left his phone in the cave. No need to worry about Duffy. If he's alone, he can stay ahead of that fire easy. If he's trying to help those people down there, he may be in trouble. They can't move very fast. There's a little girl with them, you know." Ralph was trying to sound positive, but I could hear the concern in his voice.

"Is there anyplace they can hide?" I asked.

There was a long pause before Ralph answered. "Not really. Their best chance would be where the rock chute crosses the little stream. Beyond that it's all brush and trees. If the fire jumps the rocks, as it probably will, it'll go through that stuff like a scalded weasel. They'll have to keep galloping up the trail, and those beans can't run very fast, or very far. They won't have much of a chance."

"Damn, listen Ralph. There's going to be a helicopter up here very soon. They'll take water out of the lake, and they'll drop it on the leading edge of the fire, like they're supposed to do. Would it do any good to have 'em drop it on the rock chute to cool it off in case Duffy and those people are in there somewhere?"

"Here's what I'd have them do," said Ralph, slowly. "Listen carefully. First, I'd tell them to fly right over the fire and on up the trail. Have 'em keep a sharp lookout for three people. Don't say anything about a bear, or they won't believe you. If they don't see anything, have them come back and bomb the chute exactly where it crosses the creek. After that you're on your own. I have no more suggestions and we've probably see the last of Duffy."

"Thanks, Ralph. I'll tell the ranger. He's in contact with the chopper. Can you see the fire from where you are?"

"Just smoke, dude. Lots of smoke and your crew of goofballs, who are just getting to the bottom of the hill. The guy with the flag on the end of the shovel looks like Stonewall Jackson at Bull Run; if you can picture Stonewall Jackson in short pants, that is."

"Thanks for your help, Ralph. I'll get back to you."

Ranger Borski was on his radio talking to the helicopter when I returned. "ETA is twelve minutes, right? Stay on this frequency. I'll have instructions."

I relayed Ralph's suggestions to the ranger. "Okay, I'll wait 'till they're in sight, then give 'em the word. Doesn't sound too good about the people, eh? Let's try to be positive about this, though, and hope for the best."

Fred Edd had been on his walkie-talkie with Archie, who was at the bottom of the hill.

"Archie's sending some of the volunteers back up the hill for some minor medical attention. They've discovered that Birkenstock footwear is not appropriate for fighting wildfires. Archie's got the rest of them working on the left flank of the fire. Apparently it's not too hot there, and they may actually be doing some good. Would you believe that Oddware's got the whole bunch shoveling in unison and singing the Volga Boatman song? Archie says it's the damndest thing he's ever seen. The loggers are cutting snags and working the other side of the fire up the canyon."

As he listened to Archie's report Borski looked discouraged. "Yeah, but nobody's on the front of the fire where we need 'em. Our only hope is the chopper."

The five leather-clad men with the multi-colored hair appeared from around the back of the protest bus. All were clearly overheated and three of them were carrying their heavy coats. It was the anarchist group, minus the member with the purple hair, who was in custody for malicious mischief.

"Damned old car broke down. Had to walk a mile, man," said Pink Hair, striding boldly up to Borski. "Where's the action old man? We want to get in on this gig. Moe and Gizzy used to be in the army corps, and they know all about firefighting. Cranky," he said, pointing to Green Hair, "was on the correction school firefighting crew. Give us some shovels, dude. Put us on the payroll."

A distracted Ranger Borski didn't even bother to question their motives. He briefly thought of sending them out on the point of the fire, but quickly reconsidered the idea as being much too risky. "Get some shovels and go down there and find a guy named Archibald. He'll tell you what to do. Thanks for your help."

"No problem, man, we're lookin' for action. Hey, Knobby," Pink Hair shouted at Puce Hair, "we should have brought our masks. It looks pretty smoky down there, man. Whataya think?"

"Put your bandana up, man," said Knobby, as they headed down the hill. "Watch for the bears, Moe. I hear there's lots of grizzlies around here."

"Now you tell us," said Moe, who was sporting a head of zebra striped hair.

"Hey, Cranky, don't get too close to the fire, man. With all that grease on your head you might explode."

In the distance we caught the sound of the approaching helicopter. Borski was immediately in contact on his radio. "Chopper, this is Boris Mickeilweisky, the ranger in charge down here. Just call me Borski, it's quicker. What's you name?"

"Glenn Alberg, special operations at McChord. My observer is Bill Hendricks. We were on our way to the Okanogan fire when we got short-circuited. What've we got up here?"

"You'll see us on top of the hill at the end of the road. We've got a fast-moving fire in the canyon, Glenn. You're about our only hope of stopping it now. Here's what I want you to do."

Borski outlined the plan just as Ralph had given it to us. As the chopper advanced we could see the huge bucket below, leaking water as though it was anxious to get to work. The pilot hovered briefly while expressing reservations about wasting water on a bunch of rocks. Borski explained our concern for the people who might be in danger, and the need to cool the rocks if they were to have any chance of surviving.

"Roger," he said. "I'll go on up ahead and see what I can find, but we're going to lose ground if I have to come back and unload on that rock chute. It'll take ten minutes to make a round trip to the lake. Your fire'll move a long way in that time."

"Can't help it, Glenn. Lives come first."

"Roger, Boris, I understand." The chopper accelerated to the north, directly over the Skok trail, and disappeared from view, lost in the smoke.

Less than five minutes had elapsed when we heard the chopper returning. "Nothing on the trail as far as we could tell," came the pilot's voice. "We're going to dump on the rocks as ordered." We could hear the chopper hovering briefly, and then it appeared through the smoke on a high speed run back toward the lake to the south.

Suddenly Deputy Edd's walkie-talkie radio began to crackle and we heard Archie shouting in excitement. "My God, that load of water washed two people right out of those rocks! It's a man and a woman. They look like drowned rats! I don't believe this, Fred! Stand by, I've got to go up there and help them."

"Well, I'll be damned," said Borski, in astonishment. He turned to speak to the deputy. "Fred, tell Archie there's supposed to be three people. There should be a child about four or five years old — a girl. Tell him to watch for her."

The deputy tried to relay Borski's information. "Archie doesn't answer," he said. "He's probably very busy."

Hardly able to believe his eyes, Wilmer Archibald raced across the boulder field to where the bewildered couple huddled like a pair of fugitive coal miners, blackened by soot and drenched by the unforgiving water drop, survivors of some grim underground disaster. Suddenly two of Oddware's volunteers appeared to help them negotiate the rough and rocky terrain. Amy Morlanby was nearly hysterical, asking over and over for their daughter, Meghan, while her husband, George, disoriented and guilt-ridden that this whole disaster was his fault, did his best to comfort her. Archie and his volunteers, without any real inner conviction, attempted to assure the couple that the little girl would be found safe. Slowly the group made its way across the boulder chute to the relative safety of the burned-over terrain.

Using his walkie-talkie, Archie advised Deputy Edd that he was sending the rescued couple up the hill accompanied by the two protest bus volunteers. He suggested that he break out some blankets to provide warmth for the waterlogged victims, and asked that he send any available idlers down to help with the fire.

CHAPTER SEVENTEEN
Out of the Jaws of Death

For the first time since his crazy, impulsive dash down the hillside, Duffy had time to catch his breath and reflect on what he had gotten himself into. In a matter of minutes he had gone from being a relaxed, lazy bear spending a quiet afternoon in the sunshine outside of Ralph's cave, to being an exhausted fugitive from a forest fire. As if that wasn't enough, he had become the unintended guardian of a small and terrified member of his least favorite species, the "human bean", a race of creatures that was the nemesis of every kind of animal on earth, except dogs and house cats.

Duffy had sat and watched as the little tousle-haired girl wandered away from her parents just before the fire started. She seemed to be carrying an object in her arms, which, from a distance, he imagined to be a teddy bear, the perennially favorite toy of the species. As the scene unfolded below him, Duffy saw both grownups start up the trail to look for her, leaving their illegal fire untended, and had they been the only ones in danger when the campfire exploded, Duffy would not have bothered to get involved. Ralph had often told him that the adult form of the human bean, purported to be very intelligent, actually didn't have sense enough to "pour piss out of a boot". And as far as Duffy was concerned, people who were stupid enough to put piss in their boots in the first place couldn't be all that smart.

In his opinion, the adults could look after themselves, Duffy had always viewed them as being fair game for harassment, and this was just a new kind of harassment. In fact, much of his time in the national park had been devoted to making their lives miserable, so why should he change now? Little tousle-haired girls were another matter altogether, though, especially little girls who carried teddy bears.

So Duffy had gotten involved, deeply involved, in the crisis in the valley, and when the grownup people could not run fast enough to stay ahead of the fire Duffy had dashed down the hill to pick up little Meghan and gallop on ahead. The last he heard of the parents was the mother shrieking something about her child being eaten by a bear.

Singed and scarred by his race to stay ahead of the fire, Duffy was totally exhausted by the time he reached the well-hidden cave that he hoped would be their salvation. He had discovered this sanctuary the previous year, and had marked it as an excellent place to hibernate if a bad winter ever drove him to it. He had given up the idea when he decided the cave was too close to the popular Skok trail, which had far too many hikers, even during the winter months. But he hadn't forgotten the place. Today he desperately hoped that it just might serve to save his life.

Duffy knew his position was precarious. He positioned himself across the small entrance to the deep cave so as to prevent the little girl from attempting to escape. She still wasn't sure if this large furry animal was her protector or her tormentor, and was desperate to find her parents, who had been unable to keep up with the bear, even though he was galloping on three legs and carrying the little girl with the fourth. He glanced back at her and was relieved to see that she had finally stopped crying. Her discomfort now manifested itself in small sobs and whimpers as she hugged her teddy bear tightly to her chest.

Duffy knew their chances of survival were complicated by the presence of old growth trees growing almost directly above the cave. If the fire crowned into the trees before it got to their location they were likely to be trapped by falling debris. If not that then, with the fire sweeping by on the ground, the alternative was suffocation for want of air in the back of the cave. In the meantime there was nothing to do but wait.

Duffy studied the stuffed toy held so tightly by the little girl, certain that it was indeed what human beans called a "teddy" bear. It sure didn't look like any bear he had ever seen. With its stubby little arms and legs sticking out in all directions, it resembled what a real cub bear would look like if it had been run over by heavy machinery. Its two-colored nose wasn't really long enough, either, and the bear had little beady eyes made of marbles.

Meghan's fright and anguish disturbed him. If there was to be any escape for them he knew he must calm the little girl's fears. Her full cooperation would be necessary; prompt and direct action was required. And so, for only the second time in his life, Duffy started a conversation with a human bean.

"Is that what you call a teddy bear?" Duffy asked.

Meghan showed no surprise. Humans, he knew, seemed to accept the fact that children believed they could converse with animals. It was only when grownups did it that suspicions arose.

236

"Of course, his name is Albert. What's yours?" she asked.

"Macduff Shakesbear."

"That's a funny name. Are you a teddy bear?"

"No, I'm a real bear. You can call me Duffy."

"I'll call you Mr. Duffy because you're older than I am. My daddy says I mustn't call older people by their first names. It's not polite."

"You're a very unusual little girl. What's **your** name?"

"Meghan Morlanby and I live at 3628 Laurel Drive, Beaverton, Oregon 97008," came the carefully rehearsed reply. "Albert lives there, too."

"How do you do, Meghan and Albert? Now I need you to listen very carefully. Pretty soon I'm going to take you to find your mommy and daddy." As soon as they were out of his mouth, Duffy realized that those were two words that he had never used before, and they struck him as having a particularly warm and pleasant sound. No wonder the little girl was so frightened by the disappearance of her parents.

"We've got to go up a steep hill, Meghan, and the only way we can do it is for you and Albert to ride on my back. Do you think you can do that?" Just then Duffy caught the first strong smell of smoke. He coughed twice, concerned that their time was running short.

Meghan studied Albert's black marble eyes. "Yes, we think so," she said, without enthusiasm. "We'll try."

Once again the helicopter approached, and while Duffy knew that only water was going to stop the flames, its presence concerned him nevertheless. They had heard the machine overhead earlier, but Duffy hadn't gone out to look at it, afraid that either the little girl would escape, or worse yet, that the pilot might try to shoot him. Humans, being what they were, he knew he couldn't take the chance of being seen.

The fire was hardly a quarter-mile distant when they heard the change in the pitch of the chopper's rotors. It seemed to be hovering directly overhead, and Duffy guessed it was about to dump another load. He retreated farther into the cave just as a deluge of water flooded the trail, a substantial amount of it sweeping through the entrance. It was an accurate drop, thought Duffy, and if there was ever a time to escape, this had to be it. The undergrowth was saturated, the fire had not gotten into the trees and its progress would be slowed. It was now or never.

Wrapping an arm around Meghan's midriff, Duffy dashed onto the trail carrying the little girl and her stuffed toy out into the open. He scanned the terrain for a possible route up the steep hill that would lead them away from the path of the fire. For the first fifty yards they made good progress, but he knew that he was not going to be able to climb the hill on three legs, and still make enough speed to stay ahead of the fire.

He came to a sudden stop. "Alright, Meghan, now listen carefully. I want you to get up on that big log next to the trail there," he said, pointing, "and when I come up alongside of it I want you to climb right onto my back. You'll need to lie down on your stomach and hold on as tight as you can. Grab right onto my fur, you won't hurt

me. Put Albert underneath you so he won't fall off. Pretend I'm a horse, Meghan. Squeeze your knees together as hard as you can. Ready? Okay, let's try it."

The small girl mounted Duffy's back with little difficulty and followed his directions. "Good girl, Meghan, now hold on tight. We're going up the hill to find mommy and daddy." He hoped he sounded more confident than he felt; the last time he had seen her parents they were a half a mile behind him in a losing footrace with the oncoming fire.

Duffy found what seemed like a possible route up the long hill and set a diagonal course to achieve as much forward progress as possible, without it being steeper than he could safely negotiate. He was all too aware that the fire was still moving behind him, not slowed much by the water drop that had rescued them from the cave. Fortunately the vegetation thinned the farther he climbed, but the going was dangerously slow.

"Meghan, do you remember any nursery rhymes?" Duffy asked, hoping that he could take Meghan's mind off their desperate plight. As he started to quiz her about Mother Goose he suddenly found himself laboring for breath. The smoke had affected him more than he realized. "Do as many as you can remember, Meghan. How about Little Miss Muffet?"

Now shut up, Duffy, he said to himself, and save your breath.

"Little Miss Muffet sat on a tuffet.... What's a tuffet, Mr. Duffy?"

"Thing you sit on," gasped Duffy.

"....eating her curds and whey.... What's a curd and whey?"

"Stuff to eat. Can't talk now, Meghan." The cub began to wish he'd kept himself in better shape.

"*Ride a cock horse to Banbury Cross...*What's a cock horse, Mr. Duffy?"

"Damned if I know. Ask Albert."

"Oh, oh, Mr. Duffy, you said a bad word."

Mr. Duffy began to seriously wonder whether or not he was going to make it to the top of the hill.

"*Every lady in this land has twenty nails upon each hand....*" Meghan was lying on Duffy's back, her arms now firmly circling his neck. She could hear the bear's heavy breathing. "How can a lady have twenty nails on her hand, Mr. Duffy? She would have to have four on each finger."

Kids good at math, thought Duffy, as they finally emerged from the worst of the smoke. He thought he could hear the helicopter again over the pounding of his heart, and it sounded like the chopper was hovering. God, no more water on us please, Duffy thought, as he plodded on, still aiming upward. How much farther? How much farther?

"*Barber, barber, shave a pig. How many hairs will make a wig?*"

"Damned if I know, Meghan. I'll be damned if I know."

An agitated Ranger Borski was hard pressed to find parking space for the three local fire engines that had just arrived on the scene. He got on the radio to Rumpsley at Hoodsport headquarters.

"Ron, don't send any more engines up here. I don't have any place to put 'em. There's no way they can get close enough to the fire to do any good, anyway. I need manpower and tools. No more pumpers."

Whatever Rumpsley replied was drowned out in the clatter of the helicopter, which slowed while passing over Borski's staging area as it headed back toward the lake. The pilot pointed at his radio microphone as he passed overhead, and Boris quickly switched to the chopper's frequency.

"Hey, Borski," shouted the pilot excitedly. "We've just flushed a bear out of the woods about halfway up the side of the canyon. If I'm not mistaken he's got your little girl riding on his back. Damndest thing I ever saw. He's just a half-mile past where you are. Whataya want us to do?"

"You go get your water, Glenn. I'll take care of the bear. Thanks for alerting us." Borski motioned me to his side. "Pete, I think we've found one of your bears."

Deputy Edd, who had been ministering to the Morlanbys in the back seat of his patrol car, walked over to speak to Borski. "I think I should get that couple down to town, Ski. They ought to be checked out at the hospital. The mother needs a shot of something. She's freaking out."

"Hold up just a bit, Fred. I think we may have some news..." His words were drowned out by the racket from the helicopter. "Dammit, why doesn't he get on with his water dumps?" Borski snapped, looking up in irritation. "Oh, shit, it's a damn TV station."

Sure enough, it was the "breaking news" chopper – Chopper One – from Seattle's most aggressive television station, with "FIRST ON THE SCENE TWENTY-FOUR SEVEN" emblazoned on its side in letters two feet tall.

Deputy Edd had gotten a message on his radio, and was about

to reply, when Borski took the handset from him.

"Unless you guys can hang a water bucket on that thing and help us with this fire we'd appreciate it if you would get the hell out of the way."

"We have just received a report that there is a bear molesting a child up here," came the reply. "Is that true? What can you tell us?"

Ranger Borski, beside himself with anger, improvised a reply to get their immediate attention. "I can tell you that you are flying in a restricted area, and if you don't get that damned machine out of here immediately your station will be charged with interference in a Federal Disaster Relief operation, and you two guys up there will be going up the river. Put that on your breaking news broadcast. My name is Boris Mickeilweisky and I'd be happy to spell that for you if you want me to. I'm the ranger in charge here, and I want you out of here, now! You can make that a direct quote if you want to. Now vamoose!"

"Roger that," came the surprisingly meek reply. The chopper moved away to the west.

Borski explained about the brief message from Glenn Alberg, the pilot in the water drop chopper. "Fred, Pete and I are going up north a ways and see what we can find. Radio to your people down at the causeway not to let any more traffic come up unless it's an aid car, or more able-bodied manpower. You stay here and keep in touch on my frequency, okay?" Borski turned to me, "You come with me. Pete. I may need a translator."

Beyond where the forest service trucks were parked were the faint remains of a long abandoned logging road. Borski got behind the wheel of the first truck, gesturing me into the seat beside him.

Apparently he was going to drive as far as we could go, which quickly proved to be hardly more than a quarter-mile, before a young tree blocked further progress. "Come on," he said, climbing down from the truck. "We'll have to hoof it from here."

We plunged through the dead scotch broom and second growth timber until we got close enough to the steep slope to see partway down the hill. The fire was well down in the canyon, still moving, but at a slower rate. Apparently the water drops were having an effect. I saw movement in the underbrush.

"There, look there, Boris," I shouted, pointing. "Just beyond that little bunch of trees. I think I see something. Yeah, there they are! That's Duffy, and he's got the girl on his back!"

The TV chopper was moving closer again, and I could see the flash of binoculars as the reporter scanned the ground below. I waved both arms and yelled as loudly as I could, hoping Duffy would hear me over the clatter of the rotors.

"Duffy, here! Over here!" The bear looked at me, then back over his shoulder at the helicopter. Suddenly he went to his knees and shook the little girl, who fell awkwardly to the ground. As she struggled to grab onto him again I heard him shout over the racket of the chopper.

"Go Meghan, you can make it to the top by yourself. Your friends are right there at the top of the hill. Climb, girl, climb! Don't forget Albert."

In growing alarm, Duffy looked once more at the chopper, then at me. I thought I heard him shout, "I'll call you" as he turned and ran down the steep slope he had just traversed, moving steadily away from the fire. The chopper seemed to be following him. In an instant he had disappeared from sight.

Boris went over the crest of the hill and down the slope in a clutter of dust and confusion. A dozen long leaps took him to Meghan's side. Quickly he scooped the little girl up, and displaying strength beyond what seemed possible, began an exhausting scramble back to where I stood watching in amazement. With Meghan under one arm he was halfway back to the top, when she screamed that she had forgotten Albert. Retracing his steps the ranger retrieved the teddy bear and finally made it to the summit with his burden. He didn't even seem to be breathing hard.

"Where is Mr. Duffy?" the girl asked, tearfully. "I need to thank Mr. Duffy. He saved me."

"Duffy had to go back and save some more people," I fibbed. "He'll be here later. We'll go see your mommy and daddy now. They're worried about you."

We loaded Meghan and Albert into the ranger's truck, which Borski backed almost to the clearing before he found room to turn around, and he drove out along the narrow road. The reunion of Meghan and her parents was tearful and joyous, although the little girl's breathless and disjointed story about her trip up the hill on the back of a bear who told nursery rhymes, brought a lot of "of course, dears" and "yes, yes we knows" from her distracted mother and father, who were so overwhelmed by relief that they scarcely paid attention to how she got back. Deputy Fred Edd was soon on his way down the mountain, transporting the Morlanby family to the hospital for routine checkups, where the worst injury to be found was a burn on Albert's leg where he had lost a patch of fur. By then Meghan had already renamed her teddy bear "Mr. Duffy".

At the fire line, Wilmer Archibald radioed Borski and told him that the crew of twenty-five professional firefighters had arrived from the lower trail, and he was sending his ragtag volunteers back up the hill. He reported that the helicopter water drops had corralled the blaze to a point where cooler night air, and a forecast of drizzle in the morning, should bring the fire under control.

The late summer dusk was already beginning to fall as the disheveled and exhausted protest bus volunteers came straggling up the hill. Professor Oddware Stumple, who was now using his shovel, which had lost its FREE TIBET banner, as a walking stick, limped over the crest of the hill, radiant with a glow of success.

"Mission accomplished, sire," he shouted at the ranger, executing an exaggerated salute. "We have met the enemy and bested him." His round eyeglasses, which he appeared to have tried to clean, stood out from his grimy face, giving him the appearance of a great horned owl that had spent the day cleaning chimneys.

The entire force of mismatched volunteers clustered around a late-arriving forest service truck that had brought drinking water and sandwiches. The anarchist boys showed up, most of their color having been washed away by perspiration, and their leather coats long ago discarded in the heat. They were looking for the paymaster to collect their wages, and to put in a requisition for new outfits.

When the helicopter making the water drops clattered by on a return trip to the lake the pilot radioed to Borski that about three more trips would be all they could make before dark. He also reported that "the bear was still headed north, walking." The TV chopper picked up the message and headed north itself, flying low and fast with its load of newsmen. In a matter of minutes Borski picked up their excited voices.

"Hey Flash, did you see what that bear did just now?"

"No, man, what'd he do?"

"The little bastard gave us the finger. Can you beat that? He gave us the bird, just as plain as day. Now, he's gone. I can't see him."

"That's a newsworthy bear, dude. Did you get a shot of him?"

"No, dammit, but if I had my rifle I'd a shot him alright, the little twerp."

The TV helicopter got some distant shots of Meghan and Borski reaching the top of the hill, and good footage of a terrified Duffy racing down the hill trying to escape all the noise. On the basis of that, the "BREAKING NEWS!" station concocted a story about how Chopper One had saved the child from being mauled by a wild bear, while covering a small wildfire in the Olympic Mountains.

Since it was a family station there was no mention of obscene gestures.

CHAPTER EIGHTEEN
All the News
That's Fit to Print

Ranger Mickeilweisky conducted a quick head count, and as near as he could tell all of the volunteers were out of the ravine. Now that the firefighters had arrived he decided it was safe to send them home, or at least back to wherever they had come from. There was one more obstacle to be overcome, however, before the day's adventures were done. It had become apparent that Ranger Rumpsley's campaign against bears was not yet finished.

All afternoon he had been in his office monitoring radio messages from the various rangers and helicopters. When the news report came through about a bear terrorizing a helpless little girl in an out-of-control wildfire, Rumpsley sprang into action. Shutting off his scanners, and thus depriving himself of accurate information from the "front", he immediately called his media sources to get cameras and reporters to the ranger station parking lot where he could continue operation "Off the Bears". The lot was directly adjacent to the road to the park where all the weary firefighters would gather on the way out. There would be no way of avoiding Rumpsley's press conference.

When Borski and I reached the parking lot — being the last ones off the mountain — it looked like the Ringling Bros. circus had set up for a night performance in Hoodsport. The place was flooded with high-intensity light. Satellite trucks and cameras were parked hurley-burley. At least one helicopter circled the area. Rumpsley had gotten his audience all worked up with a single-themed message about the danger imposed by free-ranging bears, which he described as being "those slobbering predators" who were a "constant menace to an orderly park environment." Biased as I was in favor of the bears it seemed to be unnecessarily intemperate talk from what should have been a well-adjusted, polite park ranger, further reinforcing my suspicions that Ronald Rumpsley's trolley had jumped the tracks. I reminded myself to tell Ralph that he was a slobbering predator the next time I caught up with him.

The busload of firefighting social protestors was the first to arrive at "breaking news central", and the stalwarts of the electronic media could scarcely wait to get their teeth into a new source of information from the scene of ursine outrage up on the mountain. Rumpsley's tirade had become tedious, and the reporters pounced on the new arrivals like jackals on fresh meat. Full of high-strung energy, Oddware Stumple bounded off the bus as though he had just finished a refreshing nap, herding his troops ahead of him, eager to give the press a full report. Pushing and shoving one another in a feverish effort to "break the story", the reporters rushed to his side, chattering into their microphones, under pressure to be the first on the air. Described as a "disheveled, owlish sort of man with all the hair singed off his stork-like legs" by one reporter, and as "resembling the unfortunate victim of a coal mine explosion" by another, his physical appearance clearly gave witness to the ordeal he had just been through. Oddware braced himself to meet the press.

Boris Mickeilweisky, "a block of a man with a moustache you could paint a barn with, and eyebrows where small rabbits could safely nest" (according to a free-wheeling scribe), introduced Stumple to a reporter as "one of the heroes of the day", and, by some osmotic process peculiar to the press corps, he immediately became the center of attention. Reporters and cameras surged forward, smelling blood and desperate to get a full report of the "horrors on the hill".

Someone found a milk crate and Oddware mounted the makeshift podium. Six and one-half feet tall anyway, he loomed over the crowd, all arms and legs and spectacles. As one who was never far from the lecture hall podium, he launched effortlessly into a gracious speech about the tremendous need for citizens to volunteer for worthwhile causes, and urged them on to a life of community involvement. He gave glowing credit to the spirit of selflessness ingrained into its students by that "great institution of liberal learning, TESC, The Evergreen State College, from whence students go forth into the world imbued with a deep sense of civic responsibility, and an abiding regard for the earth and all the creatures thereon, living testimony to all that is vital and good in America".

"Cut the blarney!" shouted a reporter. "Tell us about the slobbering bear, man. Did he kill the kid?" As the cameras moved in for a close-up, a comely lady with a large "4" embroidered under the "All News, All The Time" logo on her windbreaker, demanded to know the "mood" of the workers on the fire lines, and if there was a palpable sense of relief about escaping the bear attack.

Intent upon his message, and apparently oblivious to the

commotion around him, Oddware began to talk about the trouble his volunteers were having getting in touch with their feelings when Ranger Borski took over the rostrum in an effort to bring some order to the proceedings. The jostling crowd was beginning to have the appearance of a Michael Jackson arraignment.

"My name is Boris Mickeilweisky," he said, introducing himself, "and I'm the ranger in charge of the fire." At the request of the reporters he spelled his name three times, more slowly and more deliberately each time, and two of the reporters eventually got it right. "Just call me Boris," he said finally, his patience nearly exhausted.

"Did the grizzly carry the kid off?" demanded a stringer for the eastern syndicates. "Will you be able to find the remains?"

Just then the five members of the colored hair anarchist group arrived, having ridden down the hill in the park service pickup. All of them were seriously unkempt, their formerly colorful hairdos were a shambles, and the dye was now disbursed all over their faces and necks. Cameras moved in to get close-ups.

"Those bears been chasing you guys? How'd you get away?" shouted a reporter from the back of the crowd.

"Hey, ranger, your people shoved our car off the road up there," shouted Pink Hair. "It's down in the gully. You owe us a car, man. We're going to need new leathers, too; that's genuine calfskin leather with studs. Lugnut burned his boots off, too."

"I lost my new nose ring, dammit," shouted Variegated Hair. "Fourteen carat gold. You gotta get me a new one, man, no bull."

Sensing a growing tension the news corps moved in. "Who are you people? You see the bears? Did anybody get burned up? What happened to your heads?" they chorused.

"Hey, Mickeilweisky, when do we get paid? We got places to go."

"I have requisition papers in my office," replied Boris. "You'll have to go through channels."

"Damn channels, that'll take years," grumbled Puce Hair. "We're anarchists, we don't go through channels."

A print reporter moved in. "Who are you people? Are you with the forest service?"

"Hell, no, we're anarchists, man," he said to the reporter, who was clearly female. "We don't believe in nothin', and we're going to picket this joint until we get paid for all our stuff."

"Did you see the bears?"

"What bears?"

Archie Archibald had come back down the hill with the loggers in their monstrous pickup truck. Boris spotted him at the edge of the crowd.

"Hey, Archie come over here. Now you people listen up," he shouted to the milling reporters. "You people want the straight story here, this is your man. Meet Wilmer Archibald. Archie was in charge of the people on the edge of the fire. Without him that fire would be on its way over the mountain by now, and at least a couple of citizens would be dead meat."

The media surged forward, sensing the kill. "What about dead meat? Did you kill the bear? Are there citizens up there? How many grizzlies are there? What was the mood of the firefighters at work on the fire? Did you get a sense of the anger of the bears?"

Archie, a naturally retiring sort of man, was momentarily taken aback, but quickly regained his composure, realizing that the way to cope with such a gaggle of unruly, sharp-elbowed reporters was to give as good as he got.

"If you dudes would like to get the story straight you're going to have to back off and shut up. And you, sir, with the gigantic camera, if you want a picture of the inside of my nose I will happily pose for you later. But for now try for some longer shots, please."

Archie's freelance forcefulness did the trick, and things began to settle down. Boris watched with pleasure as Archie recounted the day's adventures briskly and accurately: the work of the volunteers, the vital assistance of the airdrop choppers and the safe return of the Morlanbys. Then Boris took over to relate the rescue of the small child by the young black bear known around the campground as Duffy, and the dash up the canyon hillside to safety. The reporters scribbled furiously, getting most of the information recorded correctly. As for the "mood" on the fire line, Archie said he really hadn't had time to poll the volunteers, but described it colorfully as being something between "abject weariness and puking exhaustion". I noticed that Rumpsley, who had relinquished center stage when Borski and I arrived from the fire scene, was skulking about on the fringes of the crowd talking to the odd reporter who might still be interested in anti-bear discussions. He vanished into his office as Borski related the dramatic account of Duffy's escape with the little girl on his back, giving me a dirty look as he left, which for some reason gave me a measure of satisfaction.

"What's become of the loggers, Archie?" I asked.

"The loggers are over at the Model T tavern," he replied. "They're more interested in rehydration than publicity. You reporters want to talk to the real heroes, go over to the saloon. Ask for a guy in a tin hat called Lugnut. He's the fellow who needs a new pair of boots."

Although I could see that the reporters at the news conference were just getting warmed up, my adrenalin had ceased to flow, and extreme weariness was setting in. As I turned to leave, a group of reporters from the Japanese National News Bureau arrived in a taxi having flown into Seattle from Los Angeles to cover the story of the "rittle gir take by bear in fire".

As I passed the park building I could see lights burning in Rumpsley's office. I later learned that he had spent the evening filling out "request for transfer" papers.

The following day I awoke early to catch the morning TV coverage of the previous day's free-for-all. As expected, the initial coverage was about as garbled and inaccurate as it could be, complete with excited "bureau chiefs" describing ravenous bears carrying off innocent children as the helicopter cameras caught occasional shots of a terrified Duffy galloping in confusion down the hillside north of the fire. Even though the facts were eventually straightened out for the later broadcasts, the bear footage was run again and again, and contributed to the "Breaking News Channel" winning the competition for viewers during the October sweeps. All the networks had good stuff from the big news hoopla in the parking lot. Professor Stork Stumple and Ranger Boris Mickeilweisky, rabbity eyebrows and all, came through nicely, both being highly photogenic characters. Most of the networks had close-ups of Oddware's singed legs.

I traveled some distance to find out-of-town newspapers, anxious to see what sort of creative coverage had come out of our meeting. As expected, the veracity of the stories produced by the print media varied widely according to their distance from Hoodsport. The New York Times, for instance, had a sensationalized version of events that an enterprising reporter had obtained from Ranger Rumpsley by calling him while he was still in his office. Somehow the facts in the article got all twisted and the story said that it was a tame bear named Duffield (sic) who had started the fire in the first place to punish the authorities for being insensitive to wildlife in the park. The ranger was quoted as having cited numerous occasions where the authorities had reason to punish the bears, and as saying that the story circulating about a bear becoming a hero by rescuing a child was simply "poppycock" dreamed up by local citizens who were trying to get their town "on the map".

U.S. News and World Report got most of their facts straight, but chose to play the poppycock angle to the hilt, claiming that there was internal strife in park management, and that the ranger, named Roger Rumstead, had resigned in protest over lax park standards concerning "drooling predatory" bears that were taking over the campgrounds. The article read as follows:

Ranger Ronald Rumsteady was reported as saying that if park authorities don't take action soon, emboldened predatory black bears will make the campgrounds unusable. He cited numerous depredations, including a time when a gang of unruly bears took over a large motor home while the owners were off hiking. They drank their beer, played rock and roll music and engaged in disorderly dancing inside the rig. Ranger Rumstedily has asked for a transfer to Yellowstone National Park where, he says, "the park people know what they're doing."

It was a while before I got a look at that supermarket favorite, the Weekly World News, which was lurid journalism at its best. I suspected that they constructed their stories by having reporters sit around a table with scissors, cutting snatches of stories from competing journals, which were then put into a tub and thoroughly mixed. Pieces were then drawn from the tub at random and reassembled with glue until a new story reappeared, ready for the presses. I noted with pleasure that there were no aliens in the Duffield (sic) story, but that omission was more than made up for by many other creative details, each guaranteed to catch and hold the interest of the most jaded of readers as they stood at supermarket checkout counters:

BEAR RECITES RHYMES WHILE CARRYING TOT TO SAFETY FROM RAGING CONFLAGRATION!

So far so good.

GRIZZLY SAYS LITTLE MISS MUFFET SAVED THEIR LIVES; CRITICIZES PRESS HELICOPTER AS BEING TOO NOSEY

Close enough.

"We were nearly decapitated by chopper blades," says Duffield, the talking bear

THOUGHT TO BE SAME BEAR WHO ONCE ATTENDED OXFORD ON FULBRIGHT SCHOLARSHIP

DUFFIELD IS REMEMBERED AS ACCOMPLISHED SHAKESPEARIAN ACTOR; DID A SPLENDID HAMLET

The World News had run right off the tracks. I couldn't wait to show this gem to Duffy.

The next day I got a call from Boris who said that the Today Show in New York wanted to get Duffy back there to appear on their show. Having no idea where the bear was, he gave them my number telling them that I was the only guy who might be able to find him.

"Thanks a heap, Boris," I said, with a measure of reprobation. "My fifteen minutes of fame at last."

The truth was I had no idea where Duffy was and had spent some sleepless nights worrying that he might still be running north hoping to escape decapitation. I thought I remembered him shouting that he would call me. Or had I promised to call him?

The message came in early afternoon. A young woman with a pleasant voice introduced herself as Olivia, an advance contact person who was responsible for booking newsworthy guests for the morning talk show. The first thing she wanted to know was whether or not Duffield was a real grizzly bear, and if I could actually talk to him. After getting her straightened out about the name and species of the animal, I assured her that I could indeed communicate with him, to my satisfaction, at least.

I could tell that she was skeptical of what she was hearing, but she launched right into a list of the perks that would be provided if we could be persuaded to come back east and appear on their show, including first class round trip air fare, limousine pickup at the airport, VIP accommodations at the city's finest hotel, and fifteen hundred bucks of spending money for each of us. Just to see how far she would go I suggested that Duffy might want to bring his grandfather along to keep him company, and reminded her that, because of their size, each of them would require two seats on the airplane. Without a moment's hesitation Olivia assured me neither request would pose a problem. Feeling the necessity to prepare her for her eventual encounter with the bears I told her that Ralph was rather opinionated and didn't put up well with stupid questions. When Olivia said they didn't ask stupid questions on their show it was my turn to be skeptical.

I could see some problems ahead for Ralph and Duffy if they decided to accept the invitation to appear on the show. I read a book once about a bear from New Hampshire who roamed around New York City trying to get a book published, and nobody ever guessed that he was a real bear. I couldn't imagine that ever happening with Ralph or Duffy. For one thing they didn't walk upright with a human-like stride, as I've mentioned before, but hopped along like crows when they were on their back legs. Two large men in fur coats hopping along the sidewalks like children riding hobbyhorses were likely to attract considerable attention, even in New York City.

I didn't want to break the news to Olivia right away, but the bears were going to have to go to New York without me. It was clear that the whole thing was a crazy idea, and I didn't want any part of it. I had a vivid mental image of strolling through Rockefeller Center with two large bears on a leash (I assume there is a leash law for black bears back there) and having a taxicab backfire nearby. There was simply no telling where we would all end up. At my age I couldn't chance it.

Furthermore, I had absolutely no idea where Duffy was, or how to get a hold of him. He wasn't answering his phone, and I assumed that either he was still on the run, or that his batteries were dead. Olivia was disappointed when I told her I couldn't contact him, and she even jacked up the spending money to two thousand bucks in an attempt to get me to try to round the bears up. I reluctantly turned her down, and suggested she might want to get in touch with the Morlanbys down in Oregon instead. I'd heard they had been on some talk shows in Portland, and assured her that they were a photogenic bunch, especially little Meghan and her ever-present teddy bear, Mr. Duffy.

I called Boris back to tell him about Olivia's call and when I mentioned the Morlanbys he said that he had just sent them a bill for the suppression of the fire they had started up on the Skok trail. According to park rules, citizens who start wildfires through carelessness are liable for the expense of putting them out. Boris said Morlanby was a fortunate fellow, who was going to get off pretty cheap, in part because Oddware Stumple considered his efforts to be a public service, and had refused to take any money. He did wonder, however, if the park service might have an old surplus bus they could give him, since he expected a big jump in enrollment in Social Protest 201 due to the wealth of publicity they had gotten from the fire story.

All the loggers had asked for, beyond their modest wages, was a credit account over at the Model T tavern where they could rehydrate themselves at taxpayer expense in the afternoons after work. Boris said that he'd had to charge George Morlanby for a new pair of boots for Lugnut, who had lost his in the fire, but thought that he could fix the anarchists up with the new car that they had demanded without additional expense. Something along the lines of a '78 Chevy van would do nicely, according to the guy with the yellow spiked hair, who had been sprung from the county jail by his buddies. Sheriff Fred Edd said he had just the thing in the weeds behind his barn — a grayish '81 Dodge that had generous side panels which would be ideal for their signs. If they could get it started they could have it, and he'd even help them get the car licensed. Purple hair reminded him that, being anarchists, they "don't license nothin'." When Boris told Variegated Hair that Oddware, in a spirit of camaraderie, had offered a TESC class ring that he could wear in his nose, the deal was sealed.

The big expense for Morlanby, according to Boris, was the charge for the helicopter, the pilots and the forest service "hot shots" who finished cleaning up the fire. George Morlanby said he'd figure out a way to take care of the bill if the park people could put the fire expenses on some kind of payment plan.

Three weeks passed and I still had heard nothing from Duffy or

Ralph. It was early November and the Olympics had their first fall dusting of snow. It was time for the bears to be hibernating, which I was beginning to think of doing myself, when Boris called.

"Got some breaking news for you, Pete."

"What's up, Ski? You hear from the bears?"

"No, not exactly, but I may have seen their tracks." He told me that he'd been up to the campground to close things up for the winter, and had seen the tracks of two bears in the new snow — one big bear, one not so big.

"They went right into the restroom," he reported. "You know we leave one open up there in the winter as emergency shelter for skiers. It looks like the bears may have spent the night in there, maybe charging their batteries. Whataya think?"

"Could be. I'll try to give them a call. What else is new?"

"Rumpsley didn't get the job at Yellowstone."

"How come?" I asked.

"They gave him some tests and said he was too excitable. Now he's counting beans back in D.C., working in a place called the Department of Wildlife Statistics, Office of Bear and Cougar Assaults and Incursions, Tabulations, Compilations and Recordings Unit. It's a make work deal just for Ronnie. He runs the place all by himself. He just called and asked me to send all his records out there so he can tabulate them He's as contented as a raccoon in a henhouse."

"Tabulation is right up Ronnie's alley, that's for sure," I commented.

"As I was going through all his junk, and believe me its all junk, I ran across another clue about Ronnie's hatred of bears. Listen to

260

this, it's his report dated July 5, 2002: 'I was humiliated in front of a crowd of tourists today. I sometimes wonder if I'm right for this job'. I'm surprised poor Ronnie wrote all this stuff down except that he was so compulsive about keeping records. Anyway, it seems Ronnie was doing an evening lecture on wildlife in the amphitheatre, and there was this rumpled character in the audience who was asking a lot of questions about bears. He had a hat pulled down over his face and he mumbled a lot. Need I go on?" Borski asked.

"Probably not," I said. "Had to be Duffy, right?"

"You got it. Told Rumpsley he didn't know diddly-squat about bears. Suggested he find a job selling shoes, and then threw off his disguise and lumbered away as casually as could be. Scared the hell out of the tourists, and needless to say, Ronnie became the butt of endless jokes. He mentions in the report that he knows who the bear is, and swears that sooner or later he'll have his hide as a carpet in his house."

"Well, anyway, Pete, here's the latest. Some of the movers and shakers down in Hoodsport — of which there are three or four, I believe — are thinking they want to put on some sort of celebration to honor Duffy for his heroism in the Skok fire, which is also now known as the Duffy Burn. They think they ought to have a 'D Day', you know, Duffy Day; a big parade, booths selling teddy bears, belt sander races at the saloon, barbequed ribs, fireworks, dancin' on the green, all that sort of thing. Naturally, they want Duffy there, too, and that's where you come in."

"Of course," I sighed wearily. "What else? The only guy who knows how to get a hold of the bears, right?"

"You're a quick study, Pete. How'd you know?"

"Mental telepathy, Boris. I'm psychic and have unusual mental powers. I also know that winter is here and those bears are about to take their long winter naps. If you want to drag them through town in a parade you'd best have a float with feather beds on it. Those bears are going to be sound asleep."

"This is all long-range planning, my boy," replied Borski. "Nothing's going to happen until next summer. I'll keep you informed. When you find the bears let me know."

"You got my word on it, Boris."

By late November we were well into our long season of dark and drizzle. Winter storms were lined up like boxcars, all the way to Tokyo, waiting to unload on us. The Olympic Mountains, which on good days were framed in my front window as if on a postcard, were nowhere to be seen.

Then on a morning when Mother Nature seemed determined to remind us that she was still in charge, I awoke to a day of stunning brilliance. I sat in awe, watching my mountain postcard, now covered with a blanket of new snow, as it changed from gray to the fabled "purple mountains majesty" of the old song, and then finally to blinding white, as the sun rose in the clear eastern sky. In forty years of watching this amazing panorama I was endlessly captured by its grandeur. The whole glittering display was enough to make an old man stand up and cheer.

As I viewed the spectacular I was reminded that somewhere up there, in a spot I thought I could almost see from my chair, were two bears I used to know, who had apparently disappeared from my life. I had heard nothing from either of them since the big Duffy

262

Burn in late September, and surely they had gone into hibernation by now, not to be heard from again until April, if ever.

"So be it," I said to myself. "If I lived up there I'd hunker down myself. It's too cold to do otherwise."

Soon I was dozing, something I can do with remarkable ease, when my catnap was interrupted by the telephone. The little window on the handset said the caller was unknown, which didn't matter to me. I talk to unknown callers as readily as any other kind.

"Old man?" came a voice from the past. I knew who it was, of course, but I was going to string the impudent fellow along.

"I prefer gentleman of mature years," I said, with a measure of feigned hauteur. "Who is calling please?"

"It's me, Duffy. I was just thinking about you, old man. The air is so clear I can damn near see your house from here."

"I was thinking about you, too. How about that?"

"Osmotic serendipity," he replied, and I thought I could detect a note of lethargy in his voice. "Wireless mental technology, or something like that. Photosynthesis, maybe."

"Whataya doing, Duff? I've been wondering if you were still alive."

"I'm sitting on a stump in the snow in front of Ralph's cave wondering the very same thing, and trying to decide if it makes any difference."

"Where's Ralph?" I asked.

"Inside, sound asleep, you should be able to hear him snoring."

"I thought he was going to move away."

"He's decided to wait for spring."

"Is he hibernating?"

"Yes, he'll be up and around in April or May."

"How come you aren't sleeping, too?"

"Wines Longfoot brought up a new supply of goochiwater last week. Ralph drank about half of it and it put the old boy right to sleep. I thought it was a shame to let the rest of it go to waste, so I just finished it off. I'm hoping it will do the same for me. By the way, did you know that goochiweed is an endangered species?"

"I didn't know that, Duffy, but it sounds like it's certainly worth saving. Its medicinal properties are legendary. I'll alert Oddware Stumple. SAVE THE GOOCHIWEED has a nice ring to it."

"The batch that Wines brought up to Ralph last week is a new and improved mixture that combines his usual fermented berries with essence of goochiweed into what he calls a 'heavenly elixir guaranteed to cure everything'. It's better than anything Lydia Pinkham ever invented, he says. I don't know Lydia," said Duffy, "but she's probably one of his lady friends from the other side of the mountains. I can testify that this goochiwater puts one into a stupefyingly reflective frame of mind."

"That's a mouthful, lad. What are you reflecting about?" I asked.

"Oh, the meaning of life. Issues about my place in the larger scheme of things. My bearhood, or my lack of it." He seemed to be slurring his words.

"That's pretty heavy stuff, Duffy. Why are you questioning your bearhood? It seems secure to me."

"Been hanging around beans too much, I think. I've been adversely affected, and it doesn't seem to be doing me any good."

"You mean human beings?"

"Yeah, beans. I'm a bear, not a bean. I'm having trouble keeping the two separate. I want to get stuff straightened out before I go to sleep."

"Listen to me, Duffy," I shouted into the phone. I didn't want my friend to drop off to sleep before I had had my say. "I want to tell you something. You're a bear who happens to have picked up a few traits from human beans, most of which are favorable. Things like what's right and what's wrong, even though your inborn sense of deviltry gets the better of you sometimes. You've got a conscience, Duffy. You might be the only bear in the world that does. What you did in rescuing that little girl from the fire is proof enough of that. A bear bear would not have gotten involved. I'm not sure Ralph would have done what you did, even if he were able to. And just in case you didn't know it, you may have single-handedly saved all the bears in your end of the park from banishment, or worse, by what you did that day. You're a hero around here, dude, and you ought to make the most of it. You are a bear with some very special qualities."

"Yeah, yeah, that's all well and good, but not very helpful. I'm still confused."

"By the way, Duffy, did you know they want to put on a parade for you down in Hoodsport?"

"Yeah, I know that."

"Who told you?"

"Sources."

"You do have very special qualities, Duff. What do you think of the idea?"

"They better not do it on the Fourth of July. We won't come. Fireworks hurt our ears." Duffy was beginning to mumble.

"Goochiwater is all gone. I'm going to bed."

"Hey, Duff," I said, "if you have questions about whether you're a bean or a bear, just remember this. I don't know of a single person in the human bean category who sleeps five months out of the year and doesn't even have to get up to pee."

The line went dead.

CHAPTER NINETEEN
Peace at Last

I often thought that the bears had the right idea. Around here, sleeping through the winter has merit. If it weren't for missing out on Christmas and New Years, and maybe the excitement of Groundhog Day, I think the idea could be adopted by human beans (now I'm starting to talk like a bear) without great harm. But I suppose it would take an act of Congress, and I don't have that long to wait. There are a couple of other options, one of which would be to go south with the misnamed "snow birds" (who should, I think, be called sun birds), and hang out in California or Arizona; and then for the truly hardy souls among us, those of us with spunk and true grit, the third option would be to stay put and "tough it out". As usual I chose the latter, and by the end of March, with the noticeable lengthening of the days, and the moderating temperatures, I knew I had survived the worst of it.

In early April I got a call from Boris. He said the "D Day" committee had been bugging him again about their proposed celebration to honor Duffy. They had to make up their yearly schedule of civic events, they said, and wanted to make sure the bear would be available.

"Apparently those people don't know much about bears, Ski," I said. "Did you clue them in?"

"I did my best. I said bears aren't big on making long-range plans, or short-range ones, either, for that matter. Told 'em I would get back to them when there was something to report."

"You seen any sign of them?" I asked.

"Nothing yet, there's still a lot of snow up high, but the ground is bare down here. It's hard to see any tracks. Bears may have been through the campground, but I haven't seen anything."

I told Boris I would try to get Duffy on the phone.

I dialed his number and got no answer. I tried again the following week with the same result. On my third attempt I got the sleepy voice of Ralph.

"Ralph, old boy, how's it going?" I was fairly shouting with excitement.

"How's what going?" he mumbled, grumpily.

"Did you have a good rest?"

"It was all right until you woke me up."

"It's spring, Ralph. It's time you were out and about." I was trying to be bright and cheerful, but Ralph was having none of it.

"I'll decide when it's time to get up. What the hell month is it anyway?" We were having our usual problem with telephones. I tried to tell him it was late April, but he was so busy telling me he didn't appreciate being disturbed that he didn't hear a word I said. "I heard the damn telephone ring two weeks ago, but I sure as hell wasn't going to answer it. You should be more considerate. A bear has to get his rest."

"Is Duffy there?" I asked. There was silence on the line and then I heard Ralph shout Duffy's name several times.

"No," said Ralph, continuing to shout.

"Where do you suppose he is?"

"How would I know? Out rutting, probably. Damn fool kids, that's all they think about."

"Well, listen Ralph, have the boy call me when he comes back. It's important, so please don't forget. We've got some decisions to make. You won't forget will you?"

"Dammit, no!" he shouted. "I won't forget." It sounded like he threw the phone down. I suspected that old bears were always grumpy and out-of-sorts when they woke up after being asleep for five months.

Duffy called that evening. Unlike his grandfather he sounded cheerful and upbeat. "I just got back from over at Mt. Rose. I had a good day."

"Whataya doing over there?" I asked, although of course I knew.

"Opening the rutting season," came the expected reply. "Getting an early start."

"Have any luck?" I inquired.

"Heck, yes! Me and Peaches spent the day together. As I said, it was a good day."

"Did Peaches have cubs this winter?" I asked.

"No, this was her off-year. She'll have 'em again next winter. I'm trying to come up with some good names. I'm thinking 'Alarums' and 'Excursions' would be good. Shakespeare used that a lot."

"Those aren't characters, Duffy, they're sound effects."

"All the more appropriate for cubs. Well, anyway, we've got plenty of time for that." Duffy changed the subject. "What's happening with you, old dude?"

I reminded him about the Hoodsport celebration, and told him the committee was bugging Boris about whether Duffy was going to take part. He didn't sound much interested, and said he'd have to talk to Ralph about it.

"How is the old bear?" I asked. "He sounded a bit testy this morning."

"The grumpiness is a normal condition, he'll get over it. When I got home he was still talking about moving. I think he's really serious about it, but he's gone back to sleep now."

"Listen, Duffy. We three need to have a serious conversation about a lot of things. What say we have a spring picnic some nice day down at that old rendezvous place where we used to leave the messages? Ralph is probably pretty hungry. Tell him I'll bring all the grub, and all he has to do is show up. Say I'll bring a case of long-neck Buds, just for old time's sake."

"Sounds like a deal, man. Beer will bring him right out of hibernation."

On a Monday morning in the second week of May, the weather was beautiful and the forecast indicated it would continue to be fine. My phone rang early. It was Duffy.

"Tomorrow's a good day, dude. Ralph says he'll come; says he's hungry as a bear, ha, ha. I'll take a day off from the rut. How about eleven o'clock?"

I checked my busy social calendar and saw that I had an appointment to get my teeth cleaned.

"I'll cancel the appointment, Duffy."

"Bring your brush. I'll clean 'em for you."

"Never mind, son, but I'll be there."

"Don't forget the long-necks, man. Ralph would be one cranky dude if you came without 'em."

"Ralph hasn't forgotten how to open bottles has he?"

"Not likely. Like elephants, old bears never forget."

I made a trip to the supermarket, loaded up on goods from the delicatessen and a sack full of nourishing fruits and vegetables. I even bought some sweet potatoes. I had read they were favorites of bears. And, of course, the full case of Bud Longs.

Strangely light-of-heart I set off the next morning in plenty of time to make the thirty-mile journey, get my car properly concealed and have the table set for the arrival of my guests. I whistled, as best I could remember it, a part of an old childhood tune called the "Teddy Bear's Picnic".

The spur road off the highway looked much the same, but perhaps a bit more overgrown, which made it easier to hide the car. I got myself turned around in a small clearing that looked to be a good spot for our pow-wow. There was even an old half-rotten log to sit on. I would have Duffy check it for ants when he arrived.

I was five minutes early for our appointment. The morning air was pleasantly warm, so I opened the door to my car and sat on the seat reading the front page of the morning paper. I had taken a cursory look around when I arrived, but knew that even if the bears were already present they wouldn't show themselves until they were sure it was really me, and that I was by myself. Even though Duffy had exposed himself to all kinds of people back during our hectic forest fire adventure, he had in no way reconciled himself to being at ease with strange human beans. Duffy was still a bear, and Ralph

271

had never been anything **but** a bear.

I heard a quiet snuffle. Without looking up I paraphrased a line from the Bard. "Come, sir, sit by my side, and let the world slip, we shall ne'er be younger."

"What's he saying, Ralph?" I heard Duffy ask.

"Macduff, you need to brush up on your Shakespeare. In his own clumsy way the old man is trying to quote from *The Taming of the Shrew*. He's telling us to get on with the picnic because we're not getting any younger, which is true."

"Forsooth," said Duffy, as he rose up from behind a huckleberry bush, his hand raised in salute. He looked like Smokey Bear without his hat on. "Beist thou alone, old man?"

"All alone and lonely, my boy. Come join me in repast. I would be pleased if one of you would check yonder log for ants. You know how they can ruin a picnic." I noticed that Duffy was wearing his embroidered fanny pack.

From the thicket behind Duffy, Ralph appeared, and he was gaunter than I had ever seen him. Even though it was quite normal for a bear to be skinny following hibernation, Ralph seemed frail to a fault. He sniffed and scratched at the punky log. "Ant-free," he proclaimed. "Where's the beer?"

"Ralph," I said. "It's only eleven o'clock in the morning. You start drinking this early, you're going to run out of supplies before this picnic is over."

"Tough, tiddy, dude. You can run down to the store and get some more." This caustic quip sounded like the Ralph of old; he might look gaunt, I thought, but he clearly still possessed the curmudgeonly old fire in his belly.

"We'll see about that, Ralph, when the time c
you been, old buddy?"

"True it is we have seen better days and I have d ......u into the
vale of years, but all things considered, I'm doing okay. A little sleep
does wonders, but I'm damned hungry. Where's the grub?"

"All in good time, Ralph."

"You always were a difficult old fart." He was sniffing around
the trunk. "You want me to open the trunk?" he asked, a note of
evil in his voice.

Duffy stood in the background grinning, enjoying a
conversation that reminded him of the 'good old days'. "Gramps,
let's just set a spell. Talk about stuff."

Ralph had his claws under the trunk lid. "When the old man
fetches me a beer, we'll talk. Or perhaps he would like to witness
how easily the accomplished *Ursus americanus* opens the trunk of
your modern automobile."

"I give up, Ralph. Don't wreck my car. I'll get your beer."

"I knew you'd see it my way."

The instant I lifted the lid Ralph found the sweet potatoes and
helped himself to several. I quickly took out a single bottle of beer,
and slammed the lid shut lest he ravage our entire lunch.

"All right, Ralph," I said. "Let's make this affair a brunch then,
not a lunch. That'll be an appetizer for you. We've got some serious
matters to talk about."

Ralph had lost none of his dexterity in opening a bottle. He
snapped off the lid and drained it with a loud gurgle. Belching
loudly and with a deep sigh, he settled himself on the log to eat the
sweet potatoes.

"A remarkable performance," I observed to Duffy. "It has lost nothing to the passage of years."

"In the area of eating and drinking perhaps...." he said, leaving the rest of the sentence unfinished. Duffy and I joined Ralph on the log while we watched him chew the mass of sticky yams.

"The townspeople have been bugging Ranger Borski about the celebration they want to put on, Duffy, and the ranger has been bugging me about it. What do you think about the idea?"

"I think it's dangerous for a bear to go into town in broad daylight for any reason. There are still redneck types around who don't like bears. I think that guy who runs the drugstore would shoot us both on sight. He comes from the Rumpsley 'slobbering predator' school of thought. Anyway, I haven't talked to Ralph about it."

"This isn't about Ralph, Duffy. I don't even think he's invited," I said.

"Well, I'm not going if Ralph doesn't go. We come as a set. Two for the price of one."

"Ask him about it then, right now."

"I think we'd better wait a minute, dude. He seems to be choking on a potato. Look how his eyes are all bugged out." Ralph did appear to be in gastric distress. I fetched another beer from the car and he downed it as quickly as he had consumed the first one. I suspected the choking business might have been a ruse to get the second beer. Ralph had lost none of his guile.

In spite of the distractions, Ralph had been paying close attention to our conversation. "I'm moving," he said with difficulty. "Like I told you last year, I'm getting out of here. There are too many people; too many rules and regulations."

"Things are going to get better, Ralph, now that Right-Angle Ronnie is gone," I said.

"I'm moving," he repeated. "Don't try to talk me out of it."

"Where are you going?" I asked.

"Mother Duckabush told me about a place up on the Dosewallips River. It's an abandoned ranger's cabin that's fully furnished. The road washed out a couple of years ago, and they haven't got enough money to fix it, so the place is empty. Nobody lives there anymore. It's perfect. I'll make it into kind of a retirement home for old bears. It's even got a rocking chair on the front porch. I'll move the COB meetings up there, and get started on a drive for new members — sign up some of those disorganized bears from over the summit."

"I know the place, Ralph, up past the Elkhorn campground," I said, "but it's right next to the trail. How are you going to handle the hiker traffic, dude?"

"When hikers get too nosey I'll just snuffle at 'em. They'll learn not to come too close. Anyway, it gives 'em something to brag about when they get home. They can tell their friends about how they stared down a bear."

"Assuming this should all come to pass, Ralph, when do you plan to move?" I asked.

"As soon as I restore my strength," he replied. "It's a long walk up there. Which reminds me, in order to restore my strength I must eat lots of nourishing food, which makes me think it's time to get into the lunch. Another of the long-necks would be helpful, too."

I gave in, opened the trunk and invited the bears to help

themselves, which they did with great enthusiasm. I remembered that bears have only a rudimentary understanding of table etiquette, and decided it best to merely stand aside and let them proceed. I only insisted that they pick up after themselves, but since bears eat anything with even a scent of food on it, there was very little refuse left when they were done; actually only empty bottles and bottle caps, which I re-stowed in the beer case.

After the meal was over the three of us sat on the ground, leaning back against the old log sipping our beer, and reminiscing about the days before the encroachment of civilization changed our way of living. Now Ralph was planning to move again, still trying to stay buffered from what he considered to be the crush of advancing humanity. My arguments to the contrary fell on deaf ears. I told him that it didn't matter how far back into the woods he went, he was not likely to find a life free of contact with the human beans he had such an aversion to. The old bear had made up his mind; he was determined to move on.

"And what of you, Duffy? Are you leaving too?" I asked.

"I'll help old gramps get settled, then we'll see. Most of my friends are down here, and now that Ralph has abdicated the job of headman in the clan, I'm the main dude. The position entails certain responsibilities."

"Well, by George, Duffy, I didn't know that. Congratulations."

"You know I took today off from the rut just to come to this meeting, and that's a dangerous thing to do," said Duffy. "Some other hot shots are probably up there on Mt. Rose right now, trying to take over. I'll probably have to fight 'em all over again tomorrow."

"I hope not, man. That could be dangerous."

"Not really, mostly it's just for show. You snort and growl, bare your canines, raise the hackles, lay your ears back menacingly, and walk around stiff-legged. Hardly anybody ever gets hurt, but it makes a big impression on the ladies." Ralph used his teeth to wrench the cap off beer number seven or eight, and with an explosively exhaled breath, lofted the cap clear over the car.

"Ralph, dammit, I'm going to have to find all those caps to tidy this place up when we leave."

The big bear's eyes were becoming slightly crossed. I wondered how much longer we could sustain our picnic.

"Suit yourself," he said.

"Duffy," I said, "we've got to make a decision about this celebration business, and we must do it soon or your grandpa is going to be completely in his cups and out of the picture. The townspeople want to have the celebration on the Fourth of July. They're going to have a parade and they want you in it. Whataya think?"

"May Day would be best."

"May Day has already passed," I said. "It has to be the Fourth of

July."

Ralph was mumbling. "Duffy, see if there's anything to eat in the car, I'm hungry."

"Nothing more in here except a large bag of peanuts in the shell and seven longneck beers," said Duffy, grubbing around in the trunk.

"Bring the beers over. I'm thirsty, too."

"Ralph," I asked, "will you be in a parade on the Fourth of July?"

The old bear ate the peanuts, bag and all, and cleared his throat importantly. "Only if I get to wear a silk top hat and ride in a big black touring car. I want to look just like Woodrow Wilson. Duffy  gets to wear a top hat too. He goes as Warren G. Harding. And here's something else, I refuse to wear a collar or any other sort of restraining device, and must be allowed to moon certain citizens along the parade route without fear of arrest." Another bottle cap flew off into the wilderness. "All the house dogs in town must be kept locked up, along with that hostile druggist. I will need to be picked up at my lodging, and returned there after the parade, and will not stay for the fireworks, which hurt my ears. I not will not submit to press conferences, and will refuse to answer stupid questions like 'what's it like being a bear?'"

Ralph looked at me in an unfocused way. "Can these conditions be met?" The old bear was doing his best to sound important.

"I doubt it, Ralph. That bit about mooning citizens concerns me, but I'll see what I can do." I began to think that this was going to be more trouble than it was worth. "Touring car? Silk top hats? What's that all about, Duffy?" I asked.

"Ralph found an old history book in a dumpster once. It had a picture of your President Harding riding in a parade with Woodrow Wilson in 1924. He was fascinated by it. Thought it made the old dudes look cool."

"Duffy, have you got your telephone in your fanny pack? I need to call Boris up at the park."

"Sure thing, dude." He handed me the phone. I got through to the ranger immediately, and began to describe the conditions under which Ralph would participate in the parade. Boris stopped me.

"Never mind, Pete, it's all off. The movers-and-shakers in Hoodsport have changed their minds. The animal rights outfits got wind of what they were planning, and let the folks know that they consider having bears ride in parades as being just another form of cruelty to animals. They threatened legal action and said they were going to get a court injunction, or something. Then the wildlife honchos in Olympia started quoting the law about people consorting with wild animals, and I told them they might as well forget the whole thing. The sheriff got involved and said he couldn't  guarantee the safety of the citizens, either, what with unchained wild animals parading through the middle of town." Boris didn't sound troubled by the news at all.

"Are there any laws against bears wearing silk top hats?" I asked.

279

There was a long silence.

"Say again?"

"Never mind, Ski, just a little joke there. By the way, do you know about the abandoned ranger's cabin up by Elkhorn? Are you guys ever planning to use it again?"

"I doubt it. The road washed out two years ago. We don't have enough money to restore it, and the tree huggers don't want us to fix it anyway. The cabin will probably stay empty until it falls down."

"Well, maybe not, but I'll tell you about it some other time. Thanks for the help, Ski. I'll keep in touch."

I returned the phone to Duffy. "You're off the hook, gentlemen," I said. "The bear portion of the Independence Day parade has been scrubbed. There will be no need for your participation." Neither bear showed the slightest disappointment.

"That's just fine with me," snorted Duffy. "I think we'd both look pretty stupid in top hats."

"The drugstore guy's gonna be pissed, though. He won't be able to get a shot at us," mumbled Ralph. The old bear seemed about to doze off.

"Well, gentlemen — if that's what you are — we seem to have settled the main reason for calling this meeting." I looked in the trunk of the car. "Duffy, will your super-size fanny pack hold five long-neck bottles of beer? That's all that's left in here."

"Probably not, dude. Why not put 'em in the hole under the stump. Maybe we'll have another meeting someday."

Ralph belched loudly. "Are you going to be able to get your grandpa home?" I asked. "He looks like he might need help." Then, without giving the matter a second of thought, I made a suggestion that could only have been induced by a sense of euphoria over not having to worry about bears in a Fourth of July parade, or by having had just one beer too many. In any case I regretted the words as I soon as they left my mouth.

"Why don't you guys get in the car, and I'll drive you home?" In an instant the deed was done. It was too late to retract the words.

"Sounds good to us," piped Duffy, without hesitation. He went to rouse the old bear. "Come on Ralph, our taxi's waiting."

"Gotta pee first," he mumbled, as he shuffled to a nearby bush where he raised his hind leg, dog fashion.

I watched in amazement. "I didn't know bears did that," I said.

"They usually don't," replied Duffy. "I think he's just showing off, or maybe he thinks he's a dog today. Tidy up before you get in the car, Ralph. We don't want to muss up the old man's car." Ralph smiled crookedly, and shook himself.

"You get in the back, Ralph; Duffy you can sit up front with me, if you promise to keep your hands off the wheel." Ralph rolled down the back window and stuck his head out. Even though he was seriously hunched over, Duffy's head hit the roof of the car. It didn't look like it would be a comfortable trip for the bears, but off we went.

As I turned off the Staircase road onto the causeway, for what I hoped would be the last time in my life, I observed the approach of a car from some distance ahead. It had emergency lights across the top, and I supposed it must be a park official leaving the campground. It followed us across the bridge, and suddenly in my rearview mirror, I saw the blue lights go on.

I said a bad word right out loud. My good Samaritan deed was going to end with me in the pokey trying to explain why I was transporting wild bears on public highways. Ralph was sound asleep by now, his head still hanging out the window. Duffy, cramped to paralysis, had slobbered all over the windshield, impairing my vision, and the inside of the car smelled like the Budweiser brewery. The day, which had started out with such promise, was about to end in disgrace. I hung my head in embarrassment as the officer approached warily, his hand on his weapon.

"Well, Pete, you're never going to learn, are you? I can see that I've got myself a big time bust here: cohabitating, transporting, DUI, disturbing the peace, public endangerment, maybe even corrupting the morals of wild animals for good measure. It'll be a long time up the river for you, old boy."

I recognized the voice of Deputy Fred Edd, stout minion of the law in northern Mason County, and looked up to see my reflection in the lenses of his big black spectacles.

"Guilty as charged, Fred. I'll go peaceful, no need to call for backup."

Fred looked across me and recognized Duffy, who he had seen from a distance on the day of the big fire. "Hi, Macduff, it's a pleasure to meet the real hero of the fire after all this time. You look pretty cramped in there. You want to file charges against your abductor here?" He pointed at me.

"Who's the big dude in the back seat?" Edd asked, keeping a respectable distance from the car.

"Forgive me for not introducing you, Fred. That's Ralph, you've read about him. Ralph, meet Fred Edd." Ralph opened one eye and snuffled softly.

"How does the big bear feel about strange humans? Am I in any danger?" Fred asked.

"I don't think so, Fred. He's feeling no pain. That brewery smell in here comes from Ralph, who has consumed sixteen bottles of beer. He has very little will power when it comes to beer. Duffy and I are the designated drivers. We're taking him home."

"Where have I heard that story before?" asked Fred, rhetorically.

I desperately wanted to divert the officer's attention away from my legal problems. "Have you heard they've cancelled the Duffy Day celebration, Fred?"

"I was just talking to Boris about that very thing. We're both relieved. How do your friends here feel about it?" asked Fred, as he removed his official spectacles.

"Much relieved, as well." I told Fred about Ralph's demands. "The old bear doesn't understand parade etiquette, I'm afraid. He wanted permission to commit flagrant indelicacies along the parade route. The sheriff's department might have had a problem keeping order."

"Just as well all around then," said Fred. "Just as well." He backed away from the car. "It looks to me like you better get your old bruin home to bed, Pete. I'm off-shift and headed to the barn, so this isn't an official stop. There will be no mention of the matter in the official records. Man, if I had to write up all the infractions I see here I'd be up to my wazoo in paperwork for at least a month. You're free to go."

"You're a prince, Fred. Now I won't have to turn these bears loose on you."

"Nice to see you again, Duffy," said Fred, "and I'm pleased to have met you, Ralph." The old bear opened on eye and snorted. "He's drooling on the side of your car, Pete."

"A small price to pay, Fred, for the pleasure of the company of bears."

"Drive carefully, sir, and have a nice day," said the deputy with a wave, as we began the climb up the grade. We were quiet as we negotiated the narrow road. Duffy and I rode companionably up past the treacherous cliff above the campground, while Ralph continued to sleep, his head lolling out the window. My thoughts were on the future of my two long-time friends, and Ralph's determination to leave the area. I knew that if he actually moved to the old cabin on the Dosewallips River, I was unlikely to ever see him again. It was simply too far away. The road ended nearly five miles from the cabin, and such a long hike was a thing of the past for me. I wished that Ralph was in better shape for what was sure to be our final farewell.

I parked the car in the clearing above Ralph's home cave. Duffy and I walked to the edge of the sharp incline where we could look down on the scene of last year's wildfire. The ground was still black, although there were already signs of recovery. Green grass and new vegetation were visible in the valley.

"Are you going to be able to get Ralph back to his cave, Duff?"

"Oh sure, he'll be okay as soon as he wakes up. I'll walk him around up here a bit before we go over the edge. He'll probably sleep until tomorrow, then he'll be ready to travel."

"Are you going with him?"

"Only if he waits until the rutting season is over. This is my busiest time of the year. But I'll check on him in any case, make sure

284

he gets settled in. We know quite a few bears up there, you know, and Mother Duck will look in on him. I'll bet she might even move in with him. He'll need a housekeeper." Duffy fished around in his fanny pack and brought out the two telephones.

"You can have these, old man. Ralph and I are going back to being bears. We've had our fling at the human bean business, and decided it's too much of a bother. It was fun while it lasted. Ralph and I talked it over and, in a word, decided to hell with it. By the way, these aren't the phones that Ralph swallowed. They were the little ones. I threw them away."

"Does this mean that you'll be staying out of the campground this summer?" I asked.

"It means **I'll** be staying out, but I can't speak for Luciana and Dromio. Peaches kicked them out of her cave, you know. They're on their own now."

"Borski will be pleased to hear that, I'm sure." I said.

Duffy walked over to the car and pulled open the back door with some difficulty, causing Ralph to tumble out onto the ground. Sprawling in disarray, his eyes came wide open as though he had awakened from a nightmare. He spoke angrily in bear, not English, so I wasn't sure what he said, but it certainly wasn't complimentary.

"Up and at 'em, gramps. Time for a little walk." Duffy got his two front paws under Ralph's middle, and set him upright as easily as could be. For the first time it occurred to me that Duffy was bigger than Ralph, and surely much stronger. They walked in circles around the car, Ralph's head hanging low, swinging heavily from side to side.

"We've got to get some meat on the old dude's bones. You're mighty skinny, right, Gramps?"

"Uuumph, houghffft sleep!" was the extent of the reply.

"Well," said Duffy, "this is the time of parting." He stood before me on his hind legs, the bear's sign of equality. "Gimmee a high five, old buddy."

We must have looked like an odd pair of sports jocks congratulating each other as we slapped hand and paw. Suddenly Ralph was on his feet beside me, and I felt a heavy arm across my shoulders as he planted a wet, beery smooch on my cheek.

"I've never even seen him do that with other bears," said Duffy. "I think he likes you."

"I'm honored, I'm sure," I said, wiping my cheek.

Ralph shuffled toward the path over the crest of the hill as Duffy

 followed. I joined them at the edge of the trees.

"I'll give the old boy a shot of goochiwater and tuck him in," said Duffy. "He'll be his usual grumpy self in the morning, worst luck."

Ralph moved slowly down toward the entrance to the cave, where he turned, and looking back, raised a paw in a silent salute before disappearing into the darkness.

Duffy and I stood for a moment in silence. "I think the old boy enjoyed himself. It reminded him of the good old days back on the south shore," the young bear said.

He followed me back to the car, "Sometime, if you and your hiking friends get up on the Dosewallips trail check out the old cabin, maybe Ralph will be there."

"That's miles beyond the washout, Duff, and easy enough a few years ago, but it's a bit out of my range now. If you and Ralph ever have a message for me, leave it with Archie down at the campground, he knows how to contact me."

"It's a deal, and you take care of yourself, old dude. If you're up this way again, look me up. Just ask for Macduff Shakesbear. Everybody knows me, especially the ladies."

THE END

EPILOGUE

In late September a large envelope arrived in my mailbox from the Staircase ranger station. It had Wilmer Archibald's name on the outside. In the envelope was a short letter from Archie, which read as follows:

Dear Pete,

I have been working at the campground again this summer and I must say things are very quiet around here compared to last year. Except for a couple of incidents involving two yearling cubs, our bear problems are hardly worth mentioning. From the few glimpses I've gotten of these two – a male and a female – they both bare a striking resemblance to our friend Duffy (the same white blaze across the chest). Could this be a coincidence? If not, I guess this campground is in for trouble again in a couple of years. Like father, like son, you know.

Anyway, I was up on the Dosie last week checking on that abandoned ranger's cabin and found the enclosed letter stuck in the webbing of an old rocking chair on the porch. (The cabin is getting to be in pretty bad shape.) As you can see, it is addressed to you so I brought it back down here, looked up your address and am sending it on to you. I haven't opened the envelope but am mighty curious to know what it is about. If you have time, and if it's any of my business, I would appreciate hearing from you.

Your Friend, Archie Archibald

The envelope that Archie had enclosed was a recycled thing, soiled and tattered with age. The address simply said "Pete, bare

289

carver, Rode 106. Please forward." I recognized the lettering as belonging to Duffy, who notwithstanding his other accomplishments, had never mastered spelling or punctuation. The letter was short. There was no date. Bears don't bother with dates.

Deer Frend:

It is with regret I must inform you of the death of my grandfather? Ralph B. Shakesbear, who deparded our soil this weak. He dide as he wood have wanted rocking on the porch wile reeding his favorit author Mr. Wm. Shakespears Much Ado About Nothing. Mrs. Duckabush was caring for him in his last months. She was not with him when he shuffled off but arranged to have COB members carry him to his finale resting plaice. He will be mist but is in a beter world where bares are never hungry and the rut is forever. Do not lament his pasing. He lived good and did it his whey.

Your frend Duffy

PS I am well, Peaches is with child again. Twins. They will be R's grate grate grandchildrins.

I made a copy of the letter and sent it on to Archie and Boris.

ISBN 1-41204291-7

9 781412 042918